A SCENT OF DANGER

A Scent of Danger

Sarah Hope-Walker

HEADLINE
Liaison

First published in 1995
by HEADLINE BOOK PUBLISHING

A HEADLINE LIAISON paperback

10 9 8 7 6 5 4 3 2 1

ISBN 0 7472 5260 2

Typeset by CBS, Felixstowe, Suffolk

Printed and bound in Great Britain by
Cox & Wyman Ltd, Reading, Berks

HEADLINE BOOK PUBLISHING
A division of Hodder Headline PLC
338 Euston Road
London NW1 3BH

A Scent of Danger

Chapter One

Cursing the sudden shower, Vanessa dashed into the shelter of a doorway and turned to stare resentfully out at the rain-washed street. Peering up into the sky she could see little hope of it abating.

That morning she had been flattered to find that she had been 'head-hunted'. There was something about the phrase, with its images of predatory savages stalking their prey, that thrilled her. News of her precipitate departure from Splash had spread like wildfire. That had come as no surprise since the advertising world was small and its high-fliers well known to each other. Vanessa had established her reputation early with the controversial Darling campaign which had so shocked the media that they had given her client several million pounds' worth of editorial space, making Splash a household name. The original shock posters had been her idea, fought for against a great deal of internal opposition and, having worked out so spectacularly, they focused a great deal of admiring interest on her from other agencies. When she'd announced her intention of leaving Splash it had impacted with much the same force as if she had lobbed a hand grenade into the boardroom.

'Why?' the CEO had asked her. 'What have we done?'

It was impossible to explain to him and even more difficult to explain it to herself. Perhaps it was that she had been made too rich too soon. Maybe Andrew walking out on their five-year relationship had made her reassess her life and had forced her to consider where she was going and what she was doing.

All she knew was that deep inside her was a nagging voice telling her to do something positive for herself before it was too late. No matter how stridently feminists declared otherwise, she knew that in taking on the men, fighting her way up the corporate ladder, grabbing for the golden ring of fame and riches, she was somehow denying her true self. Added to this, Andrew's rejection of all they had shared had come as something of a watershed – a moment when she knew she must take a new direction or wither.

That morning a call had come from a New York based agency who had invited her to lunch to 'explore options'. Gerry Goldberg was a highly articulate man, intelligent and, in his late forties, devastatingly charming. The lunch had gone well and the offer had been tempting but she felt she needed more time to herself.

As she ruefully considered her options she became aware of a man watching her from the back of a limousine which had drawn to the kerb a few moments before. Vanessa was no stranger to being looked at but the man behind the smoked glass seemed to have fixed on her with a laser-like intensity that she found discomfiting. Turning away, she noticed that the doorway she had chosen to shelter in was that of an art dealer and its warm and welcoming ambience seemed as good a place as any to escape from the rain.

The moment she stepped inside she was confronted by a professionally smiling woman in a neat suit. 'Is there anything in particular that interests you?' she was asked.

Vanessa shook her head. 'Just looking,' she told the woman. The fixed greeting smile didn't waver but by the dulling of the woman's eyes Vanessa saw that she had been classified: 'Time Waster'.

'Please . . .' smiled the woman, making an invitational gesture with her hand while adding, with just a touch of sarcasm, 'Terrible weather outside, isn't it?'

Vanessa acknowledged that it was before turning to look at the pictures. Although no great connoisseur herself, she had spent enough time with creative artists to recognise the eye-catching style of the artistic 'caterer', who paints to the market rather than letting their talent and flair find its own expression. She could almost hear the first canvas she looked at shouting 'buy me' while in the background she could hear the plaintive voice of the artist himself adding, 'For God's sake – *somebody* buy *something*!'

Guiltily aware that she was merely sheltering from the rain rather than seriously intending to buy, she turned her attention to another canvas which sent instant shock waves searing through her. There, before her eyes, was the depiction of a vision that had haunted her for years.

The painting showed a double aisle of candles whose perspective led inexorably to an altar-like structure over which hovered the menacing figure of a malevolent man. The scene depicted was one of overwhelming power, heavy with mystery and potentially dire consequences for the naked girl who could be seen walking forward to whatever fate awaited her. From beyond the candles' glare, faces of many people peered foggily out at the dramatic pageant. The title, Vanessa read, was "Initiation".

Aware that she had become rigid at the incredible similarity of this scene to her recurrent vision, she was further overwhelmed to realise that the canvas showed aspects of the dream which she had all but forgotten.

In her sleep she felt she had been in that place. The stench of scented candle smoke leapt into her nostrils, the sound of drums beat in concert with her pounding heart. That long slow walk under a hundred eyes devouring her nakedness – eyes which knew what awaited her at the end of the aisle while she did not.

So concentrated was her mind that when a man standing uncomfortably close spoke to her, she all but jumped out of her skin. 'It's well drawn, don't you think?' he was asking, 'but essentially facile. Pure melodrama.'

Giving the man only the barest of sidelong glances, Vanessa suspected that he was the same one that had earlier stared at her from the rear of the limousine. The thought that he had pursued her inside rankled with her and so barbed her reply. 'I think it's quite wonderful,' she said.

'Really?' mused the man, moving forward into Vanessa's eyeline and, at the same time, obscuring the canvas. 'It looks to me more like an illustration for an erotic magazine than a work of art.'

Vanessa, having registered that the tall man was good-looking, muscular with neatly cut dark hair and piercing emerald-green eyes, broke away from the demanding glare that was making her feel slightly nervous. 'Do you know much about art?' she enquired, still annoyed.

The man turned to her as if surprised by her question. His eyes, now warm and soft, settled on her as his lips formed into a lazy half-smile. 'Practically nothing,' he said.

'Well,' said a much reassured Vanessa, 'if you did, you would appreciate the ambience the artist has created. The stark symmetry and the sharp perspective. The way the eye is led, inexorably, towards the altar. Illustrations *illustrate* – works of art are distinguished by their emotional impact and this picture, for me, does have *tremendous* impact.'

The man continued to look on with an infuriatingly quizzical expression. 'Well, you're certainly passionate enough about it. Are you intending to buy it?' he asked.

Knowing full well she wasn't, but equally determined not to back down in the face of his challenging expression, she shrugged. 'I haven't decided,' she said.

The man nodded and looked down at the catalogue he had in his hand. '"Initiation" by Steven Weir,' he said, before he mused in silence for a moment. 'Don't think I know him,' he finally added. 'Anyway, I'd say it was overpriced, wouldn't you?'

'Matter of opinion,' answered Vanessa, turning away.

In the back of the gallery she found two other canvases by Steven Weir. Both seemed to have the same heavy erotic overtones and depicted a girl standing submissively alone and vulnerable. It seemed this Steven Weir had only one theme to inspire him but neither of these paintings had anything like the impact of the first. Feeling quite uncomfortably aroused by the pictures, Vanessa reminded herself she had things to think about and options to consider.

Cautiously looking out into the main area of the gallery she saw, with relief, that the importunate man was nowhere to be seen and decided she had time for one last look at the canvas that had so encompassed her dream.

Looking at it again she felt the flat surface of the canvas become almost three-dimensional enough for her to step into. Then, just as the gentle feeling of arousal was again overtaking her, she was chilled to see the smartly-suited receptionist step between her and the picture and place a red sticker on its frame. She knew this meant the picture had been sold and was about to ask to whom, when she found the woman smiling directly at her. 'I wonder if I might have your name and address?' the woman was asking.

'What for?' asked a surprised Vanessa.

'Our mailing list. We have frequent changes of exhibits, you know. We do like to keep in touch with all our potential customers.'

As Vanessa hesitated, unsure of whether or not she wanted to be on yet another mailing list, the woman smiled and excused herself. 'I'll be at my desk when you're ready.'

Idly wondering what had brought about the woman's sudden change of attitude, Vanessa looked back at the picture and frowned again at the red 'SOLD' sticker, realising that, given another few moments for reflection, she might well have bought the picture for herself. For a moment it seemed that her dream had been bought out from under her. Determined to find out who the new owner might be she turned to the brilliantly smiling woman to find her holding out a file card ready to be filled in.

Thinking that the simple gesture of giving her details might induce the woman to say who had bought the canvas she filled in the card and was just about to enquire about the picture when the woman spoke again. 'The exhibit ends tonight. Will that be alright?'

'For what?'

'For delivery?'

Puzzled, Vanessa began to fear there had been some misunderstanding. 'Of what?' she asked.

'Why, your picture of course. "Initiation".'

This simple statement sent her mind into confusion. Had she missed something? 'But I haven't bought the picture.'

'Of course not,' said the now permanently smiling lady. 'Steven Weir did.'

'Did what?' asked Vanessa, struggling with what she saw as a rapidly developing Alice-in-Wonderland situation.

'Bought the picture for you.'

Feeling alone in a world gone mad, Vanessa shook her head. 'The artist? But I don't even know him!'

Now it was the woman's turn to look perplexed. 'But you were just talking with him!'

Vanessa looked round the gallery feeling she must have missed something. The only man she had talked to was . . .

'*That* was Steven Weir?' she asked.

The woman nodded happily as if pleased to get that hiccup out of the way.

Still confused, Vanessa pressed on. 'Do all your painters wear Savile Row suits and drive in chauffeured limousines?'

The woman's smile didn't waver but her tone became

almost coy. 'Not all, no. It's just that Mr Weir is quite different.'

'I'll say,' agreed Vanessa before gathering her thoughts together. 'But I couldn't possibly accept.'

Now the woman was looking painfully worried. 'But . . .' she started to say before Vanessa broke off from the unwanted confusion and made for the door, aware that the startled eyes of the woman were boring into her hastily retreating back.

The downpour having stopped, Vanessa decided to walk the short distance to her apartment block with a feeling that the events of the day were conspiring towards something as yet unknown. As she walked the familiar streets, she was haunted by the image of the painting and couldn't escape the feeling that some unknown force had conspired to have her enter the gallery that day. She also wondered why, having decided that she might buy the picture, she had refused it as a gift?

It was then she saw her nemesis – a French coffee shop that served the most deliciously wicked pastries imaginable. Deciding that today she needed the comfort of reckless indulgence, she salved her conscience and went to linger over coffee and a huge, squashy, cream-filled pastry, reassuring herself that even if the calories did show up somewhere on her body, there was nobody home to see them! With great difficulty she resisted the urge to order another and riveted her mind instead on Steven Weir's extravagant, and mildly ridiculous gesture.

Such musings brought her belatedly to her apartment block in Berkeley Street. As usual the lift was busy so, suddenly impatient to be home and soaking in a hot bath, she decided to climb to the third floor where she found a strange young man sitting on the stairs with a wrapped package at his side.

Excusing herself, she stepped round the bored-looking man and became defensive when he rose to face her as she fitted her key into the lock.

'You Miss Vanessa Turner?' he asked with a brusqueness bordering on rudeness. When she cautiously nodded he seemed much relieved. 'This is for you,' he said handing her the heavy package which she realised must be the picture.

'Wait a moment!' she called as the young man turned down the stairs. 'If this is what I think it is – I don't want it.'

The young man paused, his eyes flaring. 'Well, I sure don't,' he told her. 'You want them to take it back you'll have to talk to them. Me? I'm off home. 'Night.' Turning, he clattered away down the stairs.

Feeling that her life had been invaded, Vanessa turned to the sanctuary of her apartment.

The messages on her machine were the usual mish-mash of invitations and inquiries and she thought none of them more pressing than the cup of coffee of which she felt so desperately in need.

Settled with her coffee in hand, she was considering whether or not to tear the wrapping from the picture – an action that somehow had the smack of commitment about it – when the telephone rang. She let the answering machine take it until she heard Sheila's voice on the line.

Sheila was the one person in the world that didn't mind listening to her troubles, so she hurried to pick up.

'Oh, you're there!' cried Sheila's surprised voice.

'I've just come in,' lied Vanessa.

'I've something awful to tell you . . .'

From the tone of Sheila's voice she knew immediately it was going to be about The Bastard. For two years she had shared this same apartment with Andrew. They had both agreed that marriage could wait and that they had plenty of time to make their separate careers before settling down. She had managed to delude herself that their cosy routine had evolved into the prelude to a shared commitment. One day, like lightning from a summer sky, he had abruptly told her he was moving out. The announcement had left her angry and even now, two months later, she still felt betrayed.

'What about Andrew?' she asked.

'How did you know it was about him?' asked an amazed Sheila.

'I'm psychic,' Vanessa said scathingly.

'I always thought you were something of a witch.'

Impatiently Vanessa cut in on Sheila's threatened ramble down memory lane. 'What about Andrew?' she asked.

'Getting married. She's a complete air-head, apparently, but he's got her up the stick and is doing the decent thing. Surprised me!'

A sense of bitter betrayal flooded in on Vanessa. She found her grip on the telephone tightening as she fought to keep her voice even. 'Who is she?'

'Nobody anybody knows. Quite lovely by all accounts but a complete bimbo.'

'And just how pregnant is she?'

'I was told four months . . . which means he was . . .'

'I know what it means!' cried Vanessa, terrified that tears were going to flow.

'Aren't men utter bastards?' asked Sheila, as if savouring each and every syllable. 'Anyway, this weekend will prove the perfect antidote.'

For a moment Vanessa's shredded mind went whirling off in all directions before Sheila's urgent tone sobered her enough to ask, 'What did you say?'

'The weekend, darling. Holly Hill House will be the perfect place to get over him.'

Vanessa suddenly remembered her rash promise to go with Sheila on this Self-Enlightenment Weekend. She had intended to cancel the arrangement weeks ago but had forgotten and she now found herself desperately trying to think of a reason to excuse herself.

Sheila sensed the hesitation. 'Don't tell me you've changed your mind. I've booked for us both. The cheque's been sent. It's all arranged.'

With dread Vanessa realised her own passivity had backed her into a corner from which she could only extricate herself at the expense of her dearest and, possibly at this moment, only friend. Cowardice had her murmuring instead, 'No. No, of course not. You're right. It could be exactly what I need.'

'Good. We only need take one car so I'll pick you up at about noon tomorrow. OK?'

Vanessa found her throat suddenly blocked and could barely manage a muffled agreement before hanging up the phone and giving in to the tears which had threatened to overcome her since the mention of Andrew's name.

Having heard that alcohol dried the skin Vanessa avoided it as much as possible but Sheila's news had created a special need. Glad to find a vodka bottle that still held a satisfying third of its volume, she poured herself a generous quantity and drank it straight, its raw sting serving only to heighten her sense of isolated betrayal.

Wherever she looked in the apartment there was something to remind her of Andrew. The chairs, the rug, the ridiculously oversized Chinese pottery dragon; all brought instant memories of not only where they had bought them and her mood at the time, but also of the total sexual abandonment she had imagined she was sharing with the swine!

Turning again to the bottle she poured herself another glass as she considered that what she was feeling was not so much jealousy but rejection of all those tiny, half-forgotten intimacies – those times when they had lain in each other's arms and told each other things that she, at least, would never have dreamed of confessing to another living soul. Then there were their arguments.

They had, on the first day he had moved in, made it a rule that whenever a row was brewing they would both undress and conduct the argument naked. To avoid threatening hand gestures they also had to keep their hands firmly behind their backs. And it had worked out deliciously.

Facing each other in a state of total exposure had done little to moderate the spiteful words they would exchange but neither of them could ignore the fact that the more bitter the argument, the more aroused they would become. Here Andrew was at a disadvantage since his arousal was more apparent. The sight of him, spitting anger, but growing enormous would further stimulate Vanessa until they would suddenly find themselves drawn together as if by a magnetic charge. Then they would inevitably drop to the floor, a couch, bed or any other available surface, continuing to exchange verbal insults which rising passion would make ever more obscene and insulting while their bodies renewed pledges that she, at least, had thought unbreakable.

Such moments of raw libidinous pleasure, when she had felt his surging flesh deep inside her and bringing her ecstatic release, had been exciting but then, by deserting her, he had stolen the trust with which she had given herself. For all she knew, at that very moment he might be laughing about such moments with his new love.

That, Vanessa, decided was the true betrayal.

Never again, she told herself, would she open up to another man as she had with Andrew.

It was when she felt a sudden urgent need of the bathroom that she realised she had become quite drunk very quickly. Having to steady herself against the doorframe, she cursed herself for forgetting that she had no tolerance for alcohol.

The child of a serving military father she had learned self-discipline early and lapsed from it only with a sense of overwhelming guilt.

Getting herself together and making a positive effort to *think* herself sober, Vanessa went into the bathroom. A few minutes later, she heard her telephone ringing. Sure that it would be Sheila, and deciding that she didn't want to hear any more about Andrew, she ignored it.

To distract herself from this noisy intrusion she stood for a moment contemplating the still-wrapped picture. When it had been delivered she had felt herself intruded upon, but now found herself wondering if the scene depicted on the canvas would have the same impact on her at home as it had in the gallery.

She returned to the living room, where the insistent ring of the telephone was beginning to annoy her. Picking it up, she held it over the cradle for a moment before carefully lowering it back down again to sever the connection. Tranquillity returned to the apartment. Vanessa picked up the wrapped package and took it into the bedroom where she propped it up on a soft peach-coloured chair at the foot of her big brass bed before tearing off the heavy brown wrapping paper.

The moment it was exposed she was gripped by the same electrifying *déjà vu* she had known earlier.

If the delivery of the parcel had been an intrusion of her living space the picture itself went directly and incisively into the very core of her being. It was extremely disconcerting to find herself feeling as if she had shared an intimacy with a man she had scarcely met. Even more unsettling was the thought that this stranger had taken up residence in a small corner of her mind.

Finding herself shuddering with an undefined arousal she lay face down on the bed and stared deeply into the picture as if to search out every last scrap of detail.

The altar beyond the aisle drew her forward. By closing her eyes she could almost imagine herself there in this quasi-religious place. She felt herself transported into the mind of the girl in the picture. Naked, borne forward inexorably towards an uncertain destiny, it had echoes in her own present state of mind. As she studied the form and detail, Vanessa felt her affinity with the picture increasing. She had, long ago, understood the relationship between fear and excitement. It was the reason people took rides on Big Dippers in pleasure parks and squealed with excitement when, driving in a car, a headlong rush over a hump-backed bridge made them temporarily weightless.

Looking at the painting made her realise it was also the reason she had fantasies about forced submission – the only one of her sexual fantasies she had ever withheld from Andrew – an omission which now seemed to have taken on a whole new significance.

The canvas defined her dream. Somehow Steven Weir had reached through the night and stolen her unguarded fantasy.

The thought created in her an irresistible urge to satisfy a sudden longing. Turning onto her back she spread her thighs and let her hand slip down over her belly to its most tender point. Rubbing gently, she arched her back and visualised herself tied helplessly to a stranger's bed, spread and ready to be ravaged by an unknown mouth and phallus that would invade her very wholeness – someone who would take responsibility away from her, take charge of her independence. Imagining a tongue reaching back into her throat with the same depth and searing she was creating with her fingers, which now penetrated her with such ferocity that she came with an intensity that sent waves of pleasure washing over her body.

Lying there, emptied now and a little ashamed, she fought to keep the image of the painting, and the emotions it aroused, in her mind as she slipped quietly into sleep.

The dream came rushing at her with such vivid force that it seemed more real than waking reality. Unlike her previous dreams, this one was clearly defined. Even sleeping, she was surprised to find herself in a forest, naked and this time bound by some unknown means that restricted her arms behind her.

It was night so she should have been afraid but, instead, was tingling with excitement as if within the next step she would discover a wondrous new place where all would be revealed, and all questions answered.

She suddenly saw that the path she trod divided before her. One road led across an endless desert, bathed in the golden glow of dawn light, while the other led into a mysterious and foreboding darkness. Vanessa hesitated, waiting for a sign – something or someone to appear and direct her onto whichever path she should take.

The sign finally came in the form of a voice – quietly insistent, vaguely recognised, but warm and inviting. 'Come to me,' whispered the voice in tones that made her whole body shiver. 'Come forth and join me that we shall revel and know the unbounded joy of the truly free.'

The voice had come from the darkened path and, as tempting as it was, she found herself in a turmoil of indecision. Her instinct was to go to the glow of the dawn light but nevertheless she felt herself strongly drawn to the voice that spoke out of the darkness, tempting her towards the unknown and the unseen.

Suddenly she was overcome with the need to face and conquer the dangers the night concealed. As she turned towards the darker path she felt a sense of tremendous release.

The voice, insistently repeating the same mantra, grew closer and much clearer until she had no doubt that it belonged to Steven Weir!

Chapter Two

Vanessa woke late and confused. The first thing she saw was the canvas which brought both her fantasy and dream back into a quite frightening, vivid reality.

Lying in bed staring at the picture, she wondered why it all seemed so real. Was the place shown in the picture somewhere she had been in a previous life or was it a harbinger of what was to come? Either way, she realised with a shudder, Steven Weir had been there with her, or even before her.

It took an effort to remember Sheila's impending arrival to take her away for the weekend. As she went about getting herself ready, she reflected that it was probably a good thing. Slipping into a pair of well-cut designer jeans, she consoled herself with the thought that she was well rid of Andrew. Yesterday's news of his impending parenthood had shocked her but now she could see that she had been spared the hopeless prospect of spending her life with such an obviously weak man.

Eying herself from head to toe in the full-length mirror she felt liberated. Stroking her long black hair and staring at the reflected pale blue eyes, sculptured delicately between sharply defined cheekbones, Vanessa felt something new stirring within her. To hell with Andrew. He had only known a fraction of the woman she really was, and even less the woman she intended to become.

Characteristically, Sheila was late and in a hurry to pick up Vanessa's bag and get down to the car – until Vanessa found her standing transfixed before the canvas.

'Steven Weir,' she murmured in answer to Vanessa's reminder that they were supposed to be in a hurry.

'What about him?' asked Vanessa as she shrugged into a perfectly styled soft leather flying jacket. She had the curious feeling that she was about to be called upon to defend herself.

'You bought a Steven Weir?' Sheila asked.

'Not exactly, no. It was given to me. I'm not sure I'm going to keep it though.'

Sheila turned, flicked back her blonde hair and stared at Vanessa in amazement. 'Are you crazy? Steven Weir's work is shooting up the scale of "must-haves".'

Vanessa shrugged. Sheila was an interior designer and knew about these things. 'I'd never heard of him until yesterday.'

Sheila's laugh was short and scoffing. 'That's because you rarely leave that office of yours. What you need is a damn good broadening of your horizons.'

Vanessa remained silent. If her best friend had a fault it was a tendency to be matriarchal – a disposition to imagine that she always knew best. Slightly overweight, she was always clucking on about her new diet and cursing her boyfriend, Rupert, who, it seemed, was more absorbed by his vintage cars than Sheila's fussily complicated social arrangements.

Steven Weir wasn't mentioned again until Sheila, having sworn at every other driver on the road, somehow managed to manoeuvre her ancient Peugeot convertible, without fatalities, onto the M3, heading west.

'Who gave you that picture?'

'He did. Steven Weir.'

'But you said you'd never heard of him before yesterday. Does that mean you met him and, right off, he gave you a picture? What did you do for it?'

'Nothing! I went into this gallery to shelter from the rain. I saw the picture and was admiring it when this obnoxious man sidled up and started talking to me. I didn't know him from Adam. It was only when he'd gone that the gallery told me who he was and that he'd given me the picture.'

'And it was Steven Weir?'

'I suppose it must have been.'

'And you thought he was obnoxious? Darling, you need to get your eyes tested. I'd lay down naked in Piccadilly Circus if I thought that would get him for me.'

Ignoring Sheila's ridiculous allusion Vanessa asked, 'Do you know him then?'

'Not half as well as I want to! Every other woman I know simply drools over him. Not only is he handsome, and a gifted painter but he's also one of the richest bachelors in London! If you thought he was obnoxious I would say you are in serious need of therapy.'

Vanessa considered her one sighting of the man. True he

was attractive but he'd caught her off guard and she hadn't known then who he was or that the picture she had enthused about was his. A sense of lost opportunity flooded through her. 'Anyway, I don't suppose I'll ever see him again,' she offered.

'Oh, I doubt that!' cried Sheila. 'He often drops in on these weekends. Gives lectures on visual realisation.'

'You're joking!' cried Vanessa and wondered why a deep-seated shiver ran through her.

Holly Hill House stood aloof from the world behind iron gates and a half-mile-long driveway. Watching it coming ever closer through the car's windshield Vanessa felt a rising excitement.

Knowing Sheila's enthusiasm for saving the planet at every possible opportunity, she had been afraid that she was in for a weekend in a draughty converted army barracks in the company of earnest, thunder-thighed, tweedy ladies and weedy young men with even weedier beards. Instead, Holly Hill, Georgian by design and partly clad in ancient green ivy, looked not only habitable but positively up-market.

The interior had been preserved as it must have been when it had been a prestigious country house and only just fell short of being "stately".

Vanessa's fleeting hope that the service might be closer to that of a well-run hotel than a 'Return to Nature' experience was somewhat dampened when, having checked in, she found they were expected to carry their own bags up three flights of stairs which diminished in grandeur the higher they climbed. Finally arriving in what must once have been the servants' quarters, she was shown into a sparsely furnished room which she saw with sinking heart contained six beds standing on bare floorboards. Not having slept in a dormitory since school – also in the company of Sheila – Vanessa found herself morosely wondering how much homework they were to be given.

Sheila, blithely unaware of her friend's misgivings, heaved her suitcase onto the creaking iron bed and enthusiastically started stripping off her clothes. 'We've just about got time for a shower before class,' she told the still thunderstruck Vanessa.

'Are we really expected to share this room?' she asked.

'What's wrong with that?' Sheila asked. 'It's your fault for dithering. If you'd made up your mind sooner I could have booked one of the double rooms on the first floor. Come on, let's get the City dirt off us. You're going to love it when you stop moaning!'

Sheila, wrapped in a dressing gown, was gone before Vanessa could formulate any further protest. Looking around at the other beds, she cursed herself for agreeing to come in Sheila's car. There was no easy way to turn around and go home alone, especially when she remembered the dauntingly long driveway and the fact that they were probably ten or so miles from the nearest railway station.

Once more filled with foreboding at the coming two days Vanessa pulled her toiletry bag from her case and, having undressed, was preparing to follow Sheila to the showers when Sheila herself came bustling back into the room. 'No time for that now,' she cried. 'I've just been told that the class has been brought forward by half an hour. They've brought in this special guy that everyone says is marvellous.'

Vanessa watched as Sheila stepped into a leotard. 'What class?' she finally demanded.

'Tantric dancing, darling. You'll love it but you'll have to get a move on; they lock the doors. See you downstairs – room fifteen,' Sheila called over her shoulder as she hurried out of the door.

Vanessa sank onto the cot bed she had claimed as her own and thought of the dreadful mistake she had made. You may *think* you know your friends, she told herself, but the real question was did *they* know *you*?

Having changed into an extremely high-cut, hot-pink leotard which emphasised rather than covered a body which she felt could convulse men at twenty paces, Vanessa laced her feet into a pair of white canvas pumps and went to present herself at the door of Room 15 only to find it locked just as Sheila had warned. From inside she could hear the heavy insistent throb of Gothic music and felt perversely frustrated. Ten minutes previously she couldn't have given a damn about the Tantric dancing class but now she felt excluded from something very important to her.

'Problem?' asked a quiet male voice beside her.

Turning, she found herself looking once more into the smiling face of Steven Weir. Startled, she stared at him and was beginning to wonder if he was forever going to steal up on her when he spoke again. 'I saw you dashing through the lobby . . .'

'And followed me . . .?' she asked.

'I suppose you could say so, yes.' His smile stayed infuriatingly calm.

'I shall be sending the picture back on Monday,' she told him.

'You don't like it?'

'I like it very much but I can't possibly accept it.'

'Why? Too intimate? Would a set of lacy underwear have been more appropriate?'

Vanessa found his bantering tone was beginning to annoy her. 'Certainly not,' she said, adding hurriedly, 'Now, if you will excuse me, I have a class to attend.'

'Me too.' Steven smiled. 'I'm afraid I wasn't following you, it's just that we were going in the same direction.'

'Then we share the same problem,' observed Vanessa drily.

'Which is . . .?'

'The door is locked.'

'Have you tried knocking?'

Feeling slightly stupid Vanessa stepped back to allow Steven to step forward and bang peremptorily on the door.

There was a momentary pause and then the sound of the door being unlocked and then opened. A pale-faced girl with wild red hair stared silently out through an inch or so of door.

'The reason we're late,' Steven told the girl, 'is that we weren't told of the changed time.' Then he stepped forward to push the door open wider, politely stepping aside to allow Vanessa to precede him.

Inside the dimmed-out room Vanessa's ears were

assaulted by the high volume of the music chanting out from a bank of amplifiers. Her first impression was that of a palpable sensuality blanketing the air, mingling with the pleasant musky scent of arousal. Quickly flicking her eyes about the room, Vanessa saw that it was completely unfurnished and that a scattering of both male and female student dancers were swaying steadily from side to side. All, she noted, were blindfolded which made it that much more difficult to identify Sheila among them. Never having felt comfortable in discotheques, Vanessa found the noise level almost painful and might have thought of leaving except for the amazing sight of the assembled dancers.

As she scanned the company she suddenly became aware of a man, obviously in charge, staring at her from his raised position above the heads of the dancers. His uniform of black skintight dancer's leggings, complemented by a matching T-shirt, mapped out every muscle of his athletic form while his dazzling eyes, under a mop of blond hair, seemed to be beckoning her forward.

There was something about the man – apart from him being the most impossibly handsome man she had ever seen – that seized her gaze and held it transfixed. At her side, Steven Weir said something and moved off, leaving Vanessa to be drawn inexorably forward through the dancers, uncaring that their random movements brought them bumping into her. Finally she stood, arms held loosely at her sides, before the Class Master.

'You are?' he asked in a faintly Spanish accent which somehow managed to penetrate the wall of sound.

'Vanessa,' she said.

The man looked at her steadily until she felt naked before him. 'Have you experienced Tantric dancing before?' he asked.

'Not really. My friend and I have experimented on our own, but . . .' Vanessa's words trailed away as she found herself losing interest in anything she already knew. All she wanted was to hear what this man might say.

'It is very simple. One might say primitive. First you wear a blindfold. This is for two reasons – first that you shall not be distracted by anything going on around you and, secondly, so that you may concentrate on your own feelings and emotions knowing that no one is watching *you*.'

Vanessa nodded sagely as she watched him produce a velvet band. He stepped down from his podium and reached out towards her head. Had this gesture been an embrace Vanessa could not have been more thrilled. Her stomach clenched tight as she felt his hands flitting briefly about her hair as he tied the band in place. Her unbidden thought was to hope he would do more than simply blindfold her.

He did. Having eliminated her sight he took her hand – already quivering to his touch – and led her forward to a place where she could sense the heat of writhing bodies in close proximity.

'You must let the music penetrate your consciousness,' he told her. 'You must feel it vibrating in your soul. You must not fight it and gradually you will feel all your tensions, all the detritus of inhibition, slipping away from your body. It is a liberating process but also a cleansing. There are no

27

boundaries and no penalties. Let your instincts lead you to wherever they want you to go. Just so long as you don't interfere with your classmates.'

Standing before him, Vanessa was overcome with a feeling of total vulnerability. It was, for a moment, as if her dream was speaking directly to her. She had been led to the threshold of a new and exciting experience that her recurrent dream had so long promised but never delivered. Meanwhile his voice dripped like honey into her ears.

'Now you really should not miss this opportunity to further explore yourself.' He was already rearranging the blindfold around her eyes when he spoke again. 'Perhaps we might meet later tonight? After the evening meal?'

'I would like that,' she murmured, aware that she had become enormously, yet unaccountably, aroused. She could not contain the gasps that escaped her lips as his hand, perhaps accidentally, flicked across her aroused nipples as he lowered them from arranging her blindfold. 'Go forth,' he urged, 'and find yourself.' Vanessa felt herself turned and gently propelled into the midst of the dancing company.

Vanessa's only previous experience of Tantric dancing had been once in Sheila's apartment where they hadn't used blindfolds. Now, with the electric, vibrating rhythm, the feeling of private isolation within the velvet blindfold and the insistent presence of many other bodies similarly engaged, she could feel herself sinking slowly into a world where she stood alone – as she had in her visions – but supported by like, wilful minds. A rising excitement grew in her, heightened by the thought that she might, that very night, meet with the Class Master. Vanessa felt her inhibitions slipping from her as she swayed to the music and let the mood take over.

Slowly moving at the dictate of the music, her breathing became relaxed as she swayed this way and that, stretching her limbs. She stepped forward as if into another dimension, aware that she had so penetrated her inner self that all awareness of time or place or even the presence of others was totally lost. Within her heightened state there might have been no other living being.

She had gone into a private world where, as the Master had promised, anything was possible and nothing denied. Within the framework of that self-created world she experienced an excitement she had never truly felt in an act of love. She had glimpsed, in sharply defined detail, her sexual self, naked and joyously aware that she was on the brink of entering a garden of unbounded delight.

It was this glimpse of that other secret world that had so challenged her when she had stood before Steven Weir's painting. He had given her fantasy a setting with boundaries and definition, and now, in this room, she realised that it was the canvas world, and not her dream, she wanted to visit.

With the music throbbing in her ears and all sight of the other dancers eliminated, Vanessa felt herself rushing headlong into a new experience, exhilaratingly aware that this was because she was no longer seeking an indeterminate place but knew precisely where it was to be found.

Within minutes the distraction of the cries and gasps from the others faded and, with her arms clasped behind her, she could easily imagine herself transported into the painting. Out of the darkness of her blindfold came the looming image of the imposing man that awaited her on the forest path and, in dread joy, she forced her heavy legs forward to meet him.

There she was taken by unseen hands that forced her forward to lay on the soft, leaf-strewn forest path and then surreptitiously caressed her with a touch like the sting of a serpent's fang. Then came the readied man, to whom she opened herself and was instantly pierced by a thrusting solid, icy firmness that seared through her open flesh with an agonising but exquisite pleasure . . .!

Sheila's voice was insistently calm. 'You were screaming.'

Vanessa opened her eyes to see her friend looking down at her with concerned surprise. She knew at once she was lying on the floor of the dance-class room. 'What?' she asked.

'You got a little carried away.' Sheila's reassuring smile had such fragile uncertainty about it that it frightened Vanessa. Even more disconcerting were the many concerned faces of the others peering down at her. But most frightening was to see, on the face of the Class Master, a smile which suggested triumph. She tried to sit up only to find Sheila's hands pressing her back down to the floor.

'Not a good idea. Just rest a while and you'll be fine.' Again Vanessa tried to assert herself by sitting up. It was then she realised she was covered in a blanket and nothing else.

For a moment she had difficulty with this apparent time

shift. The dank tangy smells of the forest still lingered in her nostrils and she felt suddenly vulnerable. 'What happened?' she asked nervously.

'Nothing for you to worry about,' said Sheila in that hasty tone parents use when brushing aside a question they'd rather not answer.

'Sheila!' Vanessa kept her tone even and warning. 'I want to know what happened!'

'I can only tell you what I saw. I was off on a trip of my own when I suddenly realised the woman screaming was you. I took off my blindfold and there you were lying on the floor – you'd stripped off everything—'

'What . . .?' interjected a horrified Vanessa.

Sheila nodded her confirmation. 'Your leotard was in tatters – you must have had a very intense experience. I hope you remember it. I shall insist on hearing all the details.'

'What did I do?' insisted Vanessa.

'Well, by the time I looked, you were lying on the floor completely spread-eagled and screaming blue murder – among other things.'

Vanessa felt a shiver run through her body. 'And everyone saw that – heard that?'

'Not everybody . . .' smiled Sheila carefully. 'I mean people do come here to heighten their own emotions – it's just that you seem to have broken some kind of record, but don't worry about it. It's not the first time anything like this has happened and you're among friends.'

Those 'friends', Vanessa reflected, included both the Class Master and Steven Weir! Both men must now think of her as a dangerous lunatic. 'How?' she asked. 'I mean what came over me?'

Sheila stroked her hair in an infuriatingly patronising manner. 'From what you were screaming – just about everybody "came" over you!' She smiled. 'Really, you did put on a bit of a show. I had no idea you could be so passionate – or so explicitly demanding.'

Vanessa flushed red as she heard the echo of her words screamed out in what she had thought to be her private dream world – a dream now rapidly taking on the dimensions of a nightmare. Aware of the many faces peering at her Vanessa made a more positive effort to sit up. 'For God's sake get me out of here!' she pleaded.

In response Sheila helped her to her feet, wrapped the blanket carefully about her body and led Vanessa from the room.

On the way back up to their room Vanessa was overcome with the enormity of what she had done. 'I can't face anybody!' she said. 'Will you drive me to somewhere I can get a cab or a train or something?'

'Vanessa . . .' drawled Sheila. 'The last thing in the world you should be right now is alone. Anyway, no one was shocked. In fact, most people were a mite envious of the obvious intensity of your experience. It is, after all, what we were all aiming at.'

Coming to their shared room Vanessa started to feel a little calmer. 'Maybe,' she said as she inspected the hopeless rag she had made of the leotard, 'but I've never felt so humiliated in my life. I have to get out of here – now!'

'Before meeting your secret admirer?' Sheila asked.

Startled, Vanessa remembered the instructor saying he would like to meet with her after the evening meal. It must be him.

'He still wants to see me?' asked Vanessa as she felt her spirits reviving on a warming tide of intrigue.

'*Insists* would be my word for it.' Sheila said drily.

'Why?'

Sheila fixed her with a withering eye accompanied by a long drawn-out sigh that stopped just this side of exasperation. 'The mind boggles!' she told Vanessa.

'Where? When?' Vanessa asked, aware that she sounded too eager.

As Sheila hesitated, Vanessa saw in her hand a tightly folded piece of paper. 'Is that for me?' she asked.

Nodding, Sheila handed it over with a show of great reluctance.

Eagerly scanning the note Vanessa read: '*I wish you to be naked in the Hall at Midnight. No one else must know.*'

'You're not going to go, are you?' Sheila asked, unashamedly admitting to having read the note.

'Of course I'm going. He's just about the most exciting man I've ever seen.'

'Dangerous . . .' mused Sheila.

'What's wrong with that? Dangerous men are often the most interesting.'

Sheila uttered a short scornful laugh. 'I didn't mean *he* was dangerous. I meant it would be dangerous for you to meet him naked in your present condition.'

'What condition?'

'Vanessa, you are obviously in a state of hyper sexual

33

repression. Your little cabaret in class demonstrated that. That's what makes it dangerous.'

'If that's true then this may be just what I need.'

'You're crazy if you do.'

Annoyed by Sheila's remarks, Vanessa felt a rare stab of anger toward her oldest friend. 'Jealous?' she asked.

Sheila looked affronted. Rising silently to her feet, she turned to the door where she hesitated a moment, as if having thought of something more to say. Then she obviously changed her mind and left the room.

Vanessa lay on her bed and indulged herself in a moment's reverie. *Tonight*, she thought. Midnight. It could mean only one thing and, as she had earlier told Sheila, it was precisely what she needed. She just hoped she would not be disappointed.

Finding the opportunity to prepare herself for her midnight rendezvous presented a problem. She already knew that she was to wear nothing and so it was the communal bedroom that bothered her. Having no intention of letting the other women see her readying herself for what she was certain was to be an exciting encounter, she had to pick her time carefully.

The opportunity came when everyone sat down to dinner. Vanessa, too nervous to feel hungry, went upstairs to the otherwise deserted attic room and, with a feeling of delicious abandon, showered in the full knowledge that the body she was preparing would soon be open to a lover's touch.

Back in the dormitory she carefully anointed herself with

a perfumed oil before slipping on a loose gown to cover herself on her way through the house. She was then left only with brushing out her long raven hair to leave it wild and wanton before applying a gentle lip gloss to accentuate her already excited and provocative lips. It was then that Sheila found her. 'Good God, girl, you're behaving like a bitch on heat!'

Unmoved, Vanessa retorted, 'Funny you should say that. That's *exactly* how I feel.'

'I've been asking about him . . .' said Sheila portentously.

Vanessa turned to her, protesting. 'Stop it, Sheila! I'm a grown woman! Not some starry-eyed teenager going on a date. I know precisely what I'm doing *and* I know all I want to know about him!'

'I'm not so sure you do,' Sheila drawled.

Infuriated, Vanessa turned on her friend. 'Well if it turns out badly I promise I'll come to you so you can have the pleasure of telling me you told me so! Alright?'

Heaving the sigh of the misunderstood but well intentioned, Sheila rose to her feet and went off to leave Vanessa to herself. Ordinarily, Vanessa might have regretted her outburst and gone after her but at that moment felt it was pointless.

Vanessa knew that Sheila was afraid she was putting herself into danger without realising that that was, possibly, the most exciting element in the whole scenario. Looking at herself in the mirror she realised, perhaps for the first time in her life, what she had been missing. For too long she had been forced to be more aggressive than her male colleagues. Maybe that's what had finally cost her Andrew.

Maybe it was time to rest her mind and let her body out to play!

Pausing only to add a pair of high-heeled slingbacks to her outfit she took one last long hard look at herself. The thought occurred to her that if playtime was what he had in mind, she would be presenting him with the perfect toy!

Chapter Three

The hands on the clock had dragged themselves towards the magic hour with infuriating tardiness, giving Vanessa much unwanted time in which to question what she was doing and why. Rationally she knew that this melodramatic assignation made little sense but she could not find the will to resist its temptation.

Even as she approached the door of Room 15 at the appointed hour she was still unsure. Suppose he merely wanted to talk? Suppose she had allowed her own fantasies to hear promises that he had never intended? Was it destiny that brought her here or simply misunderstanding? There was only one certainty: whatever lay beyond that door – whether ecstatic fulfilment of a long-cherished fantasy or crushing humiliation – she knew that she had totally committed herself and there was now no going back.

Pressing down the ornate handle of the door she half expected difficulties – as if the Fates would intervene and she would again find it locked – but no. It opened easily on well-mannered hinges and Vanessa felt her body tightening into a knot of expectation as she saw the room was in almost total darkness, lit only by a single candle standing on a table. It was an ordinary enough candle yet she was drawn to it, as if its simple column of white topped by the brightly flaming light was of great magical significance. She might have then felt herself transported instantly into her dream except for the overpowering awareness that this was reality and no fantasy.

Closing the door, she leaned back against it as if seeking reassurance in its solidity. The single candle fell short of illuminating the shadows about the walls and she could see no one. Nevertheless she sensed that she was not alone.

Remembering she was to have come here naked, she slipped nervously out of her gown and bared herself as she sensed that somewhere, beyond the reach of the light, someone was watching her. Involuntarily, she felt herself begin to shake with an uncontrollable mixture of fearful apprehension and consuming excitement. Suddenly she knew she had not misunderstood. Her unseen watcher knew that what he was doing was exactly what she wanted.

Her instinct to call out was suddenly cut short when the sound of quietly insistent music began to play. This was not the wild music to which she had danced earlier, more a heartbeat which insinuated itself into her, pulsing through her body, urging her to follow her dream and live her fantasy.

Whatever lay ahead for her in the next few hours she knew that the music had signalled its beginning.

Conscious that every move she made could be seen as significant, she straightened herself away from the door and carefully and precisely placed the back of both hands flat against the small of her back.

This gesture, so familiar from her fantasy, caused a convulsive shudder of excitement to pass through her from head to toe, leaving in its thrilling wake a feeling of total liberation. She now had no need for pretence. She had come into this room for one purpose only and in so doing had surrendered herself completely to the will of a stranger. Suddenly she experienced the exhilarating release of the condemned in recognising the inexorable onward march of a process in which she was central, but over which she had no control.

It was this thought which gave Vanessa the courage to move forward towards the light.

The closer she came, the more the light filled her eyes until she found she could look nowhere else but into its intense heat. Later she would swear that she could feel it reaching out to caress her. She had never felt such total commitment to anything before in her life. Her head was spinning and the blood pounded in her ears, seeking control of every one of her impulses.

With an effort, she focused her mind enough to see, laid out before the candle holder, a strip of velvet which she knew was to be used to mask her eyes.

Reason made a vain attempt to break through. Was she truly about to blindfold herself in this darkened room with an unseen watcher lurking in the shadows? This plea for rationality went unheard in a body now devoting all its resources to its fleshly senses.

With trembling hands she reached out to the sinister strip of cloth and tied it about her eyes. Suddenly she was enveloped in a world of sensory isolation in which she could now hear nothing but the insistent pulse of the ritual music.

With hands once more placed to the small of her back, Vanessa was now acutely aware that she was the centre-piece of a ceremony into which she had fallen as if rehearsed. She waited in silence, her body coiled tight like a watch spring, until she sensed the warmth of a presence immediately behind her. When his hands finally touched her, she could neither control the gasp of surprise that escaped her lips nor the rasp of intaken breath that followed it.

Now he – for there was no doubt it was a man standing behind her – drew his hands first over her belly and then to her breasts. Swaying slightly, she let herself lean back towards him, feeling against her naked skin the softness of the silk shirt he wore, through which pulsed the heat and scent of his body.

When his hand sought out the firm points of her nipples, she strained her head back towards him, seeking perhaps the reassurance of his lips on hers. Instead he thrust his mouth deep into the junction of her throat and shoulder and there, with bared teeth, bit deep into her skin.

'Mmmmm! Yes!' she cried as his arms closed around her, bringing her into a tight embrace. Her fumbling hands found him hard and erect beneath the soft material of his trousers and she turned to kneel before him. Her hands sought the hardness for which her lips were hungering.

Even as she found him and drew him out towards her lips, she felt a soaring sense of having asserted herself – of having taken control.

Impatient to taste his fullness, she plunged him deep into her excited mouth, revelling in the choking, gagging sensation which only added to her excitement at having committed herself to pleasure. So urgent was her need to draw his essence, to know him fully, that she felt something akin to anger when she was lifted bodily and thrust back against the hard rim of the table. The momentary sense of loss was short lived when she felt him enter her. She cried out as he brought her instantly to orgasm. To demonstrate her own total surrender she threw her hands over her head and found the firm phallic base of the candlestick in her hands.

Grasping it as if tied to it, the table rocking and banging rhythmically with each of his thrusts, she heard herself screaming in ecstatic certainty of her second orgasm as he thrust deeper and more firmly into her.

When he began to pulse, and then spill, she wrapped her legs around his thrusting hips, trapping him tight against her own spread loins to beg his pleasure.

Desperate to reach her own climax she pounded against him blow for blow, pleading for every last drop of his seed. Suddenly she felt yet another wave of pleasure strike her with such force that she knew he had taken the last of her strength.

Bringing her hand forward over her head, she sought to embrace him, to sit up and press her ravaged body against him. Gently, he pushed her back to lie once more with her upper body on the table. Taking both her wrists in one hand, he pushed them firmly back to rest above her head.

Vanessa had never felt more vulnerable – more deliciously

helpless. She tried to control her breathing, tried to find words to express what had passed between them, but there was only emotion and she remained silent.

When he stood back she understood without being told that she should stay as she was. Her hands, now freed from his grasp, sought out the reassuring firmness of the candlestick once more and she lay there, aware that she was spread and totally exposed, but uncaring of anything other than that he should find her worthy of the moment.

When she felt the warm breath of his mouth between her thighs she lost control totally. She heard a muffled voice speak but could only understand one word. The word was worship.

'Yes!' she cried into the darkness. 'Worship me!' She screamed in ecstasy as his tongue sought out her most sensitive flesh and proceeded to drag it from its protective hood with the most excruciatingly tender teeth.

Tormented, she abandoned all as his expert probing pushed aside her outer lips and plunged deep into her, searing her senses. She writhed in pleasure, feeling as helpless as a rag doll as yet another wave convulsed her body. One strong hand rose from between his thighs and, reaching upward, lay between her swollen breasts to push her more firmly down onto the table. Groaning with protest and pleasure she cried out to him, 'I can't stand it!'

She felt herself lifted and turned onto her stomach – an action so unexpected and violent that she felt the candlestick slip from her grasp and crash to the floor. Now she had no thought for anything as she felt him, renewed and firm, once more penetrating deep inside her frantic body. The ecstatic waves became melded into one continuous whole as nothing in the world mattered but the bombardment of sensation he was creating.

She heard her own voice cursing him for the havoc he had wreaked in her along with the fear that she would never know anything like it again. Consciously she tried to focus her mind so that it might store up every precious grain of this moment of complete self-abandonment to be savoured again and again. But it was as impossible for her ravaged brain to concentrate as it would have been to juggle in an earthquake.

As she begged for pain to counterbalance the unbearable pleasure, he took her flailing arms and, in a secure one-handed grasp, pressed them high up her back. Then, seemingly without warning, it was over. His relentless pounding of her had ended and she felt herself released. Unable to stop herself, she slid from the table to her knees, hair hanging over her face, caring for nothing. Thinking he had moved away, she raised her hands to the blindfold and tore it from her eyes only to see that the falling candle had extinguished itself and left them both in darkness.

'Are you there?' she whispered. 'Say something.' But her plea went unheeded into the still blackness.

Scrambling to her feet she faced first one way and then the other in an attempt to sense his presence, but she could not. With hands outstretched she groped forward like a blind man, until she found a wall. Using it to guide her, she started moving sideways in search of the light switch she knew must be there. The wall seemed endless to her increasingly anxious touch and she found only a corner.

Breathless with frustration she called out again but got no answer.

Following the wall, she moved from the corner and then, with a sense of overwhelming relief, felt her hands on the panelling of a door. It was then only a moment before the doorframe guided her to the light switch.

Pressing it down in triumph, she found her eyes stung by the flood of light which showed the room to be eerily empty except for the table, the fallen candlestick and a stain of colour where she had left her gown. Feeling bereft and deserted, a surge of hurt resentment welled up for the man that had taken such pleasure and then fled with it like a thief.

'You bastard!' she shouted into the empty room which was no longer the place of mystery and magic her confused mind had made of it. Angry with him and herself, she picked up her gown and stepped into it, buttoned it, and then looked around for her shoes which she couldn't remember taking off.

One was lying off in one direction while the other was nowhere to be found. Obviously she had kicked them off in the throes of passion.

With one last speculation as to what might have happened to it she left the room, carrying her one remaining shoe as she padded up the grand staircase.

There was no one about to see her agitated progress until she reached the first floor. There, standing outside an open door, stood a smiling Steven Weir. She would have turned away to conceal her confusion but there was something about his stance that held her.

'Lost anything?' he asked and then, with slow deliberation, he held up the match of the shoe she held in her own hand.

For a stunned moment she stood rooted to the spot until realisation dawned on her. 'You?' she demanded.

Steven Weir nodded. 'Your Spaniard had to leave earlier this evening. I couldn't bear to think of you being disappointed.'

'You animal!' Vanessa yelled at him and followed her words with a badly aimed shoe which rattled harmlessly off the walls to roll at Steven Weir's feet. Infuriatingly unmoved, he bent to pick it up and again smiled in her direction.

'I think you are very beautiful,' he called to her.

'You already know what I think of you!' she yelled back at him before turning towards the stairs.

Pausing for neither breath nor thought, Vanessa rushed to the door of her shared room. It was only the thought of facing Sheila, let alone strangers, that gave her pause.

Turning away, her mind calming, she began to wonder what it was she was angry about. He had deceived her, of that there could be no doubt, but he certainly had not disappointed her.

All that had happened was that she had been taken by one stranger instead of another. The memory of what they had shared still burned deep within her loins and she was further calmed to realise the extent to which her needs had been anticipated and catered for.

Having defined her fantasy in his canvas, Steven Weir had then recreated it into a searing experience which, even now, she knew was branded onto her consciousness forever.

She was startled to realise her meandering mind and body had taken her back down the stairs where she again found herself standing before Steven Weir's door. With sudden resolution she went forward and threw it open.

The artist turned in surprise, his penetrating eyes narrowing with amusement as he saw who his visitor was.

'I've come for my shoes,' she told him defiantly.

Steven looked down at the shoes still in his hand and then slowly extended them towards her.

As he did so, Vanessa understood that it wasn't the shoes she had come for. Raising her fingers to the buttons which secured her gown, she held his gaze and, with slow deliberation, opened each one before shrugging free of it to stand naked before him. Then she murmured, 'But there's no hurry.'

Chapter Four

Vanessa woke slowly with a warm glow of contentment. Last night she had offered herself up to Steven with a boldness that came from the need to savour everything that had been missing from his initial savage taking of her – tenderness, the aftermath of caress and embrace, the things that, to her, made the sexual act complete. Steven had proved himself the lover she had sought and they had come to a gentle, blissful exhaustion before falling asleep in each other's arms.

As she lay in his loose embrace, she felt him stir and almost resented it – she wasn't quite ready to lose the closeness they shared at that moment. So when he murmured, 'Are you awake?' she grunted and was glad when he lay still and said no more. She needed time to think.

How to categorise this man? He had unhesitatingly pierced, directly and intimately, her sexual psyche, reducing her to the emotional being she had sworn never again to be in front of a man. For that reason, if no other, she needed time to prepare her defences. She felt it important that tenderness be established as a fundamental part of their relationship – if that was what they were going to have –

but there was another, more exciting, prospect that demanded consideration.

Did she really want to contain his vivid imagination and capacity to eroticise? Would it not be more exciting, just for once in her life, to declare no boundaries and let his imagination run riot to do what he would with her?

As these thoughts began to fire her loins, she was having increasing difficulty in containing a sexuality which had so recently emerged from hurt famine to riotous feasting.

When the arm which had been resting lightly across the roundness of her hips began to gently explore first her belly and then her breasts, she could no longer contain the contented groan that escaped her half-opened lips.

Though her blood quickened to his touch she felt no immediate urgency but instead, as she felt him firm against her, she eased herself sightly to allow him admission without acknowledgement. It was a simple, unpressured coupling, which so precisely matched her need. Even as he began to move deep inside her, it was not uncontrollable passion she felt, more a gratifying renewal.

How had this man come to know her so completely in so short a time? Her mind began to race as she appreciated that he was not only taking her body but piercing her soul, and there arose inside her an irrepressible need to match him surrender for surrender, followed swiftly by a compelling need to voice her commitment.

'Harder!' she demanded.

Like a stallion spurred deep in its flanks, he responded with a quick movement that forced her face deep into the pillows as he mounted her from behind and thrust more forcefully into her willing, open body.

'Yes!' she moaned, lifting her head and arching her body back to make her scream more plain. 'Fuck me!' she urged as he pounded into her.

The transition from a gentle exchange of pleasure into this dominating siege added spice to the fire and soon all attempts to rationalise were lost as they joined in a helter-skelter rush towards mutual orgasm.

The moment he had pulsed his last into her she drew herself off and turned towards him knowing that what they now shared could not be broken. 'How did you know?' she demanded, her breath hissing at him.

'You told me,' he said, 'First in the gallery, then in the class.'

'You saw your "Initiation" in me?' she asked as a small seed of doubt came into her mind.

He shook his head. 'I saw myself.' Seeing her eyes flicker with doubt, he went on, 'Or perhaps I should say a more perfect vision of what I would want to be.'

She searched his eyes for any sign of irony but found not a trace. 'You mean it?' she asked.

'I would defend you,' he said simply, as if making a confession.

'Against what?'

'Whatever beset you.'

'Against myself? I'm more afraid of myself than anyone else,' she murmured.

'Afraid of what? Of letting go? Don't be. You must trust me.'

'I don't know you well enough yet. Once given, my trust will be total.'

'Then I have to make sure I earn it, don't I?' he smiled.

Later that day they emerged from the bedroom with the uneasy feeling that they now had to face an unsympathetic world and so made their departure as swift as possible.

Sheila's reaction couldn't have been more marked if Vanessa had returned from the dead.

'You must have taken leave of your senses!' she told Vanessa – a hypothesis with which Vanessa happily agreed before packing the few things she had brought with her and joining Steven beside his curiously modest car. 'No limousine?' she asked as he helped her into a family saloon.

'Only in town,' he told her. 'Traffic terrifies me.'

They drove for a while in silence before he began to speak. 'I have wealth,' he began, 'for which I did nothing but get born to the right family. I cannot justify having it but on the other hand haven't the courage to reject it.'

Feeling a perverse need to defend him against himself she offered, 'But you have your painting.'

'My sole justification for living,' he said portentously. 'That is, until I found you.'

'You didn't "find" me,' she retorted, allowing her tone to be scathing. 'I crawled on my hands and knees and surrendered to you.'

He laughed outright. 'Not true,' he said. 'You may have gone on hands and knees but it wasn't to me. You surrendered to your fantasy.'

'What do you know about my fantasies?' she asked sharply.

'You forget,' he told her. 'We *share* them.'

Vanessa settled back and let the miles unwind beneath them with the comfortable feeling that this man exuded nothing but "white" energy and that she could trust him wherever he would lead. She already knew his imagination was boundless and she had discovered in herself a love of mystery and ritual. Mentally she gave herself over to him and found it tremendously exciting to know that this man could make of her whatever he wished.

'Do you like surprises?' he asked, breaking their comfortable silence.

'I *love* surprises!' she told him.

Then he let one long mile elapse with simply a smile, before adding, 'Then you'll like my studio.'

On first sight there was little out of the ordinary to be found in the substantial double-fronted Edwardian villa to which he brought her. It stood, four square, in a street of almost identical houses. Even when the front door was opened, the hallway – grand and semi-imposing – promised nothing unusual. The ground floor consisted of two sitting rooms on either side of the hallway and had been furnished some time ago with a hand that she suspected was not his. It was only as they mounted the curving staircase that the Edwardian portentousness began to fall away and she sensed his hand in the lighter colours and ambience they created.

The real surprise was left to last as they climbed from the second floor into a huge space that had been created out of the roof – one half of which had been all but replaced by a huge expanse of opaque glass that drenched the space in diffused light. The air was soaked in a stimulating aromatic mix of oil paints and linseed oil.

Moving around the studio space, Vanessa felt as if she had been transported from the dull light of London into another climate entirely. The exotic atmosphere was enhanced by the vibrant colours of the numerous canvases that were stacked around the room and hung from the walls.

Excitedly, Vanessa plunged herself into an orgy of visual stimulation that she found so rich, she didn't know where to look first. Steven left her to it and went into a gallery kitchen to make them some tea.

Vanessa's eyes greedily flicked from one canvas to the next. It was as if Steven had opened his diary and his innermost feelings to her, and she felt both privileged and empowered. It was only as her inflamed senses calmed that she was able to see the content of the pictures objectively.

Almost all depicted a similar foreboding ambience to the one he had given her. One lone figure was always centrally placed, surrounded by an aura of the unknown.

One painting in particular struck her the most. It was of an androgynous figure alone in a glade of tall trees through which the light fell, focusing on the wary vulnerability of the person at its centre. Vanessa found the confluence of light – the way in which he had almost succeeded in creating the illusion of a light 'clash', with one ray seemingly interfering in the progress of another – most stimulating. The light haze obscured the dark area of the forest beyond and Vanessa was reminded of her dream, not so much by what was depicted, but more by the clashing beams of sunlight which, to her eye, looked more like the diffuse light of candles than that of a summery sun.

Hearing the rattle of cups behind her she turned to see Steven coming from the kitchen with the promised tea. 'This one,' she told him, 'is particularly beautiful.'

'It's yours,' he replied as he set the tray down on a table ranged before a paint-splattered leather couch.

Guiltily she gushed out her disclaimer. 'Oh, I didn't mean you to think I was begging it!' she protested.

Steven looked up and for a moment seemed as if he was about to make some humorous retort, but instead he said simply. 'Let's have our tea.'

She sat next to him, cup and saucer in her hand, but made no attempt to drink as she scanned the walls once more. A question that surprised her came unbidden into her mind. 'Who was she?'

For one heart-stopping moment it seemed that Steven might prevaricate by asking inanely 'Who?' But when he saw the question was important to her, he smiled. 'The girl that modelled for me, you mean?'

Vanessa nodded. Seeing the pictures, no one could doubt the intensity with which they had been painted or fail to understand the passionate relationship which had given rise to them.

'Her name was Imogene,' he said as if that was a full and sufficient explanation.

'She obviously meant a great deal to you.'

'Yes,' he said in a carefully balanced voice. 'She did.'

'And . . .?'

'She died.'

The two syllables lay like lead for some moments before he went on, 'It was all some time ago now – three years, in fact.'

Vanessa could see the pain in his face and had to fight off an impulse to tell him it didn't matter, because it did. She could see instinctively how important Imogene had been to him and knew she would never rest until she found out how and why the girl had died.

In the face of his continuing silence she prompted him with a question. 'Was she ill?'

Steven shook his head. 'We'd had a fight about something – I can't even remember what. Imogene was, to say the least, a feisty girl. She was forever declaring that our relationship was all over and storming out, only to come back two days later and be more committed than ever.'

The silence was threatening to grow again as Vanessa spoke again, aware that she was perhaps being cruel. 'But not this time?'

Steven shook his head. 'Nobody knows for sure what happened. She took my car – a performance car which she had always said frightened her – and drove off. There was an accident – I can't bring myself to believe she did it deliberately – but anyway, the car crashed off the autoroute . . .'

'Autoroute?' interjected Vanessa.

Steven nodded. 'For some reason she'd crossed to France . . . it seems she just veered off the road, rolled down a steep slope and the whole thing just exploded. The only consolation I have is that she couldn't have known much about it.'

Aware that she had intruded into what was obviously a very painful period in his life, she could think of nothing to say and fell back on platitudes. 'I'm sorry,' she murmured. 'It must have been dreadful.'

Steven nodded. 'It was,' he said. 'Particularly since her friends blamed me for what happened.'

'That doesn't sound fair,' said Vanessa.

Steven smiled and stood up. 'It wasn't,' he said. 'But, as people keep telling me, life goes on.' He looked at her cup of tea which had now gone cold. 'Would you like something stronger than that?' he asked.

Only just realising that she still held her cup in her hands, Vanessa smiled. 'I like my tea cold,' she said and, as if to prove it, took a long drink. It tasted foul.

Steven meanwhile had walked across the studio and was now gazing at the picture of Imogene in the forest glade – the one she had already decided was her favourite. Rising to stand beside him, she asked, 'Do I look anything like her?'

Seemingly startled he turned to her. 'Why do you ask that?'

'Well, we never see her face. Not in any of them. Why is that?'

The question seemed to surprise Steven. 'I've never thought about it.' He was silent a moment before adding, 'I don't think I realised it until just now.'

'Well, do I?'

'What?'

'Do I look like her . . .?'

Steven shook his head. 'What you're really asking is am I looking for another Imogene in you? The answer is no.

You're quite different – both in appearance and temperament.'

Happy to find that his mood had lightened somewhat, she decided to tease him a little. 'So I wouldn't inspire you in the same way?'

'What "way" is that?' he asked.

'Naked victim,' she said flatly, with just a hint of challenge in her tone.

Steven turned to look directly at her, a light smile playing on the edge of his lips. 'Naked, certainly,' he said, 'but victim, no!'

Vanessa turned coquettishly away and, pretending to be giving his words full consideration, said, 'There's only one thing I have to know . . .'

'Which is?'

Eyes sparkling, she turned to him. 'If I'm to be naked before you for hours on end, I have to have your absolute promise that you won't fail to take full advantage.'

'It's the first rule of the Amalgamated Union of Daubers and Painters!' he told her.

'Really?' she asked. 'Does that mean you make love to all your models?'

'Only the girls,' he said, returning her banter.

Vanessa sighed. 'I do love a discriminating man,' she told him. Smiling, she added, 'Is that before or after posing?'

'Before, during *and* after. The true artiste is nothing if not dedicated.'

Feeling the pulse at her loins encouraging her towards outrage, Vanessa returned to the couch and sprawled herself indecently. 'Am I entitled to think of our present status as that of "before"?' she asked.

'You are,' he replied moving forward to stand directly before her.

'Then I'm ready to be tested,' she said, reaching her arms outward in open invitation.

As Steven sat next to her on the couch, Vanessa wrapped an arm about his neck and drew herself up into a kneeling position, her hungry lips closing on his.

The moment she sat astride him she felt his hardness and it took only the briefest of fumblings before he was freed and lodged inside her.

Astride him, engulfed in him, she tried to move slowly and deliberately, but soon the demands of her hungry body caused her to buck violently, as if to batter him. The words she had so often fantasised about, but dreaded to hear herself speak, came tumbling from her lips. 'Will I have to be tied?' she heard herself screech.

'Yes!'

'And screwed?'

'With all my strength!'

'Must I be forced to crawl and beg for your cock?'

'Yes, all of that and more!'

As the madness took her, she screamed. 'I want it all!'

Catching her mood, Steven rose, but only to bear her down onto the floorboards at their feet, the better to penetrate and pierce her.

Feeling herself helpless under him, delirious now with delight, she could only scream as she felt her lower back battered into the hardness beneath it as he uncompromisingly fucked her.

* * *

Vanessa had never felt entirely comfortable sharing a bathroom with a lover even though she enjoyed sharing the shower. The sheer wanton voluptuousness of abandoning her body to a lover's soapy caresses always stirred emotions that she suspected came from memories of childhood bathtimes – unquestioning trust, and the sheer bliss of being dried as a prelude to the warm, deep, totally trusting, sleep. The child of military parents who were forever on the move, she tended to grab at any kind of security.

The thoughts Steven stirred at this moment were of a quite different order but, regrettably, not reciprocated at that moment. It was with some disappointment that she dismissed him from the bathroom while she dried her hair.

Staring at her reflection in the mirror, she began to question her actions. Where had all this come from? It seemed to her that she had accepted everything that had happened at face value, that they had known each other for far longer than the intervening hours since their meeting. The coincidence of her unspoken fantasy with his canvas must have some deeper significance than mere chance. It was as if, in meeting him, her fantasies had found a focus – a thought which was only overshadowed by knowing that he had previously shared that same fantasy with another girl. Thoughtfully she considered that there was a great deal more to be known about the unfortunate Imogene than he had, so far, told her.

Thinking of this made her feel uneasy and she turned her mind to her own motives in so wholeheartedly committing herself to this interesting man.

With the instability brought about by her father's

profession she had never dared to do anything more than take each day at a time and had always been careful to lend little weight to future plans – experience had told her that things could change dramatically at very short notice. Dare she now think in terms of Destiny?

Her thoughts were interrupted by a loud knocking on the bathroom door. 'Come out!' Steven called as she switched off the drier. 'There's someone out here I want you to meet.'

'But I'm not dressed!' she protested.

'Use one of the dressing gowns.'

Slightly resenting the fact that her thoughts had been wrenched from titillating speculation to more practical considerations, Vanessa reached for a dressing gown and brushed out her hair, unprepared for the scrutiny of any of his friends. With some reluctance she finally went out into the studio, where she was just in time to see Steven handing a coffee to a petite, scrupulously dressed, very efficient-looking woman in her early forties.

'This is Roz,' Steven told her. 'My business manager.'

As the two women exchanged wary smiles and quick assessing scrutinies, Vanessa was relieved to feel no threat.

'I was just telling Steven that you might enjoy a few days in Paris,' Roz said once they had been introduced.

'Paris?' asked Vanessa, looking to Steven for an explanation.

'I wanted to keep it a surprise,' he said ruefully before turning to his business manager and adding, 'Vanessa tells me she loves surprises.'

'Don't we all?' drawled Roz, turning back to Steven.

'But you really should go. You know the French. They prefer doing business face to face – especially over lunch. Why not make it an event? What do you say, Vanessa?'

Vanessa shrugged noncommittally to cover the conflicting emotions that Roz's presence had aroused. There was something about the woman's brisk efficiency and her easy assumption that she could arrange everybody's life that grated on Vanessa. Was it simply that she was a woman in Steven's life who had obvious influence – and perhaps prior claim? Vanessa couldn't be sure but she suspected that sometime in the past Roz and Steven had been more than business acquaintances.

With relief, she heard Steven delivering a mild admonition. 'Roz, please remember that you're my *business* manager and not my social secretary.'

Smiling, Roz raised her hands in acknowledgement before rising to her feet. 'Sorry.' She smiled to them both in turn. 'Habit.' Turning to Steven she spoke again. 'I have to rush but please do let me know ASAP so I can let them know in Paris one way or the other.'

Vanessa stayed in her seat as Steven showed Roz out. 'She can be a bit heavy going at times,' he said when he returned. Then he smiled, obviously aware that Vanessa had been less than enraptured. 'But she's good at her job and keeps me on track.' When Vanessa remained silent he went on, 'What about Paris? It's a city I know well and there I could really "surprise" you.'

Inwardly Vanessa was confused. One part of her wanted to grab at anything Steven offered while another part whispered caution. She was reminded of the larger world outside, from which they had come together burdened with quite different experiences and responsibilities. Roz's short visit had heightened her awareness of just how little she knew of him. Their headlong rush into this passionate relationship now seemed to her to be more than a little foolhardy and in need of some reigning in.

'What about it?' Steven asked in the face of her continuing silence.

'I'm not sure . . .' she murmured guardedly.

'Of what? Paris is my second home and I can promise you an extraordinary time there.'

Vanessa smiled but still found herself unable to look at him.

'Is this that self-doubt thing you were talking about earlier?' he asked, kneeling close to her in his eagerness to reassure her. 'If it is then I can only repeat that you have to learn to trust me.'

Vanessa nodded. 'It's not you – it's me! You don't yet know the trouble I can make for myself. When I do decide to do something then it's without reservations. That frightens me a little.'

'You want some space?' Steven asked. 'Is that it? Some time to think things through and be sure you're not making a mistake?'

For the first time she felt able to look up and meet his eyes. As she looked at him she knew she would be lost if she tried to speak one word so, instead, she simply nodded.

Steven rose to his feet as if to demonstrate that he didn't want to pressure her unnecessarily. 'Tell you what we do,' he said. 'Let's start over.'

Startled, Vanessa found words. 'Start over?' she asked. 'What does that mean?'

'You go back to your place. Tonight I'll call and ask you to have dinner with me . . .' He broke off as she started to laugh. 'What's wrong with that?' he asked defensively.

'Too soon. Too quick,' she told him. 'We both know how the evening will end.'

'What then?' he demanded. 'A self-imposed purgatory apart?'

'I wouldn't put it quite so dramatically,' she offered, finding his urgent attentions pleasantly exciting and very flattering. Shrugging aside her instinctive urge to surrender she said simply, 'I think a period for reflection would do us both the world of good.'

'A period for reflection?' he laughed. 'Why don't you just trust me and give me this opportunity to really surprise you?'

Tempted, she hesitated. 'I've things to do,' she answered, sounding anything but convincing, even to herself. Steven was still not willing to believe she was entirely serious or beyond persuasion and reached out towards her but Vanessa avoided him neatly and headed for the bathroom to retrieve her clothes. 'Ring me from Paris,' she told him and was grateful that he wasn't pursuing her.

'Maybe,' he said allowing a deliberate teasing tone into his voice, as if still trying to entice her to change her mind.

Vanessa laughed as she firmly closed the bathroom door behind her.

Chapter Five

Vanessa realised her mistake the moment she returned to her apartment. There, lying in wait, were a hundred and one reminders of the smashed relationship that had launched her into what she still was trying to think of as a madcap interlude.

She knew little of Steven and he even less of her. They had somehow made an instant coupling of the body, mind and psyche, and it had all but overwhelmed them. Recent experience had taught her that she needed to guard against her own tendency to commit herself too soon.

Somewhere on her road to adulthood there had been implanted the notion that pleasure was something for which one paid in pain. Was it this long-sublimated masochism that had also driven her to seek sanctuary from her pleasure?

In an attempt to distract herself she started to make soup from a packet, believing that even though she had no appetite, she must surely be hungry. Looking down at the watery-looking result of her labours, she found she had neither hunger nor appetite and, without a second thought, tipped it directly into the waste disposal before hurrying to find the remains of the sadly depleted bottle of vodka.

As she sipped her drink, it occurred to her that all she was really doing was hiding. Separation from Steven had harvested no great insight into what she might do but had simply accentuated the nagging awareness that she ached for him.

She rose and stood for a long moment staring at the telephone, willing it to ring, knowing that if it was him then she would go to him.

It didn't ring and so she took this even greater burden of defeat with her to the bathroom where she started running a bath. As an infant she had been inseparable from a baby blanket which she refused to let her mother wash in fear that it might lose its magical qualities. Then, when she was five, her mother had extracted it from her grasp and she'd felt that something precious had been taken from her. Now, she found the closest approximation to the comfort it had given her was in the depths of a deep hot bath.

Her mother would never know to what unfathomable depths that incident had plunged Vanessa, nor would she ever be told of the loathing she harboured for the way in which her mother had treated her father. That solid upright man would have been astonished had he ever suspected the understanding knowledge Vanessa had harboured about him. She had seen a man respected by the regiment he commanded reduced to a quivering jelly by his domineering wife. How often had she wanted to take him by the shoulders and shake him until he understood it was alright to fight back and that his wife did not rule the world as she ruled the house. She now understood that he was the reason she had always sought out the strong assertive man as a lover –

everything her father had not been. In her own submissive willingness she saw the mirror of the mother she had come to despise and had, in childhood, determined never to emulate.

Vanessa lay in the bath until her skin started to wrinkle and then stepped from it and started to dry herself. She had barely finished when the telephone rang. Thinking it must be Steven, she decided, even as she hurried to answer, that she was ready to go with him to Paris – tonight, if he insisted.

'Hello?'

It was Sheila. 'OK,' she said in that tired tone she adopted when at the end of her patience, 'What are you using for bait?'

'Bait? What are you talking about?'

'When two of the most drop-dead gorgeous men in London are both in hot pursuit of you I have to consider that you probably know something the rest of us don't!'

'Sheila, could you slow down and tell me what you're talking about?'

'I'm talking about Steven Weir – remember him? That's the guy you've been fucking non-stop for the past twenty-four hours.'

Vanessa felt a feline grin spreading over her features and curled up on the couch, preparing herself for the pleasure of listening to her best friend consumed with jealousy.

'That's *one* drop-dead gorgeous. Who's the other?'

'The Count!' said Sheila. 'He doesn't have your number so has been calling me all day trying to get it. I lied. I told him you'd just moved and I didn't have your new number yet.'

Guiltily Vanessa remembered that the Count had been the Tantric teacher she had thought she was submitting to on that first night. Mention of him aroused unworthy thoughts which she had difficulty in keeping out of her voice. 'Why should he want my number?' she asked.

'Dear God!' yelled Sheila so forcibly down the line that Vanessa had to hold the telephone away from her ear. 'What do you think? That he wants to try and sell you double glazing? Grow up, girl. He's running around armed, dangerous and dripping testerone. Question is, do I give him your number and start another fiery blaze or not?'

Vanessa thought quickly. That this incredibly handsome man wanted to find her was flattering and, but for the past twenty-four hours with Steven, she might well have welcomed it, but right now . . . 'Please don't,' she urged Sheila. 'Tell him you haven't got my number.'

'Things are *that* good with Steven Weir, huh?' Sheila asked quietly.

'Pretty good.' Vanessa smiled.

'I hate you!' said Sheila with enough good humour not to be offensive before putting the phone down.

Vanessa sat for a long moment listening to the dialling tone before she broke the connection. Sheila's question had started a whole new train of thought for her. Things weren't just 'pretty good' with Steven, they were, she now understood, perfect.

She thought of their first meeting, when she hadn't known who he was but had realised immediately that whoever had painted the canvas had access to her innermost fantasies. Then there was the way she had totally abandoned herself to the first experience in the dance class and in an even more direct way later in that same room at midnight and then in his bedroom and again in his studio. Vanessa now appreciated that it was only her own self doubts that had been keeping her from him.

Fighting off a barely resistible urge to call him, she climbed into bed determined to try for obliterating sleep.

Sleep came easily enough but Vanessa found herself immediately ambushed by a series of highly charged dream images of such overpowering force that when she woke in the morning she was shocked to discover the full extent of her long-suppressed fantasies. It was an element of her emotional make-up that had long lurked in her subconscious which she had both resented and wanted at one and the same time.

It was for that reason that she hoped the responsibility would be taken from her by him calling her first. By mid-afternoon that hadn't happened and unable to think of anything powerful enough to distract herself, she finally dialled his number.

An unknown voice answered, 'Roz Colman's office.'

Vanessa was so startled that she almost hung up but then remembered Roz was his business manager. 'I'm sorry, I thought I was calling Steven Weir,' she told the girl.

'You were,' she replied. 'When Mr Weir is away his calls are automatically routed to us. May I ask who is calling?'

'It's just a friend . . .' she offered lamely.

'May I have your name? I have instructions to log all callers.'

Confused, Vanessa gave her name but added the rider that "it wasn't important . . ." before hanging up and feeling desolate. Obviously Steven had decided to go to Paris, probably thinking he wouldn't hear from her for several days – or maybe he didn't care one way or the other.

Feeling abandoned, Vanessa cursed herself for her own stupidity at not being honest with herself in the first place. Desperate for distraction, she went for a walk in the park and made herself miserable envying the canoodling lovers. Thinking of Steven in Paris she had convinced herself that he probably wasn't giving her a thought and so, when driven home by a sudden shower of rain, she let herself into her apartment determined that whatever happened she wasn't going to get into a downward spiral of depression.

When she saw the message light flashing on her answering machine it was almost as if she already knew that salvation was at hand.

And it was.

Steven had called her! 'Roz's office told me you'd called. I'm moving about quite a bit so I can't ask you to call me in Paris – besides I couldn't stand waiting so I'll call again in fifteen minutes.'

And he had.

'Still not back then? Never mind. I just hope you're calling to say you want to play games with me. Speak again in fifteen minutes.'

He'd also called twice more in the time she had been out. Vanessa sat by the phone with a warm glow of expectation about her. Steven was the man! Of that she was now totally certain. She didn't care what he wanted her to

68

do. His positive response was all she had needed.

The telephone had barely enough time to ring before she snatched it up. 'Steven?' she demanded.

'Finally!' he said. 'Well, what do you want to do . . .?'

'About what . . .?' she asked even though she knew perfectly well.

'You want me to surprise you in London or in Paris?'

'Paris, please,' she said, a rush of emotion so softening her voice that he had to ask her to repeat it.

'Tonight?' he asked. 'Roz will arrange everything – a car to take you to the airport, everything. And don't bother packing too much. Paris is a wonderful place to shop and I want to buy you everything.'

Her murmured protest that he didn't have to do that was instantly dismissed and he urged her to wait for Roz's call.

Hanging up, she stared down at the telephone and tried to tell herself that she could perfectly well afford to buy her own ticket to Paris but another voice told her to relax and let him take charge. That way provided greater excitement!

Armed only with a ticket and no address to go to in Paris, Vanessa stood in the Arrivals Hall at Charles de Gaulle and wondered what she would do if something had gone wrong. She had repeatedly told him of her love of surprise and thought he might be confusing that with the practice of practical jokes! She fervently hoped not.

When her bag did appear she snatched at it with hands suddenly lifeless. Praying that there was some sensible logic behind all this, she walked out of the baggage hall where a throng of people were pressing forward to greet the arriving passengers and, just as she had begun to think that Steven might be a dangerous lunatic who had maliciously forgotten about her, she noticed a man in chauffeur's uniform holding up a card with her name on it.

Identifying herself to the chauffeur brought about an immediate change in her confidence. The man took her bag and led the way out to where a Mercedes limousine was waiting.

Settling back into its cushioned interior, she mentally forgave the recently condemned Steven. Whatever else he might be, he certainly wasn't dull.

Winter was hardly the optimum time to be visiting Paris but when night fell, as it had, the season became an irrelevance. There always seemed to be a hum in the air – something that had already invaded her body and set it alight with expectation. As they got free of the frightening ring road and started bowling through streets alive with brightly-lit cafes and restaurants she was able to define that hum. It was excitement!

She had half expected the limousine to bring her to one of the more prestigious Parisian hotels – The George V, perhaps the Meurice, even the Lancaster – so she was a little puzzled when the limousine turned off the Place Pigalle, dominated as always by the garish Moulin Rouge neon, and stopped outside an anonymous hotel that looked closed and abandoned.

'Are you certain this is the address?' she asked of the driver.

The man shrugged expressively as only the French can do and continued to hold open the door for her.

Stepping out into the noise of the street, she felt her uncertainty flooding back. It was difficult to believe that Steven would bring her to such a shabby looking place – there had to be something else! She followed the driver as he carried her bag to the front door of the hotel where he stopped to ring a bell.

What kind of hotel, she wondered, was it that kept its front door locked at this early hour?

The door was opened by a smiling dark-skinned girl dressed in a traditional maid's uniform, complete with starched cap and apron.

'You are meeting M'sieur Steven?' the girl asked.

When she nodded the girl leaned forward to take the bag from the driver and invited her in.

As she stepped over the threshold she was immediately assailed by the hot-house atmosphere, laced with perfume, cigars and the heavy musky scent of mystery.

Steven had struck again!

The maid paused only to place her bag behind a counter before returning with another broad smile and indicating that she should follow her.

Led into a dining room where tables seemed to be arranged entirely around the walls in wooden pew-like enclosures, she followed the maid to one of the tables where Steven was rising to greet her.

Grinning broadly, he pulled her into a hugging embrace and whispered that he was overjoyed that she had come.

'Did you doubt it?' she asked.

'I've had moments . . .' he murmured before turning her to be greeted by an elegant woman in her late forties who was looking at her with the expert eye of a woman who knows women.

'Madame Gallia,' Steven said by way of introduction and as he spoke Vanessa felt her last remaining doubts draining away. She now knew for certain she had been brought to a bordello. She had always wondered what one would look like – even fantasised about being made captive in one – but the reality seemed much more prosaic than her fantasy. Madame Gallia's establishment – the locked front door aside – resembled more a middle-class restaurant than a house of wicked delight.

'We were just looking through Madame Gallia's book,' Steven said, turning a large volume towards her as she slid into the seat opposite him. She saw immediately that it was an album of smiling girls. In a restaurant, it might have been the menu.

Her brain reeling with thoughts of where the night might be leading, she felt her cheeks burning as she fought for composure. Now she was glad to be able to avoid the two pairs of eyes closely watching for her reaction as she leafed through the book of characters.

Some of the pictures were straightforward portraits and others were girls lounging naked over a couch or bed. It took her a moment to realise that each of the girls was shown both in family portrait style and then in seductive undress.

Still avoiding their eyes, she didn't even dare look up as Steven pushed a glass of champagne across the table towards her. Just what reaction did this man want of her? Did he want her to make a choice from among the girls, or was he merely trying to shock her?

For the moment she wasn't sure what her true reaction was. She was daunted by knowing that if she said anything she might find herself in a situation where pride would demand she followed through. But to what conclusion?

Madame Gallia finally forced her to look up. 'You find my girls attractive?' she asked.

Desperately searching for a neutral pleasantry she could finally only manage, 'Very nice,' and hated herself for the nervous tremolo that had sneaked into her voice.

'Champagne alright?' asked Steven in an amused tone which she instinctively resented.

Inclined to give him a glaring, challenging look she suddenly realised she had been here before. This was a repeat of the scenario with her shoe! Immediately she relaxed. The pattern was suddenly transparently clear to her. First disconcert her, let her imagine the worst and then comfortably, skilfully, reduce it to proportions she could handle!

Lifting the champagne, she spread her lips into her brightest smile, offered her glass to him in toast and, in the sweetest possible voice, murmured, 'Bastard.'

Steven smiled back but Madame Gallia exploded with Gallic indignation. 'Bâtard?' she cried. 'Non! M'sieur is a gentleman!'

Ignoring Madame Gallia's pursed-lipped disapproval, she smiled again at Steven. 'Do you come here often?' she asked him.

Steven leaned forward, nodding. 'Don't you think the ambience is stimulating?' he asked.

Her smile now sugary, she agreed. 'It certainly is. I'm

73

rarely stimulated to thoughts of murder.'

Answering her challenging stare with a stone-walling one of his own, he made it clear that he was not going to be the first to look away. Vanessa, equally determined to hold the gaze, was only vaguely aware that a girl had come to stand at the end of the table.

Glad of an excuse to break the locked glances, she looked up to see a tall smiling blonde who was well groomed and quite attractive – in this light at least, she thought to herself.

Madame Gallia addressed the girl. 'Ah, Michelle, perhaps you would like to show our guests to their room?'

Unable to contain her shock, she now glared openly at Steven. 'We're staying here?' she asked.

Steven was already rising. 'I thought it would make a change,' he said, reaching out a hand towards her.

Stunned into silence, Vanessa followed Michelle as she led the way to a lift which would have been a squeeze for two but was positively intimate with three.

'Are you mad?' she whispered to Steven as the ancient machine protested its way upwards.

'We won't be eating here,' he told her, as if he imagined that to be her only concern.

'What *are* we going to do here?' she asked, and was infuriated when the elevator groaned to a bumpy halt and Michelle opened the door, releasing Steven from the need to answer.

The upper hallway was narrow, hung with velvet-and-gilt-framed pictures depicting overweight naked ladies. More worrying to her was that the floorboards creaked under her feet with every step she took.

Michelle led them into a surprisingly spacious and well-furnished suite of rooms, seemingly intent on giving them a conducted tour of the facilities.

Ignoring this, she turned to Steven. 'This place is a fire trap!' she seethed.

Bemused, Steven looked around as if considering a point that had never previously occurred to him. 'I suppose it is,' he said finally, then murmured, 'But then fire is the least of the dreadful things that could happen to a girl in this house.'

Michelle was standing before them offering a key on a phallic key ring. 'Will you require anything immediately?' she asked, carefully directing the question solely at Steven.

'Not *immediately*,' Steven replied with heavy emphasis.

Michelle dazzled a smile on them both and made for the door where she turned and told them she would see them later.

'This is a brothel!' Vanessa said the moment Michelle was gone.

'Dear me,' sighed Steven, 'first it's a fire trap, now a brothel . . . Can it be that you don't like it here?'

'I might like it better if I knew why I've been brought here!'

Steven spread his hands as he walked into the bedroom where she saw a magnificent four-poster bed, dressed over in fine embroidered silken hangings.

'But I told you – for the ambience. You said you enjoyed a surprise, did you not? Don't you find this place fascinating? Just imagine the raw sex these walls must have absorbed.' Moving towards the bed he sat on it and gazed into the overhead panel. 'Have you noticed the mirrored canopy?' he asked in languid tones.

Suddenly struck by the thought that she was reacting in precisely the manner he had planned, she forced herself to change her attitude. He was not going to have it all his own way, she thought. It takes two to play games and, though a late starter, she was now determined to catch up – fast.

'Well,' Vanessa said as she made for the open door of the bathroom, 'I suppose I'd better shower and get changed. I trust the clothes I brought with me will be suitable?'

'For what?' asked an amused Steven.

'For joining the other girls downstairs. That's why you brought me here, isn't it? To show me what a whore has to do?'

Overjoyed to see her change of tack had thrown him completely off balance, she continued, 'I'm only sorry I didn't bring any suitable photographs for Madame Gallia's book.' She just managed to slam the door shut before the protesting Steven could reach it.

Leaning back on the door she listened to him through the sturdy woodwork. 'I didn't bring you here for anyone else but me,' he was saying.

'Pity,' she called back. 'As you said, it would make a change and Madame Gallia might even give you a cut rate on the room – that is, if I work really hard!'

'Now you're being silly!' Steven called.

She turned the water full force on the magnificently ancient shower and was rewarded with a downward deluge of monsoon proportions which satisfyingly isolated her from Steven's further protests.

Naked under the downpour Vanessa revelled in the knowledge that she now had *him* off balance.

Steven had awakened in her the desire to search well beyond the boundaries of conventional behaviour and, in retrospect, had made the treacherous Andrew seem tame by comparison. Steven had removed a boring lump from her life and appeared to be replacing it with an unbounded source of surprise and adventure. With life seemingly, and suddenly, filled with infinite delight, Vanessa was thrilled to find herself willing to accept whatever surprises Steven had in mind. But she was equally determined not to let him know that too quickly!

As she stepped out of the shower cabinet and wrapped herself in the meticulously clean towels provided, she felt sure the surge in her blood was not entirely due to the stimulating shower – something much deeper had seeped into her body. Brushing out her hair, she imagined she could see a new personality emerging. She felt totally confident with this man. There was an undeniable thrill in knowing that he had brought her to lodge in a superior brothel and that she, unfazed, was free to enjoy it! It was extremely arousing to contemplate herself with a partner who could be so unpredictable, yet reassuring to know that he was also concerned and protective. As she opened the locked door, she felt ready to match him thrust for parry but instead, to her excruciating disappointment, she found the bedroom and the room beyond it empty.

What was he up to now? What was she to do? Suddenly

the quiet satisfaction of having been brought, under protection, to a brothel was gone. Instead she was faced with a quandary. Should she passively wait in the room until he appeared to explain his absence or should she boldly assume he was downstairs in the bar waiting for her?

Had this been any ordinary establishment she wouldn't have hesitated to dress and go in search of him. In this place, however, there lay a minefield of potential embarrassments and misunderstandings.

Suddenly she had the answer. All she had to do was consider what he might expect her to do and then do the opposite!

Going to her bag she discovered that someone – Steven? – had already unpacked it.

Opening a closet door, she found the few outfits she had brought with her hanging neatly on display. Winding herself into a red velvet wraparound dress she'd bought from Ungaro two seasons ago, she couldn't help but remember that her main reason for buying it was knowing how easily she could be stripped of it when the occasion arose. It was a facility that had completely passed the notice of boring Andrew but one, she was sure, would not long go unnoticed by Steven.

With that thought thrilling her, she slipped her feet into a pair of black velvet Manolo mules and went in search of the lift.

The time-expired machine responded to her third press of the O button and started downwards. It got as far as the next floor where it bounced to a halt. Through the latticed ironwork door, Vanessa saw a somewhat overweight florid-faced man staring in at her as if she were an animal on exhibit.

Having fully assessed her, he slid open the door and brought his immense bulk into the already confined space and, with alarm, she felt the floor of the lift shift unsteadily like a mounted weighing machine.

She was startled, and even a little shocked, to realise that the man's strained fly front was gaping open.

Looking directly ahead, trying to ignore the unmistakable essence of a man who had recently availed himself of the house facilities, she understood that they weren't moving. Obviously the lift had no memory of her previous button pressing instructions and, to make matters worse, she realised that the bulky man was grinning at her with complacent boldness.

'*Wie heißt du*?' he enquired.

'Sorry?'

'Your name is?' he asked. 'Perhaps you have newly come?'

Forced now to look at him, she realised that she couldn't reach for the control button without asking him to move. Not sure whether she liked being mistaken for one of the house girls, she smiled. 'Odette,' she replied with visions of an old black-and-white movie she had once seen playing in her head.

'Odette?' He seemed to be savouring the name, obviously committing it to memory for future use. '*Ist schön!*'

'Excuse me,' she said. 'But the lift isn't going anywhere unless we press the button.'

The man's belly rose and fell as from somewhere deep inside his weight-ridden flesh came a rumble of laughter. 'And where does it *wish* to go?' he asked.

Losing patience, she reached out and forced him to one side as her fingers pressed the downward buttons.

'*Schade*,' he said as the machine once more stirred itself from lethargy.

Aware that he was still lubriciously studying her, she spoke again. 'Also your flies are open,' she told him.

'*Bitte*?'

'Your flies.' When he still looked puzzled, she impulsively reached a hand under the balcony of his protruding belly and, taking hold of the material of his trousers in one hand, tautened it as she found the zip and closed it herself!

Otto, as she had mentally named him, eyes bulging and face flushed to the colour of her dress, showed signs of approaching orgasm and murmured, '*Ja, mein Gott, bitte . . .*' Reaching out, he tried to grab her hand and return it to his errant fly.

With sudden embarrassment Vanessa realised that Otto probably hadn't seen his trouser fly in years and had misunderstood her helpful assistance.

With relief the lift bumped to a halt on the ground floor and she hastily tore her hand from the German's fleshy grasp and ripped open the ironwork door.

Otto pursued her from the lift as if anxious to prevent her escape. 'Please,' he was gasping. 'I am a rich man, yes? We make each other happy, yes?'

She was about to turn on him in no uncertain terms when

she caught sight of Steven rising from one of the booths and coming towards her.

'You look delicious,' he said, planting a proprietorial kiss on her cheek as Otto let his disappointment at Steven's intrusion show by letting out a long and loud exasperated sigh.

Pausing only to give Otto a puzzled look, Steven steered Vanessa away from the disappointed German. 'We're late,' he said.

'For what?'

'We're expected elsewhere.' he replied, and turned her towards the hotel's locked front door where she found Michelle looking expectantly ready to leave. Turning to Steven, she asked, 'Is Michelle coming with us?'

Steven smiled confidently. 'She's a surprise for later.'

Still mulling over what he might have in mind and debating with herself whether or not she could consider Michelle a surprise, Vanessa found herself being hustled out onto the street where the same uniformed chauffeur that had brought her from the airport sprang forward to open the car's rear doors for them.

Settling into the limousine's capacious rear seat Vanessa knew she was now committed to what lay ahead in the yet to be unfolded drama of the night. Whatever it was she was on her way!

Chapter Six

Sitting in the rear of the limousine, Vanessa was beset with a confusing mix of emotions. Starting out as they had from a brothel in the company of a prostitute, she could only conclude that she was being borne relentlessly towards another new experience. She found that worrying but, undoubtedly, exciting. Steven had mentioned 'a surprise' and, when she thought of the surprises he had previously engineered, she felt she should prepare herself for something far more radical. But what?

She was looking at Steven's profile when he suddenly turned to her. 'Here,' he said. 'You'll need this.' He was holding a black velvet cat mask of the kind she associated with pantomime highwaymen, reviving memories of the blindfold she had worn at Holly Hill House when he had anonymously seduced her. At least this one would allow her to see what was coming!

Vanessa had to turn slightly sideways so that he could tie the mask's silk ribbons about her head. As his gentle hands worked she thought she saw an opportunity to glean a little more information about the night ahead. 'Why do I need this?'

'We're going to a costume party,' he said.

'Then where's your outfit?' she asked.

Steven, turning her to him, smiled. 'I'm going as me,' he said and then laid an infuriatingly patronising finger to her lips. 'No more questions.' When a flicker of resentment crossed her face, he added lightly, 'Besides I don't want to spoil the surprise.'

With her questions still unanswered, she turned back and, despite her resentment at his casual assumption that she would acquiesce in anything he might care to impose on her, she felt her loins starting to tingle as if they, at least, had made up their mind to enjoy themselves. Added to this, it was also more than a little intoxicating to feel out of control for once in her life.

The limousine finally drew to a halt in an anonymous street somewhere close to Versailles. Vanessa could see an iron gate set into a high and dense hedge which completely prevented any view of whatever might lie behind it.

Steven asked the two girls to stay in the car while he got out to press a bell set to one side of the gate. As he waited for a response, he turned and smiled reassuringly at them.

Seeing this as possibly her one chance to prepare herself for what might be to come, she turned to Michelle. 'Do you know this place?'

Michelle nodded. 'It is a famous place.' She smiled. 'Very expensive,' she added, as if that was all a girl needed to know.

'But *what* is it? I mean what goes on here?'

'Ah!' Michelle said. 'We must go!'

Looking to Steven, Vanessa saw that he was holding

open the iron gate and waving them forward. An eager Michelle was halfway out of the car before she followed.

Beyond the gate was a short path leading to a darkened, apparently silent, building and yet another equally solid door which, she noticed, was monitored by a closed circuit TV camera.

This second door was opened by an elegantly dressed woman who greeted Steven familiarly before inviting them to step into a small, thankfully warm, lobby. Once again, Vanessa noted that they were under the scrutiny of closed-circuit cameras. Such surveillance by persons unknown always made her feel uncomfortable and she was glad that her mask made her anonymous.

As Steven tended to the lengthy business of signing them in, she was even more grateful for the disguise since it covered the flush of excitement she felt at seeing a man, naked but for a few leather straps about his torso, come out of a door and cross nonchalantly to another. As the door opened she heard a swell of music, the sound of many subdued voices and caught a glimpse of a naked woman sitting on a stool sipping at a cocktail while an equally naked man knelt worshipping between her open thighs.

Still bemused by what she had just seen, Vanessa was only vaguely aware that Steven had returned and had been saying something to her. Apologising for her inattention, she asked him to repeat himself.

Taking her hands he said, 'I asked if you wanted to go to the bar or if you would like to eat first. The food here is excellent.'

With the word 'first' sounding particularly ominous to

her fervent brain, she murmured that she was ready to eat. Immediately they were led into the most extraordinary restaurant she had ever seen.

The walls and ceiling were totally covered with black mirrors pierced by tiny pinpoints of light. The effect was like walking into an eerily boundless space beneath a brilliant starry sky. The ambience only added to her feeling that she had wandered onto another planet.

They were greeted by a tall dark maître d', who led them to one of the banquettes which lined the walls. There, feeling as if she had found sanctuary in a mad world, she slid behind the solid table.

Still trying to make some connective sense between the exotic happenings glimpsed in the bar and the subdued, sophisticated atmosphere of the restaurant, she found the words on the menu swimming before her eyes and refusing to be read.

'Suppose we start with a light vegetable soup then continue with the lobster and truffles?' Steven was asking. 'An aperitif of champagne and a dry white Burgundy with the lobster, I think. How does that sound?'

Having caught the approach of a curious luminescence swaying towards them out of the darkened interior, Vanessa's mind was busily engaged elsewhere, so she simply nodded. The luminescent strip finally turned out to be the fly front of a coal black waiter who had come to take their orders. Aware that she was staring fixedly at the young man's crotch, she looked up to see the waiter almost arrogant in his pride at finding his groin so fascinating to her. Averting her eyes, and her thoughts, she found herself face to face with a smiling Steven who seemed to be reading her mind.

'It's so the lady guests can more easily find him in the dark.'

'Find him?' Vanessa asked, fearing that she already knew the answer which Michelle enthusiastically provided.

'His cock,' said Michelle. 'Here a woman's word is law and she may indulge in anything she wishes. Even the waiters.'

This information sent her thoughts reeling even more. A few days ago she would have considered herself a fairly successful career woman, at ease and able to cope with the world and almost anything it could throw at her. Steven had succeeded in placing her in situations where her own self-assessment was thrown into serious doubt.

With a start she realised Steven was speaking. 'In this club,' he was saying, 'the woman is supreme. It's one of the few places in the world where she decides everything. No man can touch her unless she wants him to – no matter what provocation she may choose to impose. I thought it would make a change for you,' he added helpfully.

To aid the digestion of this information, Vanessa reached for the glass of champagne which was now standing before her and took a large gulp as Michelle continued, 'You could walk naked through the bar and no man would dare touch you. If he did he would be banned from the premises for life.'

The arrival of the soup brought a welcome respite from the thoughts flooding her mind. Steven had done it again! He, who so far had been assertive and offered her no choice, had brought her to a place where apparently she could do anything she wished totally free from the need to have any escort's permission. Being suddenly presented with the limitless opportunity to indulge her fantasies, she found herself equally oppressed by the thought that she might be expected to actually carry them out. Once again she felt as she had when looking at Madame Gallia's 'menu' of opportunities and not knowing what to do with them!

Her disquiet at her own unpreparedness for this situation was heightened when her eyes were riveted by a most astonishing creature.

'Creature' was the only word to describe the tall, lissom black girl who seemed the very incarnation of self-confident beauty. A quality which Vanessa, at that moment, felt she sorely lacked.

Wearing a dress fitted so tightly it might have been an outer layer of her ebony skin, the girl now stood calmly aloof, waiting for her escort to catch up with her. No man could expect to be noticed in the company of such a woman and Vanessa didn't register him as she watched them move out of sight to one of the other tables.

Hearing Steven utter an appreciative oath she turned to see he had reacted to the girl's dramatic appearance in exactly the same way as herself.

The girl's beauty undoubtedly transcended mere gender. She was fire in the loins of both men and women alike.

Curiously her own reaction was not jealousy or resentment at his instant lust for another woman, but challenge.

'So what do you intend to do with me?' Vanessa asked.

'Nothing,' said Steven. 'Nothing you don't want to do.'

Noting that the corollary of his words was '*anything* she *wanted* to do', she suddenly remembered something her mother had once told her. Rationing, having starved her mother – along with every other child in Britain – of sugar, she had celebrated the end of sweet rationing with an orgiastic binge of chocolate that had left her reeling with nausea for weeks afterwards. It was only now, sitting in this exclusive Parisian club, she understood how her mother had felt. Liberation, she decided, could be as oppressive as starvation.

These thoughts occupied her throughout the rest of the meal, until she was once more aware of the approach of the luminescently striped trousers of the beautiful waiter. When Steven enquired what she would like for dessert it was as if he was provoking her to further temptation. Then she heard Michelle speaking words that might have been stolen from her own mind. 'I know what I want,' said the French girl, and Vanessa could only watch hypnotised as she saw Michelle's hand reach out to lay flat on the young waiter's groin.

Excited by Michelle's presumption, Vanessa saw the waiter thrust himself forward as the professional, showing her expertise, unzipped him before reaching in to produce the most unreal erect penis she had ever seen.

Already prodigiously proportioned it became even more swollen as Michelle caressed it.

Steven chuckled encouragement to Michelle as her lips delicately encompassed the young man's organ, before swooping downward in a determined, but foolhardy attempt to swallow him whole.

A very American voice intruded to say, 'Go for it, girl!' Looking up, Vanessa saw the visionary black girl standing over their table watching Michelle fellate the waiter with brilliant black eyes. When the woman's gaze momentarily rested on her, Vanessa felt as if she had been struck with lightning. 'Your wife?' the black beauty asked of Steven.

'Just a friend.'

'Hi,' said the girl, extending a hand to Steven. 'My name's Grace. Mind if I stay and watch the action?'

When Steven moved slightly to allow Grace to slide onto the banquette next to him, Vanessa found herself suddenly needing space. 'I must go to the Ladies' room,' she told him, and, feeling confused for no reason she could immediately identify, she blundered her way past Steven and the now seated Grace.

In the Ladies' room she locked herself into one of the cabinets and tried to restore some calm to her racing mind. She felt herself abandoned in a stormy sea. She had never dreamt that the first time she would ever see a woman fellate another man would be in the semi-public arena of a restaurant. It was an experience, she assured herself, that would have disturbed the most jaded and experienced woman.

Finally resolved to avoid Steven's challenge with as much dignity as possible, she determined to ask to be taken back to the hotel.

Even as the thought occurred to her she realised that it was nothing short of ludicrous to ask to leave an orgy only to be returned to a brothel!

'Damn him!' she muttered, only realising she had spoken

aloud when an answering voice called from the other side of the door.

'Damn who?' asked the voice she recognised as that of the American girl, Grace.

Vanessa's embarrassment at being overheard caused her to hesitate a moment before she slid back the bolt and opened the door to see Grace smiling at her. 'Hi, pussycat! Why the mask? You famous or something?'

Feeling suddenly foolish she replied, 'No. I was told I was going to fancy-dress party.'

'Interesting. When does it come off? Midnight?'

'Now if you like.'

'Hey, I'm the last person to come between someone and their fantasies. Who were you "damning" in there? Your guy?'

'No. I'm just a little confused. It's my first time here.'

Grace nodded and turned to a mirror where she needlessly patted her immaculately dressed hair. 'Mine too,' she said. 'Real bitch, isn't it? I mean we girls have to spend most of the time watching our arses and then suddenly find ourselves let loose in a candy store.'

Grace's words so precisely matched her own thoughts that she felt an immediate affinity with the girl. 'The trouble is I don't know what I want to do,' Vanessa murmured.

Grace focused her brilliantly sparkling eyes on her. 'Well, isn't that the point? Here a woman can do anything she wants to do.'

'So they keep telling me.'

Grace's laugh came from somewhere deep down and

dirty. 'Hey, girl, this may turn out to be the best opportunity you'll ever have.' Grace turned from the mirror to look directly at her. 'What a woman needs in a situation like this is a friend who knows how to play the game, OK?'

'Are you volunteering?' Vanessa chuckled.

Grace's shrug was expressive. 'If that's what you want.'

'But you said this was your first time too!'

'My first time *here*. I've been "here" at other times and other places, believe me. You want a friendly hand? Here's mine.'

Grace extended a hand and Vanessa found that, as she took it, she felt a surge of renewed strength flowing into her. 'You must think me pathetic.' She smiled.

Grace shook her head. 'Temptation can make cowards of us all. If you're nervous imagine how all those men out there must feel.' Grace broke off into another of her laughs. 'They're at our mercy, girl. Let's go bite ourselves off a few prime chunks!'

Emerging from the Ladies', Vanessa had intended to tell Steven that she was going off with Grace to explore. When she saw him in intense conversation with Michelle she decided not to bother and followed Grace into the daunting depths of the bar.

All worries about Steven ended as they came into the bar. Unlike the quiet sophisticated atmosphere in the restaurant, here all was loud voices and frenetic activity, much like any other cocktail lounge – except for an intriguing surplus of men.

The appearance of the two newcomers brought a flattering amount of interest and, not for the first time, she suspected that buried deep inside herself lived an exhibitionist dying to be let out. The men, while intensely interested in them, lived up to the club's reputation and made no attempt to approach or speak directly to them.

The bar was crowded and dimly lit so there was little opportunity to differentiate between one face and another as Grace led her ever deeper into its depths, but there was one area of isolated activity which immediately took her eye.

A tall, totally naked girl, slim to the point of androgyny, was dancing on a tiny circular glass dais, which, lit from underneath, made her weird gyrations even more dramatic looking. The girl had a mane of long blonde hair which she used to 'whip' across the faces of the eager men who crowded round the raised dais. There was something unearthly about the girl – as if being naked before so many lusting men was a matter of complete indifference to her.

'See that?' asked Grace. 'How many chances would a girl have to do something like that without fear of rape?'

Watching the faces of the men, Vanessa saw repressed raw lust and wondered at the rules that could hold it in check. If the barriers were ever breached she could see how dangerous this game could be. Maybe, she thought, that was the point. The real game was to play provocation to its limit to see which of the women could cause a man to risk losing his privileged place in the club.

Despite a lifetime's conditioning to think otherwise, she could see how such a game could be thrilling. Because of the rules laid down by the club a woman gambled less here in being extremely provocative, than she would in the outside world.

Maybe, she decided, this is how things should really be. Outside it was the men who gambled the least in a display of sexuality while here all that was reversed in favour of the female.

'Do you think she's beautiful?' asked a purring voice beside her.

Startled, Vanessa looked round to see an elegantly attractive woman in her fifties smiling at her. She looked vaguely familiar but Vanessa's mind, so full of new sights, sounds and experiences, could not place her. She noticed that Grace had disappeared somewhere into the crowd. Looking back to the woman, she found her still patiently awaiting an answer. 'Yes. She is,' she murmured out of politeness.

'Her name is Sylvie and she belongs to me. She's Dutch and barely half trained but very amusing.' The woman smiled. 'My name is Helge. I feel you and I should have met many years ago.'

Troubled by this unexpected intimacy, and the uneasy feeling that she should have known her, she took the woman's offered hand. 'My name is—' Vanessa started, but the woman interrupted.

'I know your name,' she said portentously. 'Your *spiritual* name.'

'Really?' she asked, casting a slightly uneasy look around for Grace.

The woman, unfazed, went on. 'I saw you with Steven Weir – have you known him long?'

94

Startled, Vanessa turned her attention back to the still smiling woman. 'No. Not long, actually.'

'A most interesting man,' said Helge with a tone that hinted that she didn't entirely approve of him. Then with another dazzling smile, she asked, 'Would you like to meet my little friend, Sylvie?'

Vanessa found herself growing increasingly uncomfortable at this woman's close presence and sought to excuse herself. 'Well, no. I seem to have lost sight of my own friend for the moment and think I should go and find her.'

'Please,' Helge said, ignoring her mild excuse. With the slightest of gestures, she summoned the naked Sylvie to join them. The raised dais meant that Sylvie, open-mouthed and seemingly anxious to please Helge, loomed over them, bringing her pubis level with their eyes. She knelt down to hear what Helge wanted to say.

'Sylvie, my dear, don't you find our lovely new friend reminds you of someone?'

Sylvie's blue eyes opened wide as she turned to stare at Vanessa, who was even more embarrassed when the kneeling girl took up her hand, not to shake it, but to kiss it!

Bewildered by this intimacy, she pulled back her hand and murmured, 'I'm so sorry, but you seem to have mistaken me for someone else.' Then she pushed through the surrounding circle of admiring men and blundered into the area behind the bar. Here the lighting was even dimmer and, from the darkness, she heard murmurs of endearment mixed with urgent entreaties rising above the background of subdued music. As Vanessa's eyes became adjusted to the low light level she was astonished to see a woman stretched backwards across a platform-like table, her legs dangling from one end between which stood a man energetically fucking her. Two other men stood either side of the prostrate woman kissing her breasts and suckling her nipples, while her mouth sought out their cocks, first favouring one and then the other.

Suddenly Vanessa became aware of a man openly staring at her while he breathlessly manipulated the erection that stood out from his opened trouser front. Her instinctive reaction was to avoid his gaze until she remembered that here the woman ruled, and decided this was as good a time as any to test the rule. Deliberately holding his gaze, she moved her eyes coldly downwards to watch what he was doing. When he turned away, hiding himself, she felt a surge of triumph.

She hadn't backed down – he had!

It was then she heard Grace shouting, 'Suck it, bitch!'

Locating the source of the sound, she found the young woman, dress hiked up, thighs spread wide, kneeling over the face of a man who was, it seemed, desperately fighting for air as Grace ruthlessly bore down on him.

Her astonishment at seeing her newfound friend so completely abandoning her sophisticated poise drew her forward until she could even hear Grace's murmured threats to the man. 'Use your tongue, bitch! Get right in there! If I don't come in thirty seconds I'm going to beat the shit out of you!' Looking up, Grace saw Vanessa staring at her and her fevered expression broke into a relaxed broad smile even as she continued to torment the man. 'Just letting off a little pressure,' she said conversationally. 'I've been a virgin since I was thirteen.'

Unaccountably, Vanessa found herself able to continue the conversation as if nothing untoward were happening. '*Since* you were thirteen?' she asked. 'What does that mean?'

'I was raped. Since then I haven't let a man inside me.' Then as the man tried to come up for air, Grace reverted to her Bitch Goddess persona. 'No, you don't. You gotta pay your dues. Do it or I'll whip your arse!'

Grace's cries had attracted an admiring audience but Vanessa was surprised to find a man kneeling at her feet and pleading in the manner of a begging dog, complete with soulful eyes and raised 'paws'.

It was then that a transformed Michelle appeared at her side. Vanessa was still taking in the fetishistic leather costume as Michelle spoke, 'Steven sent me to look for you,' she said. 'It's nearly time.'

'Time for what?' she asked as she registered that Michelle's blatantly erotic costume had patches cut out of the torso through which thrust her naked breasts.

'The pageant.'

'What pageant?' she asked, but got no answer since the man who had so recently been begging her had switched his pleas to Michelle.

'Mistress!' he was crying. 'Please . . .'

Michelle produced a whip. 'Excuse me a moment,' she said before pushing the man down onto all fours and delivering several searing lashes across his rear.

Having taken toll of the man, Michelle smiled again at

her. 'Come,' she said. 'Steven is waiting.'

With one last bewildered look at Grace, who seemed to have found yet another victim anxious to be punished, Vanessa followed Michelle out of the back rooms and into the relative sanity of the bar.

There she found an anxious Steven, obviously relieved at seeing her. 'Where did you disappear to?' he asked.

Amused to find him so concerned she smiled. 'Just taking in the sights. Isn't that why you brought me here?'

Steven still looked dubious which she found startlingly endearing. 'I suppose,' he was saying, 'that was *one* of many reasons.'

'And what are the other reasons?'

His conscious effort to sound casual was all too obvious as he spoke. 'Well, there's a tradition here. A sort of parade . . .'

'Michelle mentioned it. What is it exactly?' Vanessa asked.

'It's a kind of jokey thing where the members show off their partners. Trouble is, given the rules of the club, only women can be the dominant partners. That's the reason I brought Michelle.'

'And I'm to be the submissive partner? You want me to parade like that in front of all those drooling men?'

Hesitantly, as if half afraid of her reaction, he nodded.

Noticing that the tiny spotlit dance floor had been cleared and that a knot of fetishistically dressed men and women were already starting to assemble around it, Vanessa looked back at Steven. 'And do I get a costume like Michelle's?'

'No. That's the point. Everyone else will be trying so

hard that you, demurely dressed, will make a complete contrast.'

Vanessa took a moment to savour his anxiety as she made him wait. 'And you won't interfere no matter what I might do?' She was delighted to see his face cloud with sudden uncertainty.

'I'm not asking you to do *anything* you don't want to do.'

'That's only because under the club rules, you can't,' she said pleasantly. 'But how do you know what I *might* do?'

He looked momentarily perplexed before deciding to call her bluff. 'That's the chance I'll have to take,' he said finally.

'There's just one question before you get my answer.'

Warily he asked, 'What's that?'

'When Michelle went down on the waiter was that something you told her to do?'

'Absolutely not!' his denial was filled with indignation. 'That was entirely her own idea.'

'Good,' she said. 'In that case I'll do it!'

'Great!' Then he turned to peer into the surrounding gloom. 'Now, where's Michelle got to?'

As if in answer to Steven's query, there came an uproar from the far end of the bar. Turning they saw an argument had broken out between Michelle and Helge. It seemed to be centred on Sylvie. Helge was telling Michelle to get her 'filthy hands off her'.

'Oh, my God,' cried Steven as he hurried forward to intervene.

Staying where she was, she saw Grace coming from the rear rooms. 'What's that all about?' she asked.

'I've no idea. That woman tried to talk to me earlier. Who is she?'

Grace's tone was scathing. 'If you mean that Swedish dyke, Helge, she's in the fashion trade. I did a catwalk show for her a couple of years ago. She's bad news.'

At that moment Steven returned, bringing with him a truculent Michelle. 'That bitch!' she was saying.

Grace asked the obvious question. 'What happened?'

At that moment the woman who had greeted them on arrival came over to Steven. 'Please, m'sieur, I must talk with you.'

Grabbing Steven's arm she took him to one side, leaving the three girls alone for a moment.

'So what did happen?' Grace asked the still-seething Michelle.

'I was talking to Sylvie when Helge came up and started to shout at me to leave her alone. If I had known Sylvie was with that bitch I wouldn't have touched her with a shitty stick.'

'Why?' asked Grace.

'Because I know that Helge. Something happened between us a year or so ago.' Michelle was suddenly unwilling to talk about a distressing moment and, making an effort to reassert her self-control went on, 'No. Forget it. It's alright now.'

'She recognised you – from whatever happened before?' Vanessa asked.

'I don't think she did. Girls like me are dirt to Helge.

But I remember her! I hate her for what she did.'

Intrigued, they might have pressed further for an explanation but for the return of a worried-looking Steven. 'The management wanted us to leave,' he said.

'But why?' demanded Michelle. 'She was the one who started it.'

Steven raised two placatory hands. 'That's what I told them. I think it's all straightened out now.'

Despite Steven's assurances, a depressing pall had descended on them which was only partially relieved when attention was diverted to their hostess, Hardie, who had mounted the dais and was calling for silence as she announced the beginning of the pageant.

With mixed feelings, Vanessa watched as a long line of women, in a variety of fetishistic costumes, mounted the dais dragging with them their submissive male 'slaves' to varying amounts of admiring applause.

When Steven nudged her to indicate she should go with Michelle to take her place in the line up, she protested.

'How am I going to follow that dressed as I am? I'll look ridiculous!'

'Trust me.'

Once more glad of the anonymity offered by her mask, Vanessa followed Michelle to where the others were waiting to parade. Looking at the resplendent Michelle she felt increasingly conspicuous in her 'ordinariness'. Nevertheless deep down in her womb, were the beginnings of a throbbing awareness that her long-suppressed need to be dominated might be due for an airing.

When they were called forward the contrast between the

disappointment of the onlookers at her dress and their appreciation of Michelle's couldn't have been more obvious. Suddenly hating Steven for exposing her to their scorn, she scanned the crowd of watching faces, searching him out.

It was when Vanessa saw him standing some way off and noted the self-satisfied smirk on his face that she knew exactly what she was going to do. Taking hold of the neckline of her wraparound and not caring that she might ruin it, she tore it open, revealing herself naked as the dress slid down her arms to the floor.

The applause which greeted this gesture grew even louder when, taking Michelle's arms and wrapping them round her, she backed against her body and executed some overtly sexual moves even she didn't know she knew.

Michelle was playing up to this sudden development by dragging the whip she carried across Vanessa's naked breasts, when they were both startled by the appearance of Steven standing before them. 'Punish her,' he seethed to Michelle. 'Spank her! Here! In front of everybody!'

Michelle reacted immediately, turning Vanessa with surprising ease. She found herself held tight against Michelle with her naked back exposed to the watching crowd. The sting of Michelle's hand falling on her exposed buttocks was nothing compared to the humiliation she felt at how easily Steven had turned the tables on her!

Trying to twist away from the stinging blow, her foot slipped and she would have fallen heavily to the underlit glass floor but for the rescuing embrace that caught her.

'My dear, I hope you're not hurt?' asked a concerned Helge.

'I don't think so,' Vanessa muttered as she felt Steven reaching for her.

Helge turned on Steven indignantly. 'How could you trust such a precious creature to that whore?' she asked.

'None of your goddammed business!' said Steven huffily, and hurriedly took Vanessa away as Michelle came to wrap the remains of the red dress about Vanessa's shoulders.

'What you need is a drink,' Steven said and started her towards the bar.

'What I really need,' she told him, 'is to visit the Ladies' room.'

'You know where you'll find me,' he said, adding lightly as she moved off, 'And don't talk to any strange men!'

Holding the ripped dress around her, Vanessa started towards the Ladies' when she saw something that diverted her into the back rooms. What she had seen was a wild-eyed Grace giving a man a severe beating with what looked like Michelle's whip.

'Hi, pussycat,' Grace greeted her. 'Meet Henri,' she said, indicating the man she was beating. 'He's a good friend of mine, but he gets out of line sometimes.'

Keeping the table between herself and Grace's victim, Vanessa added yet another first to the many she had experienced that night and watched fascinated as she saw Henri's penis becoming harder and more erect with every stroke of the whip.

Grace broke off for a moment. 'You ever ass-whip a guy?' she asked. When Vanessa shook her head, she saw the haft of the whip being thrust towards her. 'Come round this side and give him a couple. Henri would love it.'

On a rising tide of temptation she was almost about to accept the invitation when she felt chilling hands on her shoulders. 'Don't say anything,' purred Steven's voice in her ear, 'I'm going to fuck you.'

Frozen with a surging tide of excitement, she leaned back into him. 'Here?' she asked.

'Here.'

Her breathing quickening and her mind racing, she felt the dress stripped from her. Then, gently but firmly, she was pushed forward, her elbows resting on the table to within inches of Henri's throbbing cock. She had little time to savour her position before she felt Steven, fully erect, entering her with welcome savagery.

Vanessa's own ecstatic cry almost matched the moans that were coming from Henri and it soon became apparent that Steven was timing his thrusts to the beat of the whip cracking into Henri's buttocks until Vanessa cried out, 'Fuck me! Harder! Please!'

Steven increased the power of his thrusts rather than their tempo and she found herself pushed even further across the table to where she could almost reach out and take Henri in her mouth.

Henri took time out from his pain to notice this and edged himself closer until he was touching her lips.

Suddenly, to Vanessa, it seemed the most natural development in the world to reach that extra inch and swallow Henri whole. While Henri reacted to her hungry mouth with ecstatic cries, Steven leaned his weight across her back and whispered into her ear, 'Dirty bitch! You strip naked, let yourself be fucked in public and then suck a stranger's cock. What does that make you?'

Vanessa would have liked to tell him just how wonderfully abandoned she felt but her mouth was otherwise, and quite delightfully, engaged. She closed her mind to the tiny part of her brain which was demanding rational explanation for her conduct.

It was then Vanessa felt Steven's teeth sinking deep and painfully into first her shoulder and then her neck. He seemed to be intent on controlling her but she didn't care. Pain or pleasure – it was all the same to her body, bombarded with sensations she wouldn't have believed three hours previously. Never before had she felt so joyously wanton or so completely alive as she felt her old life and values being thrust further back into the past.

Vanessa's eyes were now masked by Henri's belly but she could hear that the tempo of his beating had increased and sensed that others had gathered around her exhibition and were murmuring appreciatively. Knowing this added immeasurably to her own excitement. Now she wanted to be filled by both men at the same time! Anything less would be an anti-climax. She knew she was now totally out of control and wouldn't have cared if two, three or four men were to take their place in her after Steven. This was fantasy made real!

Feeling Henri's cock throb violently in her mouth, Vanessa heard his scream of pain at the peak of his pleasure and then felt him pumping into her mouth, filling her and all but choking her. Riding out her own mounting ecstasy, she felt Steven surging and, as she reached her own orgasm, was sorry that this unique experience was ending and that she must now face the man who had so comprehensively fucked her.

It was only when Henri slipped from her mouth that she saw Helge among the many spectators that had gathered around them. She seemed to be scowling disapproval of Vanessa's recent conduct. Confused for no reason she could define, she turned into Steven's comforting arms and was then astonished when some of the voyeurs started to applaud her. Others looked to Steven, hoping he might cede his place to them.

Amidst all this attention Vanessa found her mind filled only with the curiously omnipresent Helge.

Meanwhile Steven had put the discarded dress around her shoulders and started shepherding her from the room. Their progress was interrupted by Henri who hurried up to clasp both her hands to his lips and murmur his gratitude. Looking up, Vanessa saw Grace smiling at her and mouthing the silent, but unmistakable, word 'cocksucker', before coming forward to embrace her and plant a light kiss on both her cheeks.

'Let's all go and get that drink,' said Steven.

Vanessa hesitated as she felt her swollen bladder demanding attention. 'I forgot to go to the loo,' she told an amused Steven and ran off quickly.

She was totally unshocked to find a girl sitting on one of the basins screaming ecstatically, her legs wrapped about the buttocks of a naked man who was ferociously fucking her. Suddenly such a sight wasn't worth even a second glance!

Squatting in the comparative sanctuary of the cabinet,

Vanessa listened to the highly vocal girl outside and assessed just how much had happened in the past few hours.

She felt a tingle of fulfilled excitement when she realised that, a week previously, had she heard about a girl behaving as she had tonight, she would almost certainly have condemned her as beyond redemption. Experience, Vanessa decided, was illuminating!

Coming out of the cabinet she washed her hands in the basin next to the still active couple and even managed to elude the man's arm that reached out to bring her into a three-sided embrace. It was while she was using the hot-air hand drier that the persistent Helge walked into the tiny lobby.

'Ah!' she cried, 'there you are. My dear, I feel we really must make time to meet again. Where did you say you were staying?'

Despite herself Vanessa found her interest in the woman quickening but, too embarrassed to mention Madame Gallia's, she said instead that they were with friends.

'Then,' smiled Helge, 'that makes it all the more important that you be sure to call me.' Helge was thrusting a gold-lettered visiting card at her. 'Promise me you won't lose my number and believe me when I say it's vitally important to us both that we meet again. Incidentally, I thought you looked quite the most beautiful of women here tonight. That's not something I say lightly, you know.'

Embarrassed by such compliments from another woman, Vanessa could only smile back, assure Helge that she would be sure to call her, and then flee from the Ladies' room with the feeling that Steven was somehow manipulating all these 'coincidences'. Returning to the bar she found everyone looking unexpectedly depressed. 'What's wrong?' she asked.

Before Steven could answer Michelle burst out, 'That bitch!'

Turning back to Steven, Vanessa saw he was embarrassed. 'Someone told our hostess that Michelle was a working girl. It's against the rules to bring a professional into the club. We have to leave and I'm barred for six months.'

'Fuck 'em,' said Grace. 'Let's all go and finish the night somewhere else.'

'It's not even midnight yet,' complained Henri.

'Henri's invited us back to his place,' Steven said.

Filled with a sudden sense of daring Vanessa smiled. 'I've got a better idea,' she said. 'Let's all go back to Madame Gallia's!'

Steven looked askance. 'You really mean it?' he asked.

'The night started crazy, we might as well end it that way!'

Steven looked as if he was about to object to this proposal when Grace moved to stand in front of her. 'There's one thing I've got to do before we go anywhere!'

'We've seen every other inch of this lady,' Grace said, reaching for the ties of the black velvet mask. 'It's time we saw the rest!'

So saying she pulled the mask from Vanessa's face.

'Well?' asked a smiling Vanessa.

Grace gave her a long assessing look before jokingly shrugging. 'Yeah . . .' she finally said with deliberate mock heaviness. 'Well . . . maybe the mask wasn't such a bad idea!'

Only Henri, confused by the spoken English, took Grace seriously and spoke indignantly. 'What are you saying?' he demanded. 'The lady is beautiful!'

He seemed further confused by the laughter his remark created but, as they headed for their respective cars, each felt that a strong bond had been established between them.

Madame Gallia's promised to make for an interesting end to the night!

Chapter Seven

'It's a fucking whorehouse!' Grace's joyous cry of discovery rang about the hotel lobby the moment they stepped through the guarded door.

Madame Gallia was not a woman to be easily shocked but she looked positively ashen-faced as she took in the explosive presence of Grace. She hurried forward as if anxious to preserve the decorum of her establishment.

Seeing her coming, Grace spread her arms wide in greeting. 'Mama!' she cried. 'I'm home!'

Watching her friend, Vanessa thought it was the funniest thing she had ever seen. Normally she would have been embarrassed to see someone behaving in such a way. But, as Vanessa thought about it, she realised that, given the context, Grace was doing nothing wrong. She saw the beautiful girl as on the same elevated plane of exuberance as herself. Vanessa was intoxicated – not with mundane liquor but with the sheer joyous awareness of being alive at a time and place where all things were possible. It was not an emotion with which she was familiar but nevertheless she welcomed it into her armoury of experience as a cherished addition.

Meanwhile Madame Gallia had turned, open-mouthed, to make a silent appeal to Steven. To Vanessa's disappointment, he stepped forward to play the diplomat. 'Its alright, Madame Gallia. My friend is a little overly excited, nothing more.'

Hearing this caused Vanessa her first unsettling doubts about the man to whom she had all but abandoned herself. Why did he not see, as she did, that it was inappropriate with the prevailing mood to try and placate the hard-faced brothel keeper? Why not simply present themselves as the highly aroused and liberated sophisticates Vanessa, in that moment, thought themselves to be? Why did Steven feel any need to explain or even apologise? Watching him, Vanessa was disappointed and somewhat brought down from the excited high which had carried her this far. Unaccountably she thought of it as something of a betrayal.

Madame Gallia looked unconvinced as, with pursed lips, she watched Grace start a tour of inspection of the ground-floor restaurant and the clients and girls sitting there.

The sun broke through for Madame Gallia when Steven mentioned having four bottles of champagne sent to his rooms. 'Why, certainly, M'sieur Steven.' The outrageous profit she would make on four bottles of champagne made her brave enough to bear a little disturbance.

'So what are you ladies going to do with us poor guys tonight?' Steven asked.

'What would you like us to do?' Michelle asked.

'Surprise me!'

Vanessa watched this innocent exchange with mixed

112

feelings. Suddenly she saw Steven as an alien person, a feeling she could not account for. When he turned to her with the same question, bright-eyed and obviously unaware of the newly arisen conflict in Vanessa's mind, she turned to Grace for inspiration.

Using the capacity of the tiny lift as an excuse, Grace told Steven and Henri to wait in the bar until called for. She told them the girls needed time to prepare.

The moment the three girls were squeezed into the lift, Grace assumed control. 'OK, now a place like this has to have equipment, right?' Turning to Michelle she asked, 'Where is it?'

Michelle was puzzled. 'What is it we are trying to do?'

'We're going to twist those guys' balls off till they don't know whether they're coming or going!' said Grace. 'That's what! Michelle you go dig them up. Vanessa and I will set the scene.'

The moment Vanessa was alone with Grace in their suite she voiced her doubts. 'I don't know what you've got in mind but I don't think Steven will want to play the same game as Henri.'

Grace grinned. 'Trust me, honey. I think I can claim to know more about men than you.' She paused and a frown replaced her smile. 'Unless, of course, you've something more romantic in mind?'

Vanessa was taken aback by the unintended challenge. She had that night done many things she would have previously thought inconceivable. She had allowed herself to be lodged in a brothel, been naked in an orgy club and been publicly humiliated by an unashamed whore. Was she now to balk at this last claim to be as wild and free as, so it seemed, Grace was?

Much against her instincts Vanessa smiled. 'Of course not,' she said. 'You're in charge. We'll play it anyway you want.'

Grace's smile returned. 'No matter what happens, just remember that you said that.'

Vanessa immediately regretted having so readily conceded control but her thoughts were interrupted by the return of Michelle, dragging a large wicker hamper of costumes and 'toys' and she was soon preoccupied with dressing up. She chose a leather basque and fishnet stockings, then excitedly compared notes with Grace who looked utterly, savagely, magnificent, but practically naked in a leather thong, thigh-length high-heeled boots and wielding a whip. Curiously Michelle had chosen the comparatively demure outfit of a pink gingham dress, which to Vanessa's untutored eye, looked like a milkmaid's costume.

'Ready girls?' asked Grace in challenging tones.

Michelle nodded enthusiastically and Vanessa, her doubts resurfacing, felt she had little choice but to go along with the prevailing mood. 'Ready,' she agreed.

Reinforcing her authority Grace despatched Michelle to summon the men and, meanwhile, had Vanessa pose in a threatening and dominant manner in which she felt uncomfortably theatrical.

The slightly heady feeling of taking part in something staged and unreal was further increased when Michelle returned with Steven and Henri – both goggle-eyed at the openly sexual display awaiting them.

114

Vanessa was amused at the way Steven had looked at her and even began to feel that, maybe, Grace had judged the moment better than she. It was even possible for her to feel lust filling her loins as Grace issued peremptory orders to which both men were only too happy to submit.

Grace strode up and down before the two men like an ill-tempered prison guard looking over new prisoners. 'Stand up straight!' she rapped out, and Vanessa was amused to see the way the men warily straightened their backs. 'You're going to be thoroughly searched,' Grace told them. 'Get naked!'

Trying to tell herself that she really ought to be enjoying this as much as Grace and Michelle obviously were, Vanessa tried to imagine that this was no more than a play in which they all had assumed characters behind which they could hide. Reality however impinged itself the moment she saw Steven naked with a soaring erection. In that instant she felt a sense of loss. It wasn't only her that induced such excitement in him – Grace and Michelle, she suspected, were making a much better job of it!

Doubts flooded through her mind as she saw Michelle waved forward by Grace's whip, and then ordered to kneel before Steven. 'Suck cock!' Grace murmured as she turned, smiling, towards Vanessa. 'You do the same for Henri,' she told Vanessa.

Feeling that her body was filled with ice, Vanessa forced reluctant legs forward and knelt before Henri, her mind more interested in the sounds emanating from Steven as Michelle blessed him with her undoubtedly talented mouth. She, meanwhile, had taken hold of Henri's solid flesh but, as she addressed it to her lips, felt reluctant to repeat something she had earlier done without the slightest hesitation. She was startled to feel a burning sensation on her exposed buttocks and hear Grace snarl, 'Do it, bitch!' She realised then that Grace had laid the whip across her. Quieting her instincts, which told her to refuse, and using the stroke of the whip as compelling motivation, she took Henri fully into her mouth and only wished she didn't feel quite so humiliated by doing so.

The sounds of Grace's whip falling on naked flesh brought the return of some sense of erotic arousal which was quickly dispelled when she realised that the whip was falling on Steven and that his groans indicated that Michelle was bringing him to something approaching imminent climax.

Already a reluctant participant in this sexual tableau, Vanessa's resolution to stick it out broke when there was an upheaval next to her.

Steven had borne Michelle backwards to the ground and, as Vanessa turned to look, she realised that Steven had lodged himself deep into the girl's loins and was now enthusiastically bringing himself to an unstoppable climax.

'What's the matter with you?' asked Grace's soft voice. 'Never seen a girl get fucked before?'

Suddenly angry at having allowed herself to be put in this position, Vanessa was as surprised as anyone to find herself on her feet and turning away. 'Leave me alone!' she heard herself murmur. Going into the far bedroom, her mood was not helped by hearing Steven's voice joining that of an ecstatic-sounding Michelle as both came to climax.

Vanessa sat on the edge of the bed as Steven and Michelle's lovemaking died down, the sound still ringing in her ears. When Grace came into the room Vanessa resented her presence but her voice, when she spoke, was soft and filled with understanding. 'You in love with the guy?' she asked.

Wishing she could bring her temper to flashpoint Vanessa felt even more impotent as she realised that instead she was about to burst into tears. 'No!' she managed to shout angrily.

'Then what's the problem?' asked Grace, coming to sit beside Vanessa on the bed. 'It's only flesh on flesh. Tomorrow, he'll be the same as he was yesterday.' Grace paused allowing Vanessa time to react. Vanessa remained silent so Grace went on, 'After watching you tonight I thought you were ready for this.'

An icy anger had gripped Vanessa but its focus was blurred. Was she angry at Steven for preferring a whore to herself or was she confused by echoes of her feelings after Andrew had left her for another woman? She felt cursed with an emotional burden that others seemed able to lightly discard. She felt as if she had failed some vital test, that she had climbed an erotic mountain only to lose her nerve as she looked down.

Maybe Grace was right. It *was* only flesh upon flesh and nothing more than an exchange of pleasure she might have coveted for herself. She had almost decided to return, when Steven appeared in the bedroom door, looking a little pale and worried. 'Something wrong?' he asked.

Grace rose immediately to interpose herself between

Steven and Vanessa and not only ushered Steven back out of the room with words that Vanessa couldn't hear but also destroyed Vanessa's resolution to be sensible.

By the time Grace turned back, Vanessa had determined that there was nothing to be gained from trying to prove herself a 'good sport'. She just wanted to be left alone to sort out her confused emotions. Happily, before Grace could launch into more consoling homilies, Vanessa chanced upon a form of words that would both excuse her and give her the space she wanted. 'Maybe I'm just tired.' She smiled towards Grace. 'It has been quite a night.'

A great tension seemed to leave Grace. 'I'm sure that's it,' she said. 'Listen, why don't you get yourself a good night's sleep, then you and Steven can sort this out in the morning.' Grace broke off with an unconvincing laugh. 'Things always look different in the morning. Not always better . . .' she added as if philosophising '. . . but different.'

Grace waited out Vanessa's silence a moment more before adding, 'So what shall I tell him? That you'd rather talk in the morning?'

Nodding, she added a further condition. 'Tell him I'd also rather be alone tonight.'

'Done!' cried Grace with apparent relief. She reached a consoling hand down towards Vanessa which she took to her cheek with genuine affection. 'Thanks,' she murmured.

Grace turned away as if embarrassed by the sudden intimacy that had sprung up between the two girls. 'Hey, listen, life is all a matter of timing.' At the door Grace turned. 'Things maybe moved a little too fast for you tonight.'

Vanessa felt the need to demonstrate that she was totally

naive and nodded. 'That must be it,' she said, smiling.

Grace started to speak but changed her mind and turned away. 'Get some sleep. I'll be here in the morning for you.'

Watching the door close Vanessa felt reassured that in Grace she had found a supportive friend and advocate. Meanwhile she faced a night alone with her thoughts.

As she took off the borrowed leather, Vanessa felt herself shedding a false shell. Naked, she looked at herself in the mirror and tried to connect the image of the girl she saw there with the one that had earlier done unimaginable things. As she turned away from her reflection she considered that there was something missing. Somewhere along the way she had lost the courage of her convictions and allowed herself to become merely a player in someone else's fantasy.

Getting into the bed which had been built and installed with activities other than sleep in mind, she looked up into the silky canopy and felt foolish. There were things for her yet to learn, margins of experience to be explored. As she switched off the light and turned to her side she remembered that, at Holly Hill House, she had gone forward naked, expecting to surrender to quite a different man. The Count's face filled her mind as she let a welcome tiredness engulf her wearied body.

Having spent the sleeping hours in a turmoil of confused erotic dreams – featuring Grace, and of all people, the Swedish lesbian, Helge, in the company of the incredibly handsome Count – Vanessa woke, mentally primed and ready to renew a form of gladiatorial sexual combat only to find a huge gap where her faceless jousting partner should have been.

It was at that moment that she caught the pungent aroma of French coffee coming from the other room.

There she found Grace, smiling at her across a loaded breakfast table and wearing a bath robe.

'The coffee's good,' said the ebony beauty cheerfully.

'Grace!' answered Vanessa with barely concealed surprise. 'What are you doing here?'

'Steven asked me to stay by you. He had to leave and didn't want to wake you.'

'Did he say when he'd be back?'

'Late afternoon. Said he had meet some business colleagues.' Grace gestured to the table. 'Have some coffee.'

'And he asked you to come by and babysit me?' Vanessa made no attempt to keep the incredulity out of her voice.

Grace laughed. 'No way! He said that, since he was under orders to leave you alone, he thought we might do something together. Like go shopping.'

Filled with a wary disillusion, Vanessa sat down at the table and waited, her taste buds impatient for the coffee. 'Is this his way of buying me off? Placating me?'

Grace shrugged. 'Sounds good to me.'

'But not to me,' said Vanessa. 'I don't feel like being bought off, but shopping sounds like a good idea. I think I'd like that. Especially with you.'

'Absolutely!' cried Grace. 'I know all the fashion houses and with me along they'll know better than to try and gouge you for the ticket prices.'

Vanessa already felt better and now viewed the coming

day with greater optimism. 'Sounds good.'

Grace let her short sharp laugh ring out again. 'Even better when it's at someone else's expense.'

Vanessa was perplexed. 'Whose expense?' she asked.

'Steven was adamant. You're to charge everything you buy to his account at the hotel.'

'No way!' exclaimed Vanessa. 'I told you I'm not going to be bought off. I have my own charge cards and I'll use them!' she said.

Looking genuinely downcast Grace shook her head. 'It's against my religion not to spend someone else's money when it's offered but I guess I can live with it.'

Vanessa smiled at Grace's worldly cynicism. 'I'll shower and you can show me your connections,' she said.

'Just one thing,' called out Grace, 'we'll have to stop by Henri's studio so I can change.'

'Studio?' Vanessa asked.

'Didn't I tell you? Henri's one of the most famous photographers in France.'

Shaking her head, Vanessa turned away and got under the welcoming downpour of the shower, surprised to find that her skin felt super-sensitised and that she was becoming unaccountably aroused.

Returning to the bedroom, Vanessa was drawn to the glitter of gold lettering sparkling in the sunlight. Curiosity drawing her closer, she saw a visiting card lying on the bedside table. Remembering the card given to her by the universally-hated Helge, she picked it up – and froze.

The gold lettering spelt out the company name VELLIORIA followed by a titled name: Countess Helge.

Grace looked up from the card Vanessa had thrust at her. 'Right!' she cried. 'I knew that dykey bitch the moment I saw her last night. I did a catwalk job for Vellioria about two years ago. She doesn't *work* there – she's the owner! She must be worth millions. You any idea what it costs to finance a couture house?' Vanessa didn't and simply shook her head, as Grace went on, 'So what's bothering you?'

She shrugged. 'I have no idea. There's just something about that woman that gets to me.'

Grace was dismissive. 'Seems to me there's a whole lot more important things bothering you right now and that Helge bitch ain't worth a second thought, although I got to admit their house does make some fine clothes. They got a reputation for elegant erotic stuff.' Grace looked up smiling. 'You want to check it out?' When Vanessa nodded, Grace cried, 'Then let's go.'

They found Henri looking close to death. His watery eyes, set into a white face, showed something close to panic on seeing Grace. 'Oh God, NO!' he cried. 'No more women! I never want to see another woman as long as I live!'

As Grace roared with laughter he appealed directly to Vanessa. 'Have you any idea what those women did to me last night? It's inhuman! I have to work today and look at me. No sleep, ravaged and raped – I'm barely conscious!'

Still laughing, Grace went to him, cupped his head gently into her hands and kissed him. 'Poor baby,' she cooed. 'How would you like us two girls to make a body sandwich of you?' Henri's outrage died an instant death as his expression softened into docile submissiveness. He sounded almost desperately apologetic as he murmured, 'But I have work today . . . couldn't it be tonight?'

'In your dreams!' yelled Grace and, laughing, turned away. 'Entertain my friend while I put something on!'

Henri looked ruefully after the departing Grace. 'That woman is so cruel to me, you know?'

'And you love it?' Vanessa asked.

'Adore it! She is so beautiful and the camera loves her,' he answered with as much brightness as his tired body could muster. 'Would you like some coffee? God knows how, but I managed to make some earlier.'

Coffee was the last thing she needed right then but she felt any kind of refusal might provoke an emotional crisis in the man's delicately hungover condition.

Seated at a table in the kitchen corner of his vast studio, she became aware that he was staring at her.

'You!' he suddenly said. 'Have you ever been photographed? You have a great body – with the right make-up I could do sensational things with you.'

Vanessa smiled. 'I don't think so.'

'Pity,' murmured Henri looking genuinely disappointed.

For want of anything else to say, Vanessa started a conversation she immediately regretted. 'I hope I didn't spoil the party for you last night.'

Puzzled, Henri stared at her. 'For me?' he asked. 'I had a wonderful time. Did something happen that I missed?'

Henri's genuine unawareness of any drama connected to the previous night's events put everything into sharper perspective than a day's agonising thought could have done. It had been nothing of great importance, she realised, and if there had been a failing then it was probably her own.

Henri was still enthusing. 'I do find you very exciting,' he was saying. 'I would love to photograph you if only for myself.'

Unsure of how much of this was play-acting and how much was real, she was relieved when Grace returned, making a dramatic appearance dressed in a red hat with a brim of umbrella proportions, a rib-crushing minidress that looked as it had an in-built corset, and seven inch red patent stilettos that sent her already tall figure soaring towards the heavens.

'Let's go to market!' she yelled.

Chapter Eight

Looking out from the window of the cab that bore them towards the Parisian temples of haute couture, Vanessa could only wonder at how grey and mundane the world looked. Idly she considered what these people going about their everyday concerns would think if they knew what fantasies she had so recently made reality.

Grace broke in on her thoughts. 'So where do you want to start?'

'I don't know,' Vanessa answered. 'You're the one who knows your way round the fashion houses. You tell me.'

'Let's start from the skin out. Underwear. To me there's only one choice – La Perla. By the way Steven left one other message for you. You're not to go back to Madame Gallia's.'

Vanessa looked at Grace. 'I'm not?'

'He's moving you both to the Hotel Meurice so don't look surprised when I give that as your address.'

'That's nice,' she murmured. 'But when did this happen?'

'This morning, just before he left. He didn't want to wake you.' Grace let out a rip of a laugh. 'Lucky for you he couldn't read your dreams!'

125

'How do you know what I was dreaming?' she asked ruefully.

Grace's laugh continued. 'I've been there sweetheart! Wouldn't surprise me if you didn't have a bunch of Marines in bed with you!'

Flushing with embarrassment at the memory of just how Grace – and the Swedish lesbian – had figured in her dreams, she was glad Grace couldn't read her mind either!

As they drove through the streets of Paris, Vanessa found other considerations weighing heavily on her mind and needed to share them with Grace. Turning to the beautiful girl with whom she had struck up such an instant rapport, Vanessa was reminded that she really knew very little about the girl, which once more led her to consider how little she knew about Steven. Vivid images of Michelle straddling him came sickeningly to her mind and stubbornly refused to be dismissed. She had an uneasy feeling that she ought to be able to handle what had happened the night before more easily – in a more sophisticated manner. Then she decided that the back of a cab was no place to try and order the chaos in her mind. 'Can we stop somewhere and talk?' she finally asked Grace.

Shrugging, Grace nodded and gave a new instruction to the cab driver who, within minutes, had deposited them outside a pavement cafe.

'Now what's this all about?' Grace asked the moment the waiter had moved off with their order.

Vanessa, struggling to articulate her thoughts, found instead her confusion deepening. 'I can't face him, Grace!'

Grace's expression turned from astonishment to curiosity. 'What? You can't face who?'

'Steven. Last night . . . seeing him with Michelle . . . I can't get that out of my mind.' Vanessa raised a hand as she saw Grace drawing breath to protest. 'Now, I know we're all supposed to be super sophisticated and able to handle such things . . .'

Grace broke through. 'You sure looked like it in the club last night!'

Vanessa nodded. 'I know I did. I don't deny it was exciting and I got very turned on and, maybe, sent out the wrong signals.' Vanessa paused to give Grace a chance to pick up on her arguments but instead found her friend staring at her incredulously. 'What I mean is . . . I don't know Steven that well. That is, I thought I knew him, thought I knew where we were headed. Thought I was playing a game but when it came down to it . . .' Vanessa shuddered with horror. 'I just can't rid myself of the thought that he preferred to screw a whore rather than me.'

Grace nodded non-committally and stared off into the distance before speaking. 'There's an old saying that when a man's cock stands he loses the power to think. Can't you just put it down to experience and forget it? I know he's genuinely fond of you.'

Considering her words carefully, Vanessa murmured, 'I've been trying.' Sighing she went on. 'I just can't . . .' Her words lost direction in the confusion of her thoughts and she tried changing tack. 'Maybe it's me. Maybe there's more for me to learn before I'm ready for this kind of emotional game playing.'

127

Grace nodded sagely, still not turning to catch Vanessa's eye. 'Seems to me you're not a woman who's had a lot of affairs.'

'That's true. I've had affairs but they've mostly been long-term commitments – on my part, at least. I had just been comprehensively dumped when I met Steven and had sworn to myself never to be as open with a man again.' Vanessa smiled ruefully. 'I forgot that resolution in a hurry. Maybe I grabbed for the first man to come along and did it too desperately.' She broke off for a moment as another thought struck her. 'The funny thing is the first time I did it with Steven I thought I was doing it with someone else.'

Now Grace did turn towards Vanessa, her eyes wide with surprise. 'Say that again!' she demanded.

Pleased to have shaken her friend's cool, Vanessa smiled. 'It's true. I got this note telling me to be in a particular place at a particular time, leaving no doubt as to what was to happen there. I went thinking it was from this other man. I only found out afterwards that it was Steven.'

Grace was amazed. 'You're one hell of an adventurous girl!' she said in awed tones.

Vanessa snorted. 'Not last night, I wasn't!'

Grace turned to stare once more across the busy boulevard. 'Seems to me your problem is that you think you might have made a wrong turning somewhere.' She paused and let the silence grow before going on in a more positive tone. 'This other guy – the one you thought you were going to – is he still around?'

Vanessa shook her head in denial. 'I don't know where he is. Anyway I don't think that's the answer.'

'So what is?' demanded Grace.

Vanessa shook her head. 'I just don't know.' She paused before deciding to put her trust in Grace entirely. 'What am I to do, Grace?'

'Tonight, tomorrow or the rest of your life, I don't know. What I think we ought to do right now is get our minds onto some serious shopping.'

Pleased to be relieved of her inner conflicts Vanessa agreed wholeheartedly.

Their first stop was just off the Rue de Rivoli. Here Grace led her into a small but exclusive boutique whose stock was a cascade of shimmering silks. Bodies, panties, bras and an array of other beautifully designed undergarments seemed to beckon her attention until she felt in danger of drowning in their subtle fluidity. After selecting several gorgeous numbers, she decided she wanted to add an extremely tarty garter belt and stocking set but Grace laughed and her told she knew of 'whorier' stuff than that and that she'd be better to wait.

Then they went to Fogel for, what seemed to Vanessa, ludicrously expensive stockings and tights that, nevertheless, screamed their pedigree from the house tops.

Shopping had never been simpler. Vanessa made her choice, Grace did the negotiations. She had begun to feel a little light-headed by the time they arrived at Herve Leger's. This was fairyland shopping. Here they were seated in a tiny viewing room and were served coffee and exquisite little bitter almond biscuits, while a selection of magnificent evening gowns were shown 'over the arm'. If they proved of interest either she or, if they had nothing in her size, a house model would show the gown.

Making a choice was easy. She wanted them all!

Leger had a market in clinging gowns built for the girl with a woman's body rather than the androgynous model-girl figure. His gowns did things for Vanessa's bust that would have sent schoolboys into seizures.

Grace insisted on modelling one or two of the gowns and embarrassed her by telling everyone that she needed gowns that would come off easily. 'We're dealing with a real horny lady!' she insisted on telling the unflappable fitters.

Vanessa selected two gowns. A short tight dress in power purple – the neckline plunging to give her that fabulous Leger bust line – and another long one that clung, to Grace anyway, like the shimmering coat of a sea mammal. Leg movement was only possible because the skirt was slashed on one side to the thigh. Noting that the only underwear that could be worn under the gown would be a showgirl's tanga, she made a mental note to look out for some when they got to Grace's 'tart's' emporium.

After making her initial purchases, Vanessa was taken by a tight-as-a-sheath dress. Barely decent about the crotch, with a halter top supporting a neckline cut straight across the bust, it was not something she would have bought off a hanger, but she couldn't wait to see herself in it.

As her purchases mounted so the offer of coffee and biscuits gave way to champagne and caviar.

When they came to Armani, Grace tried tempting her into buying a fabulous, but incredibly priced suit. She made a brave, but weak, attempt to call a halt. 'I'm behaving like a drunken sailor on shore leave!' she protested.

Grace was outraged. 'How can you face life without at least one Armani?' Easily persuaded, she was soon entranced by a cloud of cream and beige that settled about her like a perfumed membrane.

'You're right,' she told Grace, with a delighted smile. 'Life would never have been the same!'

Amused, Grace took them both out onto the boulevard where their combined appearance threatened many a distracted driver with disaster. She waved down a cab.

'So what do we do now?' Grace asked.

'I want something deeply erotic. Something to give me confidence – or that makes a statement of intent I can't renege on,' Vanessa answered in the tone of a child let loose in a toy shop.

'Hate to admit it,' Grace mused dubiously, 'but that means Vellioria.'

The House of Vellioria turned out to be a surprisingly modest-looking enterprise. That is until you noticed the gold-plated door furniture, the almost crystal quality of the front windows, and the uniformed flunkey who leapt forward to open the cab doors for them.

Inside, the ambience was of quiet reverence with barely an item of stock on display. Not one, but two smiling women in beautifully tailored suits and equally tailored hair cuts came forward to greet them.

Grace came directly to the point. 'We want elegant erotic,' she told them. 'Suede, maybe, certainly silk, but mostly, "different".'

With smiles undiminished, the two saleswomen conducted them to a beautifully appointed room where the designs were to be displayed on a large television monitor. No house models here, no waste of time in zeroing in on choices, here they had twelve monitors set up in banks from which a whole range of designs could be displayed simultaneously, with the customer able to interact and follow through the theme that interested them most.

Grace seemed completely at ease with the technology and, using a remote handset, quickly brought on screen the kind of sexually specific elegance she thought would most likely interest Vanessa. Having defined the theme, the two saleswomen left in search of samples of both fabrics and garments. Left alone the two girls turned once more to the video screens which they treated as the equivalent of a child's dressing up box. Some of the designs were intriguing, some hilariously inappropriate to anything other than a bizarre costume party. Grace dismissed these as the kind couture houses threw in to shows in the hope of catching the attending journalists' eyes and so getting free editorial exposure.

'Exposure is right!' commented Vanessa as they contemplated some of the more bare-breasted models. 'Would you wear something like that?' she asked of Grace.

'On the catwalk? Sure! In life, maybe only in private.'

Vanessa was still contemplating the temptation of one of the more extreme designs when her thoughts were interrupted by the return of the saleswomen.

'So let's see what you've got!' Grace cried.

From among the many suggestions they had brought,

Vanessa was particularly intrigued with an evening gown. From the waist down it was two voluminous ivory silk panels, held from an exotically gold-embroidered waistband, which allowed glimpses of the full length of the legs to be revealed. The stiffened cups of the bust were sculptured as if from two exotic sea shells, supported by an entwined gold and ivory halter band which was secured behind the neck by a real pearl clasp. It was a gown for a glittering event, a showcase for the body beneath – and an unashamed 'lustmaker'. While Vanessa's interest was aroused Grace seemed to take against it, finding all kinds of faults which would never have occurred to Vanessa. She might have protested that she would like to try it on but Grace dismissively demanded to see the design-room staff and went off with the saleswomen to discuss the 'problem' at root.

Left alone, Vanessa turned again to the video screens and, copying what she had seen Grace do, was soon delving deeply into whatever else there might be on offer.

Engrossed as she was, she didn't notice Helge's quiet arrival until she spoke. 'My dear,' said the woman whose accent was only slightly Scandinavian. 'I'm very flattered that you have come, so soon, to my little shop. But why did you not warn me in advance? I could have made some preparations.'

'I didn't know myself.' Vanessa smiled back. 'Grace is taking me round.'

Helge smiled, her eyes having dimmed only slightly at the mention of Grace. Waving a dismissive hand about the viewing room, Helge purred. 'But this is not for you. You'll be more comfortable in my rooms. There I can show you some designs that are not even on view at the moment.'

Suddenly, inexplicably discomfited, she made a feeble protest. 'But I don't know where Grace is – she'll come looking for me here.'

Helge smiled. 'I'm sure my staff are competent enough to see that she finds you. Come.'

Thinking it might be thought churlish to refuse, she followed Helge from the viewing room to a small lift where Helge was issuing quick orders to the remaining saleswoman.

Helge's 'rooms' were a spacious, sun-filled suite, exquisitely furnished and filled with photographs of Helge with some of her more illustrious clientele. Vanessa found herself drawn to one of the few photographs which didn't also include Helge. It was of a girl of wistful beauty, dressed in an immaculately cut trouser suit, her hair tumbling down over her shoulders. She was smiling in a somewhat defensive manner into the camera.

There was something about the way the girl stood that made Vanessa feel she had seen her before, even though the girl's features were completely unknown to her. Picking up the framed photograph, she studied it more closely. So intrigued was she by the girl's image that when Helge spoke she all but jumped out of her skin.

'Her name was Imogene,' Helge was saying.

Vanessa turned, her mind suddenly racing. 'Imogene? Is that the same girl that posed so often for Steven?'

Helge nodded and took the photograph from Vanessa's fingers. 'I do believe they did know each other.' Helge briefly studied the picture before placing it back on table. 'She was one of those people that are endowed with so much that the Gods envy them and so, in spite, take them early.'

Helge had spoken so quietly and with such depth of feeling that Vanessa felt uncomfortably as if she were intruding on private grief.

When Helge turned back to her, Vanessa was startled to see her eyes brightened by tears. Compassionate to her obvious suffering, Vanessa was suddenly chilled by the intensity of her gaze.

'There are few people in the world that one truly cherishes,' Helge was saying. 'Imogene was one of that precious number.' These words were heard by Vanessa as if from a great distance while she herself felt transported until she once more stood before Steven's painting. For one brief moment she felt a chilled and trembling fear. The connection between her feelings and once more seeing Imogene's image was obvious, yet the feeling of impending disaster lingered even as Vanessa was startled back to an awareness of her surroundings by Helge's cool tones. 'Come, my dear,' she was saying, 'there's something I would like you to see.'

Propelled by a gentle but insistent hand on her arm, Vanessa moved with her to an adjoining room which all but took her breath away.

Dominating the room was an almost life-size, standing figure of an exquisitely golden naked female figure. The girl was hauntingly, wistfully beautiful and, even to Vanessa, quietly arousing. It was then that the connection between the photographs and the sculpted figure was made. 'Is this that same Imogene?' she asked of Helge.

Helge nodded and smiled. 'It is.'

'She's beautiful,' Vanessa murmured as, reaching out a hand, she touched the cold hard surface. 'Was it sculpted in bronze?'

Helge was quietly shaking her head. 'It wasn't "sculpted" in the conventional sense. I made it by laying bandages of plaster of Paris over her body. The mould was then poured with bronze.'

Startled Vanessa looked over the beautifully delineated features again. 'You must have loved her very much.'

When Helge was quiet Vanessa glanced towards the elegantly featured woman and was embarrassed to see tears in the woman's eyes. 'I'm sorry,' she offered. 'I didn't mean to upset you.'

Helge turned towards Vanessa and dragged herself back to the present. 'Do forgive me. I'm forgetting myself. I haven't offered you any refreshment.'

Helge turned away and had left the room before Vanessa could protest. Lingering for one last glance at the frozen beauty of the statue, Vanessa followed to find Helge on the telephone ordering tea and biscuits to be brought. Having completed her orders, Helge turned to her with a brilliant smile. 'Forgive my momentary lapse. You're quite right. I did love Imogene with a totality that is now shaming to recall.'

Feeling herself warming to the woman, whose outer sophistication she now knew concealed a vulnerability to match her own, Vanessa felt genuinely moved. 'There is no shame in committed love,' she said.

'How clever of you to understand that,' Helge murmured in a warm tone which, for some indefinable reason, Vanessa found disturbing.

Helge seated herself on a couch and continued to survey Vanessa with a smile which, she sensed, concealed a very active assessment of her.

Indicating a chair, Helge motioned for Vanessa to sit down. 'Have you ever experienced such commitment?' Helge asked airily and, as Vanessa struggled to find a suitable answer, went breezily on. 'Perhaps not. You will have gathered that I prefer to love women rather than men. We understand each other so much more easily.'

The conversation was starting to create a feeling of unease and Vanessa was glad to have the tension relieved by the arrival of a young girl bearing a large tray, laid with the refreshments Helge had ordered.

'I trust you enjoy herbal teas?' Helge asked, reaching for the silver teapot as the girl laid down the tray.

'Very much,' she enthused, somewhat distracted to see the silent girl that had served them bobbing a little curtsey at them both before scampering from the room at a half-trot.

Helge seemed amused by her interest in the girl. 'Do you find that one attractive?' she asked.

Startled, she looked back into Helge's clear eyes and saw vividly the androgynous Sylvie from the night before – a memory which caused in her a stir of trepidation.

'Not particularly,' she answered, allowing a slight brittleness into her tone as she took the cup.

'Her name is Renate.' Helge was giving out the information unasked. 'Austrian, but very amusing.'

Uneasiness becoming something akin to panic, Vanessa questioned herself on how she could have been so stupid as to let Helge tempt her into her private apartments, placing her under the obligation of playing the part of a polite guest.

'Now,' said Helge more positively, 'to business.'

Relieved to have her mind shifted from speculation about Helge's unashamed interest in young women, she smiled and nodded.

'What I would like to do for you is something special. Exclusive, even. I have many ideas in my studio at home. Perhaps I could send them to your hotel and then we might meet and discuss them?'

'That would be nice,' Vanessa agreed, thinking she was being shown an easy and unoppresive way out of the situation.

'Good. You mentioned you were staying somewhere quiet. If you give me the address I can send my ideas there.'

'We've moved. To the Meurice.'

'Ah! Excellent.' Making a note Helge murmured, 'Salvador Dali used to stay there, you know. I would visit him often. In my youth I modelled for him. Wonderful man. An intriguing mind.' Helge once more looked up with her disconcerting, clear-eyed stare. 'Someone like yourself – a man with a positive awareness of his Destiny.'

Vanessa was embarrassed. 'I really think you've mistaken me, you know. I pretty much live from day to day.'

Helge smiled. 'A condition Nature imposes on us.'

Helge's tone became almost condescending. 'It is difficult to do other than live one day at a time. The point is to know where it is all leading. We are, most of us, all led. Occasionally one of us is destined to be a leader.'

'Not me!' she cried.

'Nor Steven?' asked Helge.

Hearing mention of his name amid her increasing apprehension was even more disconcerting. It was suddenly important to her to know something. 'Have you known Steven long?' Vanessa asked.

Helge smiled. 'Not long, but very well.' She smiled. 'He is a very charming man and fortunate indeed to have you as his consort.'

Consort was a curious word, she thought. Helge might have said girlfriend or even mistress but 'consort' suggested something regal and she found herself becoming more discomfited by the minute. Helge, though the epitome of polite charm, had not, she realised, brought her here out of simple politeness.

There was something deeper, much more incisive, in her questions and Vanessa felt impelled to counter them with one of her own. 'Did you know Steven and Imogene when they were together?' she asked.

The question seemed to disconcert Helge and she made a patently obvious attempt to avoid answering. 'Perhaps we should get on,' she said hurriedly, not bothering to disguise the irritation the question had caused her. 'I think you and I should conspire to come up with something really special if we are to please Steven.'

Uncomfortable with the implication that she was

somehow entering into an intrigue with Helge, and even more surprised to discover herself about to blurt out that none of this was specifically to please Steven, Vanessa simply smiled and answered, somewhat lamely, 'That would be nice.'

'So,' said Helge, briskly rising to her feet and apparently anxious now to end the meeting, 'I will send my ideas to you at the Meurice as arranged and perhaps you will call me when you've had a chance to look them over?'

'Of course,' Vanessa agreed, only too happy to take this chance of getting away.

Helge walked with her to the private lift. 'You still have my card, of course.'

Replying with a nod, she was surprised when Helge leaned forward to grasp both her hands in her own and deliver a kiss to each of her cheeks. 'Until we meet again then,' she said, adding, 'I'm sure that will be very soon.'

She was still sighing with heart-felt relief when the lift delivered her back to the salon where a puzzled Grace confronted her. 'Where did you get to? There's some really great stuff I want you to look at.'

Shaking her head she said, 'Forget it, Grace. Let's just get out of here!'

Concerned, Grace asked no more until they had reached the sanctuary of a nearby cafe.

'What happened?'

'That woman!' she protested. 'I don't know what it is, but she scares the hell out of me.'

Grace let out a peal of laughter. 'Helge? The grand Countess Helge? Don't tell me she made a pass at you!'

Vanessa shook her head in vigorous denial. 'I don't know what she was doing but there was definitely something.'

Grace's laughter was so scornfully loud that other customers were drawn to turn and look. 'She made a pass!' cried Grace delightedly. Leaning in she spoke more earnestly. 'You telling me you don't know a pass when a woman's making it?'

'No,' Vanessa answered. 'I don't think I do.' Ruefully she added. 'That still doesn't explain why she was so frightening.'

'She wasn't frightening you! You were frightening yourself. Be honest – weren't you scared you might say yes?'

Indignation rising, she exploded. 'Certainly not! Other women don't interest me – not that way, anyway.'

Grace looked away into the mid-distance before murmuring, 'Don't knock it till you've tried it.'

Ready to be angry, she looked at Grace but was disturbed to find there was some truth in Grace's analysis. Steven had exposed her to many new experiences in the past few days – things she would have been appalled at in the cold light of day but had, on being persuaded, enjoyed immensely. Equally, she was aware that she had a great deal more confidence in Grace's presence. Suddenly this girl's friendship was important to her. 'Are you coming with me to the Meurice?'

'Love to, but I've got to meet some magazine people who want me to do their cover. Remember, I'm a working girl!'

'That's a shame,' Vanessa murmured.

Grace looked puzzled. 'What's bothering you?'

'I don't honestly know!' Suppressing a shudder, she went on. 'That Helge woman. She was so intense. So positive. You know, when she was looking at me, I kept thinking she knew something more about me than I knew myself.' She took a long pause under Grace's curious gaze. 'I got the impression there was some strong connection between her and Steven. That there was something . . .' Breaking off with a frustrated sigh, she added, 'When I was with her, I felt that she had the power to manipulate people. That in some way she was about to interfere in my life.'

'Crazy talk!' said Grace decisively.

Nodding, Vanessa smiled but inwardly knew that her instincts never lied.

Chapter Nine

As she came into the lobby of the Hotel Meurice, Vanessa had decided that Steven should have a second chance. The raw anger of the night before had lessened and, though doubts still hovered in the corners of her mind, she was prepared to concede a civilised discussion during which, she hoped, their relationship would be better defined.

Her determined mood lasted only so far as the reception desk. There, her enquiry for the number of their room was met with a disconcerting frown and a hurried shuffle through the register, followed by a murmured consultation among the men staffing the desk. Finally one of them returned to her with a smiling deferential expression on his face.

'There appears to be a misunderstanding, madame,' he told her.

'What sort of misunderstanding?' Vanessa demanded.

Lips pursed, the man shrugged. 'We have no reservation under the name you gave us.'

Stunned at this unexpected rebuff Vanessa thought of the many parcels and packages that would shortly be arriving here for her. 'But that's impossible,' she said. 'I'm sure if you look again you'll discover your mistake.'

The man's eyes grew soulful. 'There is no mistake, madame, I assure you. Perhaps your partner is delayed,' the man suggested. 'We shall be happy to place a room at your disposal until this unfortunate error resolves itself.'

'But I've been shopping,' she protested. 'Packages are going to be delivered here . . .' Vanessa broke off as she realised that all her doubts about Steven had come back with full force and her shopping was really the last of her considerations.

'We shall, of course, keep any such deliveries at your disposal, madame.' The man was trying to reassure her but Vanessa's mind was already focused elsewhere. Across the lobby she had spotted the uniformed chauffeur that had picked her up from the airport.

Abandoning the well-meaning but unhelpful receptionist, Vanessa hurried towards the man, anxious to intercept him before he disappeared out of the lobby. 'Excuse me . . .' she called, and was much relieved when the man turned with a smile of recognition. 'There seems to have been some mistake. I was expecting to meet Mr Weir here but . . .'

The chauffeur was already smiling. 'But I was looking for you, madame. I have been sent to fetch you. The car is outside and waiting.'

With a sigh of relief and a mental apology to Steven, Vanessa returned to the desk to tell them that her problem was now solved. They, in turn, reassured her that any packages that arrived for her would be properly guarded, so she followed the driver out to the limousine which stood, as promised, at the kerbside.

Once more ensconced in the familiar surroundings of the

car, Vanessa allowed herself to think about her own emotions. Having overcome the unfortunate misunderstanding at the hotel, she felt once more disposed to remind herself of the excitement she had so far enjoyed in Steven's company. There was no doubt that he had a capacity to be something other than ordinary. Seen in that context, even his lapse with Michelle could be forgiven, though it still bothered her. In its place she let in anticipation. She was now on her way to an unknown destination where she felt – hoped even – something outrageous might happen.

Echoing in her mind, for no reason she could rationalise, was the opening sentence of a forbidden novel she had read as a teenager.

'Her lover one day takes O for a walk . . .'

That such an anodyne, commonplace beginning had led the heroine of that novel into a fantasy world where she happily submitted to everything imposed on her without question, seemed at the time an unattainable fiction.

The only parallel with her present situation was the limousine that finally picked up O and took her to the beginnings of her odyssey.

Had some sixth sense told her that all that had gone before in this relationship had been preparation?

She had gone to the hotel with mixed emotions, eager to show off her new purchases but, as the Mercedes threaded its way through a series of ever-narrowing streets, the doubts began again.

She had always prided herself on her knowledge of Paris but this was a totally unfamiliar district that she was sure she had never before seen. After twenty or so twists and turns, she gave up trying to relate these new places geographically with those she knew. She felt totally disorientated – which worried her. But she also had to admit that she was shamefully excited at being so totally at Steven's disposal.

Deciding that it was this alone which had brought the memory of that novel's first line back into her mind, she felt the comforting embrace of inevitability. Whatever was now to happen was not her responsibility.

She had once read that those who find they cannot cope with life would, sometimes consciously, escape into insanity – so making their condition and their confusion someone else's problem while they could relax as mere spectators at their own downfall.

She thought she could divine a parallel to herself since she now sought escape by disclaiming fault.

The thought freed her. In the depths of the cushioned elegance of the limousine she smiled. She had played her part. She had been summoned without explanation and she had responded without protest.

Having reconciled her fears and now able to judge them trivial, she was surprised to find herself trembling when the limousine finally stopped.

The chauffeur, with reassuring deference, leapt out and opened the door for her to step out into the narrow, dimly lit street. She had half expected to be brought to a club, a theatre or some such public place but here the street was gloomily domestic – guarded as if aware that its best days were past.

Looking at the heavy double doors, built in another era for the passage of horse-drawn carriages, she hesitated, wondering if perhaps the driver would know what awaited her beyond the door. A direct question was impossible.

Instead she asked, 'Are you sure this is the right address?' She hoped his reply might contain some clue, however slight.

'Absolutely, madame,' he replied, adding, 'Madame is expected,' before conducting her to a small access door.

Maintaining a coolly confident demeanour was difficult since her body was suddenly drenched in an intoxicating mixture of anticipation, fear and excitement. She could almost hear, above the pounding of her heart, the sound of warning bells urging caution.

The chauffeur politely opened this smaller gate for her, then, standing back, allowed it to close behind her with a smack of finality. Bidding her fear-filled mind to be quiet, she stood on quavering legs and tried to take rational stock.

Facing her was the kind of courtyard commonly found in Parisian residential property. The buildings, looming high above the quadrangle of cobbles, embraced her intrusion with disdain. They had been built to withstand a rioting populace. One trembling girl could not expect to trouble their complacent solidity.

If the manner of her delivery to this place was meant to unnerve her then, she reflected, it had succeeded.

Most of the windows overlooking the courtyard were dark. Here and there was a yellow gleam but her eye was drawn to a door which, fronted by four or five steps, was lit by a dull amber lamp. Instinctively, she knew that this was

147

meant for her and moved towards it.

Mounting the steps she was confronted with an intimidating wooden door, gleaming with a mirror-like black paint finish. To one side was a circular brass plate framing a well-worn bell pull. Many hands over many decades must have worn the smoothness into that heavy metal, but none, she imagined, had been as nervous as she felt reaching for it.

Reason dictated that what she was doing was foolhardy. No one knew where she was. Her only reassurance that Steven had imposed this surprise on her was the limousine which he had used throughout their stay.

When the door lock buzzed to announce its release, she needed every once of her uncertain courage to push open the door and step across its threshold.

Inside, Vanessa found herself standing in a small lobby. Before her were etched glass doors, made all but opaque by the engraved patterns but still with enough clear space to see through. Beyond the closed doors, she could see a sumptuously furnished hallway, discreetly lit, but glowing with promised elegance. Somewhat startled to find the door before her firmly locked, Vanessa felt distinctly uneasy for a moment, as if she were trapped. Then, through the finely crafted glass doors, Sylvie appeared, wearing what seemed to be a floor-length white silk gown. She was coming towards the door with the obvious intention of releasing her.

In the short interval between Sylvie's appearance and the door being opened to her, Vanessa felt an all but overwhelming rush of intrigued excitement. Certain that she had been manoeuvred into her unsettling condition by Steven and that Helge must have some part in this delightful conspiracy, she experienced the same heady feeling of sexual freedom she had felt in the club the previous night.

As she stepped into the hallway, dominated by the regal colours of red and purple, Sylvie's smile made her feel welcome and calmed her nerves slightly.

'Madame Helge is awaiting you,' Sylvie said.

This simple announcement stopped Vanessa's heart. It was suddenly obvious to her that Steven could not have conspired with Helge to bring her here with the intention of launching her into yet another of his erotic surprises. Feeling confused, Vanessa followed Sylvie along the expanse of the hall determined to find out just what was going on.

Sylvie meanwhile had led her to two ornate double doors and was in the process of throwing them open. It was only as the girl did so that Vanessa noticed that the gown Sylvie was wearing was actually nothing more than a double panel of silk which, without seams of any kind, flowed open from the girl's shoulders to her ankles. Apart from the heavy chain about her waist, it was obvious that this was all she wore.

The thought distracted Vanessa from immediately taking in the room which had been revealed to her. She was still only aware that there was one other person present before she saw Helge, dressed entirely in elegant black, hurrying forwards to engulf her in an effusive embrace. 'My dear!' cried Helge as she brushed Vanessa's cheek with a kiss. 'How wonderful that you were able to come so soon.'

This greeting unsettled Vanessa. Had the chauffeur

received some invitation that Steven hadn't known about? As Helge took her hand, Vanessa was still pondering the sequence of misunderstandings that had brought her here and reminded herself that she hadn't seen Steven since walking out on him the previous night. Then, suddenly, all such thoughts were pushed from her mind.

Standing before her was the gorgeous Count! The impossibly handsome man she had already mentally surrendered to in Holly Hill House and the man who had featured so strongly in her erotic dream of the night before!

'The Count Alonzo Fuego e Meducato,' Helge was saying by way of introduction. 'But then, I believe, you have already met.'

The Count, smiling, stepped forward to take up Vanessa's numbed hand and kiss it. 'Indeed we have,' he drawled in a deep voice that struck through Vanessa like an arrow. Standing there Vanessa felt helpless before an avalanche of emotion. Dumbly, mindlessly submissive, she felt no less ready for him than she had that night in Holly Hill House. Tonight he was dressed in a shimmering mauve shirt decorated with an elaborate cravat of fine black silk worn with immaculately cut trousers. But all this was nothing compared to the impact of his wide, almond-shaped eyes, which blazed an unnaturally beautiful green.

Aware that she had never before felt such instant animal lust, it was all she could do to prevent her weakened legs from buckling her to the ground and begging him to be merciful!

Fortunately Helge was there to break into her feverishly aroused emotions with a sobering enquiry. 'Did Steven not come with you?' she asked. 'The invitation was meant for you both.'

Dragging her eyes from the Count, Vanessa found herself annoyed by this reminder of Steven. 'No,' she managed. 'There seems to have been some sort of confusion. I haven't seen him all day and then there was a mix up over the hotel and . . .' Vanessa broke off realising that none of this would interest the Count. She added lamely, '. . . so he couldn't tell me about your invitation.'

Helge's eyes grew round with astonishment. 'And yet you still came,' she cried. 'What a sweet trusting girl you must be! Do you think he will be much further delayed?'

Just for this one moment Vanessa found herself not caring whether Steven ever arrived. He had, in the past twenty-four hours, proved himself to be capable of creating chaos out of complication, and images of him with Michelle made her wish for an opportunity to be alone with the Count.

'Perhaps we three should start dinner in the hope that he will soon arrive?' Helge was asking.

Vanessa agreed and she found the Count offering her his arm, his touch electrifying her. Helge led the way into a dining room with a huge table, glittering with gold and silver, and lit by two magnificent candelabra. Helge took the head of the table while Vanessa found herself seated directly opposite the Count. Feeling his eyes boring into her, she sought respite by fussing with the heavy linen napkin, but was unable to avoid looking at him when he spoke directly to her.

'You were magnificent that day,' he told her in warm

tones that seemed to trickle through her nerves like warmed honey. Helge demanded to know that meant and the Count turned his excoriating gaze from Vanessa to their hostess. 'Vanessa responded more fully to my Tantric class than any other person I have known.' The Count's voice quickened as he recalled the afternoon. 'It was like the eruption of a volcano. Such fire! So much dramatic beauty. It was breathtaking to witness. It was as nothing I have ever seen before. Totally exciting.'

Vanessa found her eyes locked into the seemingly depthless gaze of the Count. Longing to dive into them with headlong, total abandonment, she thrilled to see him returning her mesmerised glance with equal fervency and was certain that they had made a silent pact. For her part, Vanessa had never felt so totally excited in her life. The thought that Steven might arrive at any moment now seemed more of a threat than a promise.

'Sounds like something quite exceptional,' Helge murmured somewhere on the edge of Vanessa's consciousness. Then, bringing Vanessa back down to earth by addressing her next remark directly to her, she said, 'You are to be congratulated, my dear.' She raised a glass of wine in salute. 'There are few women that can so attract the Count.'

Quivering with pleasure at this compliment, Vanessa glanced again at him. In his eyes she could see mirrored the lust that now seethed in her, a lust so total and committed that she barely recognised it as her own. When the Count raised his glass to his lips, it took Vanessa a moment to understand that she was not merely a witness to these events but a player. As she returned the toast she felt reality, and its consequences, draining from her. At that moment she felt anything was possible and nothing denied.

'Do you think we should delay dinner any further?' Helge enquired of her guests. 'Perhaps Steven is critically delayed and may not come at all. What do you think, my dear? Should we wait?'

Vanessa heard this but absorbed nothing. Her mind had abandoned itself to her lust and she wanted nothing more than to hurry the inception of the unspoken pact she had made with the Count. The feeling of unreality – of taking part in a play upon a stage – overwhelmed her and she was astonished to hear herself say, 'No. I don't think we should wait at all.'

Unaccountably Vanessa found that she had risen from the table, circled it and now stood before the Count.

Vanessa heard Helge murmur a polite protest, but it meant nothing since all Vanessa could think of was that the Count had also risen from the table and now stood before her, reaching out to lay a hand upon her shoulder. Then he murmured their excuses and guided her from the room.

No longer caring what Helge or anyone else thought, Vanessa was taken to a room crowded with objects that might, in other circumstances, have intrigued her. At that moment though she was interested in nothing except the man who stood before her.

When the Count, his lips hovering teasingly close to her own, smiled and touched his fingertips to each of her temples, Vanessa felt a surging charge rage through her, leaving her arms and legs defencelessly limp. This man could do anything with her but the sense of freedom she felt in knowing that she *wanted* everything, liberated her from all restraint.

When the Count murmured, 'Undress her,' she couldn't imagine who he was talking to until she felt hands on her dress, loosening it and pulling it from her body. She found she had no interest in knowing who it was that stripped her clothes from her and only rejoiced that she would soon be naked for him.

Stripped of everything but her shoes, Vanessa felt gently insistent hands forcing her to kneel before the Count, where her eyes went at once to his bulging crotch. She would have reached for him except she found her arms had been taken by the unseen person behind her and she was held.

A tiny cry of frustration escaped her lips as she saw other hands – Renate's hands – caressing the Count from behind, moving across his chest and down over his flat stomach as Vanessa could only watch.

As the hands circled ever closed to the treasure that Vanessa was sure lay beneath the thin layering of trouser cloth, she made a vain attempt to drag her hands and arms free of their manual bondage, but she was held firmly and could only moan in protest as Renate's hands caressed the ever-growing bulge within inches of her eyes.

Feeling herself almost salivating, she watched in increasing excitement as those alien fingers she so dearly wished were her own took up the silver tag of his fly zip and teasingly drew it down.

Renate's hands sought him out and soon, rearing with awesome beauty before her eyes, she saw his aroused flesh for the first time. She wanted nothing more than to taste it, to take it, consume it and make it her own and so it was with a cry of gratitude that she felt her head pressed forward and could finally reach with her mouth for the object that, at that moment, she most desired in the entire world.

Hungrily she snapped at it, gagging as it found the back of her throat, content that she alone could service this reliquary of her desire. So intense was she on transmitting pleasure that she screamed a protest when she felt strong arms lifting her, dragging her mouth from its dedicated worship to be drawn backwards across the room.

Her protest only subsided when she felt herself being laid on a couch and watched with dumb excitement as she saw the Count stepping from his trousers, being helped from his shirt by Renate, and then advancing in breathtaking naked arousal towards her as she lay in a shameless sprawl and hopeful expectation of immolation.

His touch, as he lowered his weight between her hungry thighs, felt like a benediction – as if she were to be sacrificed to unbearable pleasure. Then she felt him fill her, his immensity only becoming daunting as it thrust home hard and fast, touching her tenderest places almost painfully until the hurt was buried under the onset of the first of an avalanche of orgasms.

Somewhere Vanessa was aware that a woman was screaming in exultation and total surrender. It was only of passing interest to her to know that the woman that screamed was herself.

His honeyed voice was whispering in her ear as she writhed helplessly under his powerful thrusting body and was cast adrift on an ocean of uncharted, uncontrollable emotions. 'Use your Tantric powers,' his voice seethed into her ear. 'You must leave your body. It is the only means by which you will be able to control the pain.'

Her mind reeling Vanessa tried to understand what was being said to her. Pain? What pain could possibly be imposed upon a body drowning in pleasure? As she sought to peer into his beautiful face and cover his mouth with her own, her wrists were taken in a firm grip before being dragged from his back. Protesting to these unseen assailants, Vanessa struggled as she felt straps being put about her while her hands were pinioned helplessly above her head. Her writhing became more intensified as she saw the Count raise his body from her own while the relentless pleasure pierced her very soul.

Aghast she looked into his eyes, once so warm and softly inviting, but now so hard and unrelenting that they had become daunting – so intense was the expression on his face.

Helge's voice whispered into her ear. 'You must not be afraid. But you must accept the torrent you have unleashed. Your lover is pitiless but you will prevail.'

Staring upwards into the wild eyes of the man who continued to pound relentlessly into her loins, Vanessa experienced the first pangs of terror. Her own body was now saturated by pleasure and ready for surcease but still he continued to thrust and delve into her soul until she feared it would never end. Her voice, which fifteen minutes earlier had proclaimed orgasmic release, now begged for respite.

Frantically she tried to use her upthrusting loins to push him away but succeeded only in making the way clearer for his deeper, punishing thrusts. Suddenly she was filled with the horrific idea that she was engaged in a mortal combat!

In her desperation she finally understood why he had cautioned her to use her Tantric powers to vacate her body. He wanted it entirely to himself!

Just at the point when she feared she would descend into a continuous scream of unsupportable pleasured pain, he stopped his relentless battering. Vanessa knew that he had come to climax and watched in triumph as she felt him convulsively throbbing deep in her womb.

The relief that flooded her as the torment ended was so intense that she felt the blood draining from her head and fell into a state of unfeeling consciousness, buoyed only by the sense of triumph and the knowledge that she had pleasured him beyond his control.

On the very brink of escape Vanessa heard Helge's voice. 'Well done, my dear.' Then the warm, velvet loss of consciousness engulfed her completely.

Chapter Ten

'Where is she?' cried Steven the moment Grace came into Henri's studio.

Grace looked from Steven to Henri and back again in bewilderment.

'You were with her all day. Where did she go?'

'What in hell are you talking about? I brought her back to the Hotel Meurice hours ago.'

'The *Meurice*?' Steven cried incredulously. 'I said to bring her to the *Lancaster*!'

Grace stared at Steven for a moment. 'Shit!' she finally exclaimed. 'How could I make a mistake like that?'

Steven sighed impatiently. 'Because I mentioned to you that I had tried the Meurice but the suite I preferred was already taken! God, none of that matters. What happened after you took her to the Meurice?'

'Well, nothing that I saw – but I did see her go into the hotel. I know she did.'

'And you didn't see her come out again?'

'No. It so happens that the cab we'd taken got boxed in by traffic and we had to sit there for some minutes before we could leave. I know she didn't come out again.' Grace saw Steven turn away disappointed and worried and called after him. 'Why don't you call the Meurice and ask what they know. She could be still there, waiting for you!'

Steven nodded and made his way to the telephone. 'Anyone know the phone number?' he asked before muttering that it didn't matter and dialling Information. Within minutes he was speaking to the Hotel Meurice receptionist.

'Yes, sir, I remember the lady well. She was surprised to find you had no reservation.'

'But what happened to her after she left your desk?'

The receptionist let out an effusive Gallic sigh. 'You understand, sir, this is a very busy hotel. I lost sight of the lady—' The man broke off as if another thought had occurred to him. 'One moment. I am almost sure I saw her approached by a chauffeur in uniform. Yes. Now I am certain. She came to the desk with him and asked us to look after certain packages when they arrived.'

'This chauffeur. What did he look like?'

'M'sieur!' the man protested. 'There was nothing extraordinary about him. He looked like a chauffeur – nothing more.'

On the brink of losing his temper, Steven found Grace at his elbow, urgently trying to tell him something. Turning to her he asked, 'What is it?'

'What about your chauffeur?'

'What, you mean the limousine driver? I told them I didn't need the car any more.' Steven broke off, his voice cracking. 'I rented a self-drive instead. I was taking her to Amsterdam tomorrow.'

'So what was he doing waiting at the hotel?'

'I don't know. I suppose he was on another job.'

Grace shook her head. 'I don't think so. Listen, I told you my cab got trapped in traffic, right?'

Steven nodded.

'Well, while I sat there I noticed the limousine you'd been using parked in front. Wait a minute! That's right! I remember thinking then that he'd been looking out for her. When she went into the hotel I saw him going in after her!'

'But you didn't see them come out?'

'No.'

Turning back to the receiver Steven thanked the receptionist and disconnected. 'I'll call the limousine company,' he told Grace. 'They'll know if he had any business there.' Even as he started to dial he hesitated. 'But why would he want to abduct her?'

As he dialled Grace had another question. 'Have you been to the police?'

'I spoke to them. They practically laughed in my face. Young, beautiful woman missing in Paris for a few hours? They told me to come back in a week if she hasn't reappeared by then.' Steven turned back his voice less excited. 'What was her mood like today? How did she seem to you? Was she angry about my stupidity with Michelle?'

As Grace went to answer he held up his hand as his number started ringing. Within seconds he had slammed down the telephone. 'Bloody answering machine! What kind of limo service is that?'

Recovering somewhat, Steven turned back to Grace. 'Did she say anything about going back to London?'

'Not to me. I told you she couldn't wait to get back to

the hotel.' Grace broke off to glance at Henri. 'You spoke to her while I was changing. Did she say anything to you?'

'Nothing very much,' Henri said.

'There's only one thought that occurs to me,' Grace said with some reluctance.

'Which is . . .?'

'She told me that one of the things that excited her about you was the way you surprised her. Put her into things without warning . . .'

'And – what about it?'

'Well, maybe she mistook some stranger's approach for the beginning of another of your adventures . . .'

'And went off with them?' Steven's tone was both guilty and incredulous.

Grace shrugged. 'I agree it doesn't sound like her. We're talking about an intelligent woman here . . .' Grace dismissed her own theory. 'No. Forget it. She wouldn't have gone with a stranger . . . unless . . .'

Steven turned to Henri. 'Look, I'm sorry to be tying up your phone like this. You understand I'm worried?'

Henri shrugged. 'I understand. Be my guest.'

Steven nodded, the telephone already in his hand. 'I need to call London.'

The phone was answered after a couple of rings. 'Roz? It's Steven!'

Roz had been on the very brink of sleep and now sat up in bed and pulled the telephone closer to her ear, totally alert. 'What is it?' she asked.

'Vanessa's gone!' he said.

'What do you mean gone? You had some sort of fight or what?'

'Nothing like that. She just didn't come back to the hotel.'

'Right . . .' said Roz wondering what she, in London, could do for him in Paris. 'You sound as if you think something sinister might have happened.'

Steven's groan resounded down the line. 'I hope not. Listen, what I want you to do is go round to her apartment – you went there, didn't you? You know where it is? I tried to ring her earlier but there was no answer. She could be there and just not answering. Will you check it out?'

'Of course, but what makes you think she might have come back to London?'

'I don't know. I don't think so but it's a possibility. Will you?'

Focusing her eyes on her clock she saw that it registered just after midnight. 'Of course, but – tonight?'

Steven was silent for a moment. 'Roz, I'm getting desperate. I have to know.'

'OK, I'll do it. Where can I call you back?'

'I've moved to the Lancaster. Call me there.'

Roz hung up the telephone and stared at it. She wondered if Steven knew what he was doing. The girl was beautiful and he was obviously obsessed but he knew very little about her. Maybe she had simply been stricken with conscience and returned to a previous lover. Who could tell? The possibilities were endless.

The girl could be anywhere . . .

Chapter Eleven

Fully aware that she was adrift in a fantastical world conjured from her dreaming subconscious, Vanessa felt she could happily remain in this place forever.

The landscape – the path through the forest with its trees on either side – sprang directly from the paintings she had seen in Steven's studio, but the figure that had featured so strongly was no longer visible and Vanessa knew that, in her vision, she had become that girl and that she now saw everything as if through her eyes.

What had seemed sinister and foreboding now became light and welcoming. She came into a forest glade where the sun glinted through the trees, its beams defined by the floating, highly coloured blossom which lent its comforting perfume to further enhance her sensual delight in this magical place.

As she moved forward she reached out to touch the fringe of trees that lined the path. Instead of the rough, bark texture she expected, she found the rearing, soaring trunks warm and soft to her touch – pliable and textured like so many huge phalluses giving song to her already enraptured heart.

This was a place out of time – an unexpected move into

another dimension of sensory perception – in which Vanessa rejoiced even though she knew that she might soon be forced to awake to a harsher reality.

For the moment however she was happy to dwell in this fantasy and store the ecstatic feeling of completeness against her inevitable awakening.

Her ears, keening for every sensual delight, picked up a crooning sound. It was every bit as insistent as the rhythms of the Tantric experience but sweeter, more pleasantly modulated, and emanating from a clearing in the forest. As she rounded a curve on the forest path, she saw before her a dell, bathed in sunshine and peopled with dancers so beautiful that Vanessa hurried forward to join them.

Joining their rhythms as if born to them, she felt hands caressing her body and face to leave trails of glowing pleasure in their wake. Emerging, forming before her delighted eyes, Vanessa saw a glowing column which as it rose and defined itself, took on the features of a smiling, approving Helge. Going forward to embrace the image, Vanessa found herself surrounded instead by other figures – those of Renate, Sylvie and the warm touch of male hands – until she felt herself brought before the deific figure of Helge who spoke softly.

'You are come to the edge of our world.' Helge's voice came as a caress to Vanessa's ears. 'Beyond this place lies a Tantric Garden of Delight. But, be warned, the path to Paradise passes through Purgatory, for none may be admitted that have not known every sensory experience which you must know encompasses pain as well as pleasure, for who can judge sweetness that has not tasted vinegar? You have already shown your willingness to explore the Nirvana that is in each of us, that waits only our discovery, but do you have the courage to proceed?'

Joyously Vanessa acceded, though she never consciously spoke. Instantly it was if a veil had lifted from her eyes as she saw the commanding face and figure of the Count Alonzo displacing the image of Helge.

With a cry, Vanessa hurried forward to embrace him but found her feet unable to find purchase on the forest glade's floor and felt insistent hands on her body holding her back, less by force than by caress . . .

'Are you awake, my dear?' asked Helge.

Startled, and a little angry to have been torn from her dream, Vanessa turned her head and stared into Helge's warm but concerned eyes.

'You were in a dream – or was it a nightmare?' Helge asked.

'A dream,' answered Vanessa, now aware that the caresses she had experienced in her dream were still with her in this reluctant wakening. Looking around, she saw both Sylvie and Renate smoothing her naked skin with oils and creams and, stretching like a contented cat, she arched herself upward from the couch on which she lay.

'It was a beautiful dream,' she murmured contentedly. 'The most beautiful I have ever known.' Smiling, careless of any implication which might be drawn, she turned to Helge. 'You were there.'

Helge's smile beamed. 'I'm flattered.'

'And everyone. It was so beautiful that I didn't want to come back.'

167

'And do you know where this dream took place?'

Vanessa sighed. 'If I did I would go back there right now.' Pausing, she recalled one phrase from the many she had heard. 'Someone called it a Garden of Delight. A *Tantric* Garden of Delight.'

Helge nodded as if not only understanding but approving. Looking up to the girls still caressing Vanessa's body, she called their attention by clapping her hands. 'Leave us,' she told them. 'Renate, you will bring us the tea.' The two girls bobbed deferential curtsies and made off with their curiously choreographed trotting run.

Vanessa sat up as Helge handed her a silken gown similar but different in colour to those worn by the girls. 'You may find this more comfortable to wear.' Turning away, Vanessa rose and found that the garment could be slipped over the head to fall into two floor-length panels which covered her but left her with a sense of quite exciting vulnerability. She looked up as Helge returned to hand her a finely worked golden belt which, cast about her waist, held the two panels in place. Delighted with the effect Vanessa looked up, smiling her approval. 'Those girls seem to be devoted to you,' she murmured.

'Indeed,' nodded Helge. 'I am very fortunate to command such affection from the many young people that gather to me.'

'You make it sound almost like a religious devotion.'

Shrugging the suggestion aside Helge smiled. 'I am no priestess.'

'But you have a philosophy?' Vanessa pressed. 'I remember you speaking of my having a destiny?'

Helge nodded. 'If there is one then it is only that, deep within all of us, there is an untapped potential for an ultimate experience which circumstances and society force us to leave untapped. My belief is that each individual should be given access to their inner potential – their fantasies, if you will – and go forth boldly in search of the ultimate they are capable of knowing.'

This statement echoed so directly Vanessa's dream that she felt, for a moment, as if Helge had shared it. She was suddenly tempted to reveal everything to this charismatic woman. However Helge's tendency to launch into large concepts continued to ring cautioning bells somewhere in the deeper reaches of her mind. 'Going "forth boldly",' Vanessa said, attempting to lighten the mood with a tentative laugh, 'is all very well but first you have to find the road that leads there.'

Helge turned to Vanessa, her eyes burning with the light of a zealot. 'That is precisely what I intend. You, above all other women, can be our guide along that path. You took the first steps last night.'

Embarrassed to be reminded of her total abandonment with the Count, especially in front of others, Vanessa wanted to turn aside from Helge's burning gaze but found herself transfixed like a terrified rabbit in headlights. '*Me?*' she managed to squeak.

Helge nodded vigourously. 'You!' she declared positively. 'There was another – known to you – Imogene. She too had the will and the courage to explore the immense power of her sensuality. She, had she lived and not been diverted, would have opened the path for other women to

169

follow. I – and the Count agrees with me – feel that you will prove to be her worthy successor.'

Vanessa stared at Helge, unable to break from the bondage of her direct gaze or dismiss what was being said to her. Suspecting that Helge could be quite dangerous, she could not forget the intensity of her sexual experience with the Count nor deny the urge to repeat it. That the experience had led her to dream and, further, into recognising the echoes of that dream in Helge's words, overwhelmed Vanessa with the thought that she might be on the brink of a great revelation.

Both transfixed and confused, it was tempting to Vanessa to consider if her dream – her fantasy – was realisable.

She finally decided a little risk along the way might be worth it. The alternative was to return to the grey-hued world she already knew too well, to spend a lifetime wondering if she had not deprived herself of a great, and possibly ultimate, experience. Suddenly it seemed transparently obvious that it was only the fear of commitment that was preventing her from taking that first step towards achieving ultimate self-realisation.

For the moment, Vanessa was able to delay her decision as Renate returned bearing a tray on which stood two fine porcelain bowls. 'Your tea, Lady,' Renate announced as she laid down the tray and, again exercising her curious deference by a tiny curtsey, turned silently away and out of the room.

Helge brought one of the bowls to Vanessa. 'It is a herbal concoction of my own devising. Most find it restorative if not a stimulant.'

170

Vanessa raised the bowl to her lips. Her first impression was of the sweet aroma and then the lava flow of tingling sensations as the brew slid down her throat. Along with this gratifying sensation came a slight headiness, as if she had dipped deep into a fine brandy. 'It's delicious!' she announced to Helge. 'What is in it?'

'Nothing harmful, I assure you. Some herbs, spices, of course, honey, ginger and the tiniest trace of alcohol. I'm glad it pleases you.'

Vanessa was unable to resist draining the bowl. With each sip, she found the wondrous effect it created not only intensifying but bringing a disconcerting glow to loins already disturbed both by the dream and the caresses of the two girls.

Emboldened beyond her own understanding, Vanessa laid down the bowl and turned to Helge. 'This self-exploration you spoke of, do you seriously think I might achieve it?'

'I have no doubt of it,' replied Helge.

'And would the Count be found somewhere along this notional exploratory way?'

Helge's smile positively beamed forth. 'He would feel himself much deprived if it were otherwise.'

Vanessa, feeling herself already committed, nevertheless hesitated as she heard a warning echo from her dream. 'And does the road to this Nirvana lead through some purgatorial forest?'

Helge's eyes arched in surprise. 'Where did you learn that phrase?'

'That doesn't matter. Only your answer.'

'Sensual enlightenment means experiencing all forms of pleasure, some of which can only be attained through pain.'

Vanessa nodded as what she had learned in her dream was being confirmed. 'You are saying that I cannot appreciate wine until I have tasted vinegar.'

Helge, delighted, came towards Vanessa with arms half raised as if to embrace her. 'You really are a most remarkable girl.'

Allowing Helge to hold her, Vanessa asked in a whisper, 'What does that mean, exactly?'

Close to her ear Vanessa sensed that Helge was smiling. 'It means the price of admission to my Garden of Delights, and your total freedom to explore all and everything that lies there, is that you come to me and acknowledge me with your submission.'

'More specific, please,' said Vanessa, still standing in Helge's close embrace.

'Nothing less than the submission you gave to that whore in the club. And certainly much more imaginative.'

Emboldened by the glowing effect of the herbal tea, Vanessa insisted, 'Are you saying I would be beaten?'

'Only with love,' cooed Helge, 'and to ensure that no sensory experience was left unknown to you.'

Murmuring appreciation of Helge's lips which now brushed against her throat, Vanessa felt that she had been shown a threshold which she must either cross or reject. Knowing full well she would in other, less stimulated circumstances, have fled from this situation, she felt herself instead propelled forward by recalling Helge's earlier words that most people rejected experience because of fear.

At this crucial moment Vanessa found she needed fear to bring forth her courage and was delighted to find both in balance. 'I agree,' she murmured into Helge's throat. 'Do with me what you will.'

Helge's voice soothed itself into her ears like velvet. 'How wonderful that you show such deep trust of me.' Helge's lips lovingly but gently sought out Vanessa's own. 'I have, in another place, a stage worthy of such delightful drama.'

'Not here, in Paris?' asked Vanessa as a feeling of total languor gripped her entire being.

'No,' smiled Helge directly into her face. 'Not here.'

Chapter Twelve

Meeting Steven at Heathrow, Roz was immediately aware that he had returned from Paris bearing a heavy burden of defeat.

They barely spoke until their car cleared the airport traffic and was speeding on the M4. 'Nothing?' Roz asked.

Steven shook his head. 'It's been two days,' he said as if that said it all.

'And the limousine driver?'

'No trace. It's obvious that he is involved – but in what? Kidnap? Murder? Then again – why? Dammit, there's no reason!' Steven gave a long heartfelt sigh. 'I'm at the point of wanting just to *know*. Know anything. Even the worst possible news.'

They rode almost into town before Roz felt able to break in on his internal anguish. 'I've compiled a cross-plot of all your movements in Paris. I've documented everyone she could have had contact with. None of it makes any sense.'

Steven looked at Roz. 'What does that mean – sense?'

'What I mean is your trip was not pre-planned. She didn't know anything about it until the last minute – no one could have known she was to be in Paris.'

'So what?'

'Well, it means that whatever happened must have started and ended in Paris – in those first two days. That's why I concentrated on her movements there. There's no sense nor logic but there is one oddity.'

'Which is?'

'There were only two occasions when neither you nor the model, Grace, can account for her movements. Time when she was alone.'

'Tell me.'

'The first is in Madame Gallia's. You left her in the room and went downstairs. You told me that when she came down she was in company of a German guy.'

'Herr Otto Rauffenstille? Nothing there. I had him checked out. He was alone with her for a total of about ninety seconds. They rode down in the lift together. He's the director of an electronics company, has three grown children and had already returned to Munich the next day.'

'So that leaves only one other window of, let's call it, "opportunity".' Roz looked down at her notes on her lap. 'During the shopping trip with Grace there was only one time when they lost sight of each other. That was at the House of Vellioria.'

Steven looked puzzled. 'Didn't she go off for a fitting or something?'

Roz shook her head. 'I haven't met this Grace girl – just spoken to her on the telephone – so you tell me, what do you think of her?'

'She wouldn't be involved in this thing. She's been as worried as any of us. She's spent her entire time doing everything she can for us in Paris,' snapped Steven a little impatiently.

'That isn't what I meant. Would you trust her judgement?'

'Certainly. She's a highly sophisticated girl. She's been around and can certainly take care of herself.'

'So you'd trust her?'

'Certainly, but where's this leading us?'

'Simply that, after visiting Vellioria, Grace said your girl seemed to be nervous.'

'About what?'

Looking again at her notes, Roz searched out the name she was looking for. 'The owner, Countess Helge.'

Steven reacted as if Roz had prodded him with a high voltage cable. 'Who?' he yelled.

'The Countess Helge. She owns Vellioria.'

Steven seemed to be about to explode. 'So that's it!' he cried.

'That's what?' asked a puzzled Roz.

'That Helge bitch . . .' Steven seethed silently for a while before turning to Roz. 'You never met Imogene, did you?'

Roz shook her head. 'I've heard you speak of her.'

'Well, when I met Imogene she was on the run from that crazy woman Helge.'

'On the run?' mused Roz. 'You make it sound as if she'd escaped from somewhere.'

'She had – from Helge. She'd held her mesmerised in some crazy castle or other for years. Little more than a slave . . . I had heard Helge had sworn to revenge herself on me. Crazy talk, I thought, but now this . . .'

'You think she's kidnapped Vanessa?'

'I'm certain of it! It's just the kind of thing she would do!'

Roz shook her head. 'That sounds crazy to me . . .'

'She is crazy! The moment we get to the office I want you to call that detective agency in Paris and get them started on uncovering everything there is to know about this woman.' Roz was still making notes when they arrived at the office. Steven continued, 'You know something? I'm in the wrong damn city.' Calling to the driver, he said, 'Take me back to the airport.'

'Hold on,' Roz said. 'Wait ten minutes. I need to pack a few things. I'm coming with you.'

While he waited for Roz, Steven used the car phone to call and confirm two seats on their next flight. Roz's analysis of the situation was a great deal more concise than the detectives he'd hired in Paris. The link between the chauffeur and Helge was the most promising lead yet.

As Roz came hurrying across the pavement to get into the car, he saw that she not only carried a small case but had a bundle of papers under her arm.

'Think we'll find her?' Roz asked as she settled into the limousine.

Steven nodded. 'Let's hope to God we do before that crazy bitch does something irrevocable!'

Chapter Thirteen

Vanessa woke into a boundless wonderland of pleasure where time had no meaning.

Soft hands were already on her body – tenderly caressing and stimulating her with warmed oils, bringing her to sensuous awareness of just how alive she was.

It was Renate that tended her this morning, her dark red hair falling in cascades about a young oval face from which burned wide brown eyes. Renate's lips created tiny explosions on her body as the warm oils seeped deep beneath her skin, adding their heat to that already being sensuously generated deep in her body. Vanessa had never known such arousal. It was, as Helge had promised, as if she were being led into another dimension of experience in which anything was possible.

She had, at some point, been transported from Paris to this place which seemed to Vanessa to be built for unstinted pleasure.

With a tiny murmur she insisted Renate's lips moved to her hardened nipples.

As she allowed her senses to envelop her, she felt herself coming to orgasm. Never had she dreamed that such pleasure could exist or that her body was capable of experiencing it. The pleasures of the flesh had never tasted this sweet. Gently guiding Renate's tongue between her thighs, she longed for the whips that Helge had promised would flash her body with even more intense pleasures.

She was determined to scream for Helge just as Renate, Sylvie and the others screamed for her.

Now nearing her pleasure peak, she urged Renate's tongue deeper inside her and laid a hand upon the girl's cheek. She smiled. 'Why is there no music?' she asked.

Renate looked as offended as deference allowed. 'But there is,' she insisted.

Turning her head she could indeed hear a low rhythmic melody insinuating itself into the windowless chamber. 'Ah, yes,' she murmured. 'But I thought that music was in my head.'

Relieved, Renate smiled. 'Shall you bathe now?'

'In a moment.' She smiled. 'First bring me my tea.'

Turning to one side Renate brought a flat silver bowl forward and offered it to her.

Lifting it to her lips she was reminded of the first time she had tasted this delicious honeyed brew which lit her mind and body with dancing lights and a feeling of exquisite happiness. The infusion burst into her blood, surging through her veins and exciting every nerve ending in her body and she now drank it three or four times a day.

The liquid, which had the consistency of a thick milk shake, struck the taste buds as sweet, but then, after sinking into her throat, left behind a residual bitterness. The aftertaste was to be dissipated by whichever of the girls attended her.

Even now Renate was dipping her long tongue into a dish of sticky honey ready to smear into the inside of her mouth. With a nod she gave her permission for Renate to attend her.

The young girl leaned forward and pressed her tongue deep into Vanessa's mouth, flicking it from roof to tongue to eliminate the aftertaste. As she completed the chore and withdrew, Vanessa's eyes were bright with excitement and she suddenly found the girl very appealing.

'Take more honey onto your tongue,' she told her. Renate bent to open the dish and came up, tongue coated and eyes bright. This was a game she obviously enjoyed.

'Give me your breasts,' Vanessa said.

Kneeling up on the couch, Renate braced back her shoulders and thrust her breasts into Vanessa's questing hands.

Taking each of the girl's nipples in her fingers, Vanessa dug deeply into them with her nails until she saw Renate wince.

'No,' she murmured. 'You must not frown at my taking pleasure from you. You should be happy. Smile for me . . .'

To obey Renate had to withdraw her tongue and, showing her tiny white teeth, did her best to smile. 'If it pleases you.' The words were uttered through gritted teeth as fire points of pain danced into her senses.

'But where is the honey?' she asked, searching the girl's eyes.

Renate flinched guiltily at the trick that had been played on her. 'I beg your pardon but I . . .'

'Then you must be punished. Isn't that how things are done here?'

Renate nodded. 'Yes, mistress.'

Letting the girl go, Vanessa cast aside the silks that had partially covered her and strode towards the screen that concealed a sunken bath, whose perfumed waters had already pervaded the atmosphere. 'While I bathe I shall see you with your pretty boys,' she said.

Renate's expression grew pale as she padded in the wake of the woman they addressed only with the greatest reverence. 'If you wish it.'

Sinking into the perfumed water, her thick black hair piled high on her head, Vanessa smiled up at Renate. 'Don't you enjoy them?'

'You know, Lady, that I prefer my own sex.'

Bringing hands cupped full of the water over her heated breasts, she smiled. 'Your preference is not to be considered in my presence. Send for two of them.'

Renate did her curious bobbing curtsey and padded away.

Revelling in the caress of the perfumed water, she again marvelled at the pleasure garden to which she had been brought. Laying back, she experienced the thrill of the explorer, feeling that all had been made new in the world and that she was poised on the brink of awakening the true self that Helge had promised lay dormant within the tingling anticipatory shell of her body.

Here, though she was pampered, with everyone at her command, none of the young men were permitted to touch or approach her, so the one indulgence denied her could only be experienced vicariously through her plaything attendants. They would report themselves afterwards and Helge would punish them severely, but that had been the rule of this place long before she came to it.

How she came to be here had long ceased to interest her and even why she had been brought here interested her only occasionally. One did not question a dream nor distrust a fantasy. In a place without time she felt she would not age and she found herself with no desire to rush forward in search of reality. Caught in the thrall of a continuing erotic dream, she had no desire to wake. All was for her pleasure and she felt no need to ask why.

Fully convinced that Steven had brought her here, she thought she saw the pattern as he had opened one gate after another, carefully leading her on her journey to this place of ultimate indulgence. In retrospect, she saw how her own cautious naivety had caused doubts when, had she known the pleasure garden awaiting her, she would have rushed forward in joy.

How could she have imagined such a place? How could she have known that Steven's careful schooling in sensory indulgence was destined to bring her here? How could mortal woman be expected to understand that it was possible to live life poised on the very brink of continuous orgasm?

The oils in the water were invading every sensory pore of her body. Though soothing they had an irritant quality about their invasion. Tingling their way deep into her blood they roused her outer body just as the musky perfume rising from the water invaded her inner senses and detonated tiny pleasure bombs.

It was then that the largest, most beautiful black cat she had ever seen landed with a soft footfall on the raised edge of the sunken bath. He wore a black velvet collar, studded with what looked like real emeralds. His huge clear eyes matched the colour of the gems as he stared unwaveringly at her with a piercing intelligence.

'Hello, lovely pussycat,' she cooed, reaching out to stroke the arrogantly proud feline. 'What's your name?'

'His name is Pluto,' said Helge who had come round the screen to stand looking down at her. 'I'm pleased you find him beautiful.'

Helge was dressed in a loose silk kaftan with a flowing silk scarf about her hair. Her appearance was, as always, commanding.

Despite the reverence which Vanessa was invariably shown in this place, Helge always somehow managed to frighten her a little. Now, however, she was smiling down on her with the indulgent smile of an aunt looking at her favourite niece. 'Are you content?' she asked.

Purring in unison with the beautiful Pluto, she murmured, 'Immensely.'

'Your pleasure is everything to us. We want you to be happy.'

Burying her head into the luxuriant fur of the cat gave Vanessa a moment to consider her situation and the question that inevitably arose from it. 'Why did you decide to indulge me with all this pleasure?'

Helge seemed amused. 'But why should I not?' she asked.

Vanessa concentrated on stroking the velvety fur of the cat as she considered that her feelings towards this woman were not so much mixed as mangled. Her own impulses had never been directly towards other women but the pleasure she found in dominating the willingly submissive Renate had shown her there were whole depths of pleasure – different, but no less worthwhile – to be shared with her own sex. The imprinted memory of what she had felt at the club Steven had taken her to was with her still. She had been on the point of accepting Grace's thrilling invitation to whip Henri and had only been prevented from doing so by Steven's even more welcome interruption. The memory of how she had, with her lover lodged deep inside her, given her mouth to another man scalded her conscience.

What was she? Until this moment she had always thought of herself as heterosexual, inclined to sexual experience with men and anything else no more than a diversion but, alone with Helge, she suspected her resolve would crumble. The woman had such presence that Vanessa could well understand how she came to command such imperious respect from both men and women.

Helge turned away as Renate returned. 'Yes?' She demanded of the girl, whose total submission made her wide-eyed.

'The Lady asked me to summon the men,' she murmured, curtsying deferentially.

'Well then,' said Helge. 'Show them to her.'

Opening her eyes, Vanessa sat up in the water, as Helge smiled down at her indulgently. 'I'll leave you now but tonight I shall send Renate and Sylvie to dress you for this evening.'

Helge's tone suggesting further delights, Vanessa found her curiosity aroused. 'What is happening tonight?'

Taking both of Vanessa's hands in her own, Helge's

eyes shone with excitement. 'Tonight you are to meet your peers. Women like yourself who have dared to seek their inner-selves.' Seeing Vanessa's eyes cloud with apprehension, Helge went on, 'But there is absolutely nothing for you to worry about. You will delight and astonish them. You too, I know, will revel in their veneration.' Helge squeezed Vanessa's hands before releasing them and turning away. 'Now I shall leave you to your personal pleasures.' Again, Helge smiled indulgently. 'Until tonight then?'

Helge waited until two young men, their naked muscular bodies oiled to gleaming perfection, followed Renate round the screen. After registering Helge's presence they knelt before her, their hands seeking out the nape of their necks, before rising with athletic grace to their feet.

'Face your Lady, not me!' snapped Helge.

The two young men turned towards Vanessa's eager eyes as she lay back in the water. She was amused to see that while both were anxious to present their well-defined bodies to the best advantage, only one of them was proudly erect. The sight of the two perfectly contoured male bodies, submissively aroused, sent waves of previously unknown empowerment flooding into her loins. Now she could barely wait for Helge to leave.

Helge obliged at once and excused herself. 'I can hardly wait for tonight,' she said as she went.

Watching Helge leave, Pluto in close attendance, she waited only until she heard the door of her room close before turning her unwavering gaze back to the two nervous men. Laying back in the bath, she cupped her breasts with both hands and allowed them to crest out of the water as her fingers sought out the engorged nipples. 'What is your name?' she asked of the one that had yet to become fully erect.

'Rolf.'

'Well, Rolf, do you not find me beautiful?' The young man shifted uneasily on his feet before he nodded. His throat worked but it was obvious to her that his fear was choking his words.

'Answer me!' she insisted.

'Yes. Very beautiful.'

'So why do you come before me limp and useless?'

His throat worked frantically as his eyes remained fixed on her self-caressing hands. 'I don't know. I think I am . . .' he broke off.

'You are what?' she demanded.

'Afraid,' he murmured.

'Of me?'

Rolf could only nod.

Looking directly at the rigidity of his companion she said, 'Fear doesn't seem to have affected your friend.'

Rolf's face reflected his panic at the comparison.

Smiling she let her hands wander under the water, stretching herself luxuriously under the avid gaze of the young men. Remembering how men loved near-naked girls to strut and pose for them, she saw the opportunity to equalise matters. 'Show yourselves to me,' she murmured as her self-caress caused desire to sear through her body like a voluptuous tidal wave.

The two young men, both dedicated body-building

narcissists, began the well-developed posturing routines designed to emphasise their impressive muscular structures.

The performance lasted some minutes before she found herself more and more interested in the contrasting state of their sexual flesh.

Rolf seemed, if anything, to have grown smaller, but the other man, despite the effort of pumping his pectorals, was still beautifully engorged. Calling a halt to the show, she had Rolf stand before her.

'Are you still afraid?' she asked, a cat-like smile playing about her lips.

Rolf nodded, swallowing hard, but still unable to speak.

'Perhaps Renate could help you?'

She watched fascinated as Rolf, eyes closed, began to shake with tension, evidenced by the cords of sinew that stood out from his throat. Every muscle in his body was now tensed, not for show but against the ordeal he feared was to come.

Renate responded to the click of her fingers and, dropping to her knees, her hands held behind her back, she reached forward with her tongue to delicately trace out the contours of his penis.

Leaving Renate to her chore, she waved the other young man forward. 'And what is your name?' she asked as he came to stand over her.

'Lars,' he told her.

'And you are not afraid of me, Lars?'

'My desire is greater than my fear.'

Sitting up slightly so she could reach him she extended her hand to take him delicately between her fingers. Lars gasped at the touch of her hand on his penis, a sound she pretended to ignore.

'Tell me, Lars, can you sing?'

'Not well.' His voice quavered as his first doubts engulfed him.

'Well, I shall be the judge of that.'

She let a silence grow between them as her fingers, now caressing his risen flesh, brought forth further tiny sounds of pleasure.

'Do you know a little children's song called "*Frères Jacques*"?' she asked.

Puzzled, Lars could only nod.

'Then sing it for me.' She smiled.

Lars was forced to concentrate his mind on the song as her hand, swift and light as a bird, manipulated him.

'Sing!' she said sharply.

Lars' voice began to falter as he fought to remember the words to the banal song, not sung since his nursery school.

Delighting in the torment of contradictory impulses she was engendering in him, she increased the tempo of her stroking fingers as, finally, Lars found his voice and began to sing.

His voice desperate, his body convulsed, Lars looked down into her smiling eyes and would have broken off his reedy singing to plead with her, but she spoke first. 'You are forbidden to take pleasure,' she said sharply, as she felt him starting to quicken under her ministrating hand.

Now Lars groaned. 'Please . . .!' he begged.

She had to force the anger into her voice since, in truth, she found the agonised body of the young man, fighting for control, extremely arousing. 'You will not come!' she said as sternly as she could manage. 'But you *will* sing!'

Lars' strangulated throat repeated the first verse of the song, which was all, it seemed, his mind could muster.

Renate's soft voice broke in hesitantly. 'Lady . . .' she murmured, drawing Vanessa's attention to Rolf. Renate's efforts had born fruit and the young man now stood hugely erect. For a moment she revelled in the transformation Renate had wrought. What she had previously described as limp and useless now stood thickly proud, erect and quite beautiful.

Waving Rolf forward, she had him stand next to Lars. 'Sing!' she told him.

His voice wavering in pain, he started to join in the children's song. She withdrew her hand from Lars' erection and replaced it with Rolf's. 'And you are to take him in your hand,' she told Lars.

The two men reached out to stroke each other as she lay back in the water and laughed delightedly at the picture they presented each trying desperately to control their own desires while trying to induce a climax in the other.

Renate was trying to appear invisible in the background, as if dreading what part she might be called upon to play in this tableau. She didn't have long to wait to find out.

'You,' Vanessa called, snapping her fingers at the anxious girl. 'Kneel before them. Do not touch them but be ready to catch their seed should either disobey me!'

Renate hurried to kneel before the now distressed men and alternated her gaping mouth between the two frantically working cocks.

'Not a drop of their seed must touch the ground, Renate,' Vanessa warned. Then she addressed the men. 'The first to come will be punished, the other rewarded,' she told them.

Both men frantically increased their efforts to make the other be first to lose and it wasn't long before their faltering voices signalled that the game was coming to climax.

Rolf was the first to break. His body shaking with uncontrollable convulsions, he began shooting out great gouts of tribute, which Renate desperately scrambled to take into her opened mouth.

Clapping her hands with glee, Vanessa stood up from the warm perfumed water. 'So, now we know which of you is to be punished, and which is to be rewarded!' Stepping out of the bath, she presented her glowing body to the victorious Lars. 'You may have the honour of drying me,' she told him.

Renate came forward to offer Lars a warmed bath towel. Turning her back to Lars so that he could begin to gently pat dry her back, Vanessa came face to face with Rolf. 'On your knees!' she ordered him.

Rolf knelt, head down, his lips hovering just above her feet.

Her voice was little more than a murmur as she spoke. 'You failed the test and must be punished,' she told him. 'Let me see . . . this requires a great deal of thought . . .' She felt her own body singing with pleasure at the power that had been delivered into her hands. At the same time though, she was presented with a confusing number of options, leaving her unable to decide on the one perfect, exquisite, torment. Her thought processes were further disturbed by Lars' gentle ministrations. Three naked slaves awaited her decision and she found that additionally oppressive. She felt constrained to do nothing that would disappoint *them*. She was discovering that the dominant partner was, in fact, at the service of the submissive and not, as she had always imagined, the reverse.

At that moment her gaze fell upon the hazel eyes of Renate. It was clear that she expected so much of her mistress that Vanessa felt inadequately suited to the role of taskmaster.

It was then that she felt the brush of Lars' urgent erection against her thigh.

Welcoming the distraction, Vanessa turned to face the shamefaced young boy. 'Did you dare to touch me?' she asked.

Lars expression flashed with bold, masculine challenge before he regained control and, dropping his gaze, mumbled a plea for forgiveness.

'Dry me,' she told him with a carefully controlled tone as she presented her naked breasts and belly to the caress of his towel.

Eyes bright with desire, Lars went about his task, unaware of how central his erection was in Vanessa's thoughts.

Abruptly she turned back to Rolf and Renate. Lars, surprised by her action stopped his gentle service but she spoke sharply to him. 'Continue.' As the gentle, fair-haired Lars hesitated, unsure of how he could do this with her back turned, she added, 'Reach around me.'

Lars' arms immediately encircled her body and almost embraced her as his towel flew about her breasts and belly.

'And my legs?' He responded by immediately dropping to his knees and gently drying her, using long stroking motions from her ankles to her fire-soaked loins.

Wanting something precious to define this exquisite moment and overcome by her own body's cry for satisfaction, Vanessa could think of only the most banal of punishments for the still waiting Rolf. 'Fetch me a whip,' she told Renate.

The young girl looked almost disappointed as she turned immediately to the concealed closet which harboured the tactile leathers.

As she waited, trembling on the brink of bodily betrayal herself, Vanessa saw that Rolf had dared raise his eyes to her.

'Get to your feet!' she ordered him, her voice now rasping. Rolf rose with careful grace to face her.

When Renate returned with a light, many-stranded whip, Vanessa knew that she had guessed her intention even before she had defined it to herself.

'Turn sideways to me,' she told Rolf, whose arrogance faded rapidly at the sight of the whip in her hands.

Her confidence growing, she reached down and tore away the towel, so presenting her naked body to Lars' caress. As he hesitated to touch her body without permission, she brought his hands up to touch her bare flesh. 'Be most careful what you do,' she told her kneeling supplicant. 'But you may caress me.'

Lars' eager hands fluttered lightly as he reached up to encircle her breasts.

Looking to Renate, she ordered her to her knees before

Rolf. 'We shall test his ardour,' she murmured to the girl. 'What you erect I will demolish. Do you understand me?'

Renate nodded anxiously and then flinched back on her heels as the light whip flashed downwards on Rolf's throbbing pride.

Renate's reaching tongue was almost eager as she leaned forwards to tongue tease the already responsive flesh.

Watching them, Vanessa leaned back against Lars and gave herself over to his reverent caress, revelling in the urgent press of him against her back.

So intense was her own pleasure becoming that she sought to increase it, focus it, by closing her eyes. It was Renate's soft murmur that brought her from her own indulgence.

'Lady?' prompted Renate.

Opening her eyes she saw that Renate was resting back on her heels proud to have brought Rolf to full erection. She had meant to play a game in which Renate would arouse Rolf and then she would whip him back to submissive impotence – a cyclical game she could have extended endlessly. But deep in the throes of the excitement created by the tableau before her and close to her own brink, she now felt unable to do anything significant and instead thrust the many-tailed scourge into Renate's hands. 'Use it!' she seethed through teeth clenched against her own internal struggle for control.

Renate, rising to her feet, looked from the whip in her hands, to Rolf and then back to her writhing mistress, confused as to which of them was the intended recipient.

'Here!' she screamed. 'Bring him to me!'

Worried now, Renate looked to Rolf as he came to stand before his mistress, a confident smile on his lips. Hesitating only momentarily, he moved forward into her beckoning embrace.

Sandwiched between the two fully aroused men, one rearing against her belly flesh and the other against her buttocks, Vanessa looked wildly to Renate who, seemingly distressed, hurried forward. 'Lady!' She spoke urgently. 'They are forbidden to—'

Feeling herself rapidly approaching climax she interrupted. 'Use it!' she screamed. 'Use the whip on them!'

As Renate still hesitated, Vanessa screeched, 'Do it!'

The young girl stood back, measured the distance and then started bring the angry thongs down onto Rolf's back.

Yelling with delight, Vanessa now abandoned all attempts to conceal the pleasure waves coursing through her. She ignored Helge's strictures that she should avoid orgasm and gave herself up to the intensity of the moment.

It was almost an irrelevance to her own consuming pleasure to feel the men simultaneously pulsing out their tributes on her heated flesh.

Their climaxes having weakened their grip on her, she pushed them away as Renate, breathless from her own exertions, stood staring wild-eyed at her.

'Have them clean me,' she told Renate. Then with the afterglow of forbidden orgasm still ravaging her, she added wickedly, 'With their tongues . . .'

Chapter Fourteen

Steven stared at the report before him with growing incredulity. Having returned to the Lancaster in Paris with his investigative team focused totally on Helge's activities, Roz had seen him reanimated. At last, it seemed, they had broken through the wall of silence that had descended after Vanessa's disappearance. For days the investigators, along with Roz, Grace and Michelle had been out talking to people, examining public and business records and building up a coherent picture of Helge's life in both Paris and her home country of Sweden.

'Is she crazy?' he asked Roz.

'Nobody that builds up that kind of fortune is entirely crazy,' she answered.

Steven shook his head. 'But a creed that declares that anything is possible through the focusing of sexual energy? In this day and age?'

Grace, who had been listening from a distance, came forward. 'More today than at any other time. Think about it. Substitute drugs for sexual energy and you get the picture.'

Steven stared at her. 'Sorry but I don't see the connection.'

'OK,' said Grace, 'some time back if you talked of drug addicts you'd think of flower power, hippies and rock musicians, right? If I'd said then that high-powered executives in suits with homes and families could get hooked you'd have laughed at me, right? Well, who's laughing now? It's the same with these religious nuts. Whether it's Jesus or sexual energy, there are people out there who've lost faith in everything and are ready to believe in anything – put forcefully enough – to the point of fanatiscm. If I'd told you, again, years back, that a Christian preacher could lead his people to mass suicide, would you have believed me?'

Michelle, who had become as concerned as any of them over Vanessa's disappearance, spoke. 'You can believe anything of that woman,' she said.

She spoke with such bitterness that they all turned towards her and were momentarily silent.

'You know something about her?' Steven asked gently.

'I know she is the most evil woman I have ever met.' Aware that everyone was listening, Michelle seemed to struggle with herself before she could continue. 'Look, I'm a professional whore, right? I make no secret of it to anyone. A girl like me can come to expect anything – but nothing like what she did.'

'What, in God's name, did she do?' asked Grace incredulously.

Michelle turned away, unwilling to meet their eyes.

'Look,' said Steven carefully, 'if it has any relevance to what we're trying to do here, I think you ought to tell us.'

Turning back, a light of defiance in her eyes, she spoke.

'I can tell you that if Vanessa is with Helge then she is in great danger.' Michelle took a moment to collect herself before going on. 'This woman has great character – what do you call it – like a prophet?'

'Charisma?' offered Roz.

Michelle leapt upon the word. 'Right! Charismatic! Like these religious fanatic people, you know? Well, she thinks of herself as a reincarnation of some Goddess of Love who believes the world is ruled by the energy created by sex.'

'We already know she's crazy,' interjected Steven.

Michelle nodded. 'The trouble is that she has many followers who also think she has great power.'

'Which she loves to exercise . . .?' asked Roz.

Michelle nodded. 'You have a word for that, too. What is it?'

'Power freak,' said Roz.

Steven was sceptical. 'There are all kinds of *crazies* in the world. People who like to get off by dressing up and deluding themselves that they can influence the world. It's all fantasy.'

'Except that this woman believes it,' Michelle insisted. 'So do her followers. If Vanessa is with her then she could be in great danger. Especially if she is to be the Chosen One.'

'What does that mean – the "Chosen One"?' asked Steven.

Michelle turned away as if struggling with words she barely dared speak. Finally she turned back to Steven. 'Look, I'm not intellectual, OK? All this is difficult for me but I have a friend who became quite interested in Helge,

199

until she realised how evil she truly was. She explained to me that Helge has an idea – a concept, she calls it – that contained in a woman's sexuality is an enormous power. That men have long known of it and, because they fear it, sought to repress it.' Michelle gestured extravagantly. 'For instance, a man who has many lovers is admired but a woman who attracts men is labelled bad. Helge claims this is part of the campaign to prevent women understanding the true power of their sexuality. Her theory is that, if women ever do understand the power they hold, then they will assume their rightful place as the dominant sex.'

Michelle's speech was followed by a reflective silence until Grace chirped, 'Sounds good to me!' When everyone turned to her aghast, she added hastily, 'Just kidding!'

Steven spoke, sounding dubious. 'I don't see what all that has to do with Vanessa being kidnapped.'

'It has everything to do with it,' said Michelle adamantly. 'You see, Helge feels that what women lack is an icon – a leader, someone to stand up and proclaim herself to be sexually emancipated from the chains that men use to bind and restrict them.'

Appalled, Steven turned to Michelle, 'And you think this is what that madwoman plans for Vanessa?'

'It might be,' said Michelle quietly.

'No!' cried Steven. 'No. I can't believe anyone could be that mad! Not in this day and age!'

Michelle's voice was gentle as she spoke. 'But you already knew such a candidate – one chosen by Helge.'

Steven's eyes widened with shock. 'Oh no!' he finally groaned.

Roz, looking from one to the other in bewilderment, demanded, 'What?'

Steven rose and began to pace. 'This is worse than I thought.' Turning back to Roz, he demanded, 'You knew of Imogene?'

Roz nodded. 'I know you painted her dozens of times.'

Steven went on. 'She came to me after running away from this Helge woman but could never bring herself to tell me why.' Steven broke off to make a dismissive shrug. 'I assumed it was because Helge wanted to get her into some kind of sex game she didn't want to play. I never dreamed it could be anything like this.' Struggling to order his thoughts, he continued. 'It might sound crazy but the fact is, the night Imogene was killed, she had left me and was on her way back to Helge. This lunatic Helge blamed me for losing Imogene at the moment of her greatest triumph – getting Imogene back from me.'

'And you suppose Helge is revenging herself on you by taking Vanessa in her place?'

'It could be,' Steven murmured. 'It's one explanation, anyway. The question is where would she have taken her? They're obviously not in Paris.' Steven mused silently for a moment before adding, 'Imogene once told me about some sort of fabulous place in Holland. The trouble is she didn't say precisely where it was.' He turned to Raoul, the head of the private detective agency he had hired. 'Have you found out anything about the properties she owns?'

Raoul nodded and opened his notebook. 'The Countess Helge has properties here in Paris, Holland, Sweden, Switzerland and on the Côte d'Azur, but the Riviera property was closed for the winter in October. Switzerland has been leased out for the past two years and there's a huge tax bill hanging over her head if she returns to Sweden . . .'

'Which leaves Holland . . .?'

'And a problem . . .' said Raoul.

'Which is?'

'Dutch law is very liberal. The SexEnergy Centre, as they call themselves there, is legal.'

'Legal!'

'It's properly registered and has even acquired tax concessions as a non-profit making organisation.'

'You're kidding?'

'I'm not. That means we have no recourse to the police unless the missing person is a minor or we have firm evidence that they are being held against their will. Furthermore, the Countess' estate there is very large, deep in forest, and security is tight.'

'That's incredible,' murmured Steven.

Raoul continued. 'But there is one chink in their armour.'

'Which is . . .?'

'They run a club in Amsterdam called the Osiris. It's a sex club which they use as a recruiting ground for the more susceptible.'

Steven was on his feet. 'So let's go!'

Raoul shook his head vigorously. 'If you rush in and make yourself obvious you'll learn nothing. The casual visitor would see nothing he wouldn't see in a dozen other places in Amsterdam. It's only if they have any interest in you that you have any chance.'

'How do they get interested?'

'If you're an attractive woman or a potentially interesting client . . .'

'OK, so we know that much. What else?'

'Showing some inclination towards a liberal attitude to sex also gets you noticed,' Raoul added.

Steven was aware that both Roz and Grace were watching his reaction closely. 'So . . .?'

'Well, that's where we girls come in!' said Roz, after a quick glance at Grace.

'To do what?' asked Steven sharply.

'I don't know. We'll go there and ask for jobs.'

'Right!' agreed Grace.

Steven looked at them for a long moment. 'I couldn't let you do that,' he said finally. 'God knows what you'd be letting yourselves in for.'

Grace chuckled. 'We know full well what we'd be "letting ourselves in for". Jesus, we're women, aren't we?'

Steven still hesitated.

Roz broke the silence. 'It might be the only way.'

Turning to them, he said, 'I can't believe you're serious.'

The two girls looked back at him, implacably silent.

'OK,' he finally agreed. 'But not as girls applying for jobs – only as two rich women looking for excitement – and only with a solid back-up.'

'Now *who* could you have in mind for that job?' asked Grace, smiling.

Chapter Fifteen

When Renate and Sylvie appeared in Vanessa's quarters to dress her, she was surprised to see what they themselves were wearing. They were practically naked except for a gold collar about their throats, a chain between their breasts, which, on closer inspection, proved to be suspended from clips attached to their nipples, and a heavier gold chain which hung from their hips, masking their pubis but leaving their buttocks bare. The effect was bizarre but also disturbingly exotic. They looked like creatures emerging from a highly imaginative erotic play.

'Aren't those clips painful?' she asked as she looked at their crimped nipples.

'We do not feel them,' answered Renate enigmatically.

'But surely—' Vanessa began, but Sylvie interrupted.

'Lady we must prepare you and there is little time.'

Aware that the status of the girls was little better than that of slaves, she knew that to question them further would probably result in their being punished.

First, she was offered the heavy herbal concoction on which she found herself increasingly dependent. Recognising that it must be narcotic, she nevertheless welcomed the warming glow, even if its effects were curiously ambivalent. It calmed her as she drank it, then, as it seeped through her system, she felt her body opening up, strengthening itself and becoming ready for any new experience. Whatever it was, it certainly helped and tonight she suspected that she would need all the help she could get!

The girls showed surprising skill in styling her hair and applying make-up before having her stand while they hung the heavy chain loincloth about her hips and then put garlands of chains about her breasts.

Delighted with the effect created by the costume of gold, she showered them with congratulations, but they were not yet finished.

Over her head they carefully lowered a headband creation which sparkled with fine diamonds giving the effect of a riotous explosion of dancing light.

She stared at the image this final touch created.

Gone was the earthly girl she felt herself to be, and in her place had appeared this resplendent vision.

Now she could confidently be the creature of fantasy everyone about her wanted her to be. Safe within the 'armour' of her costume she could be anything she wanted – even, as they insisted, an object of worship!

Turing to her attendants, she now felt prepared for anything.

When she declared herself ready, she really meant it. Ready to go forth and astonish!

Sylvie and Renate led her along a labyrinthine hallway of passages to a part of the château she had never before seen. There, waiting for her in what seemed to be an underground antechamber, was the statuesque figure of Helge, resplendent in a green gown so translucent that her body glowed through its gossamer threads. Enhanced with a gleaming necklace of jade coloured stones, she was both magnificent and daunting.

In attendance on Helge were two muscular young men whose only adornments were broad bands of gold about their biceps, wrists and ankles. As Vanessa came into sight, they dropped to their knees, as did Sylvie and Renate after bringing her to face Helge.

'My dear,' smiled Helge, 'how totally stunning you look.'

Still trying to formulate a reply, she was further embarrassed when Helge took up her hand, lifted it to her lips and kissed it, before looking up into her eyes and smiling.

'There is no need for you to be fearful. You are to be presented to your peers – your sisters – who have all undergone a similar ceremony to that awaiting you. There will be no men,' Helge added with some satisfaction.

On hearing this, Vanessa had not been able to prevent herself glancing at the two naked men already in attendance. Helge smiled indulgently. 'Save, of course, your attendant slaves.'

If Helge's words had been intended to reassure Vanessa, they had precisely the opposite effect. To be paraded before the critical eyes of other women was a frightening prospect and she was about to voice her fears when Helge turned away and clapped her hands twice. Immediately the two young men hurried to their feet and went forward to a heavily studded double door and threw it open. From inside, the murmurings of half a hundred voices could be heard. Gradually, they became silent.

Turning to her, Helge held out a courtly arm for Vanessa to take. 'Come, my dear, they await your arrival.'

Her head buzzing with uncontrolled thoughts, Vanessa took Helge's arm and moved forward, nervous as a bride entering a chapel. She was stunned by the sight that greeted her.

It seemed there were some fifty or sixty women in the chamber, all dressed in an assortment of avant-garde fashion designs – and all silently facing the door where she was making her entrance. Although they were of all shapes and sizes, the women looked beautiful and at first Vanessa was disconcerted by the collective low moaning sound that arose from their throats, until Helge reassured her it was meant as an appreciative greeting.

Had she been more attired, less obviously disrobed, Vanessa would have been a little intimidated by the heavy ambience created by the sweeping arches of the vaulted ceiling and tapestry-draped walls. Instead, led by Helge's outstretched hand, she went towards a dais on which stood two throne-like chairs. One was placed at a higher level than the other.

Helge led her towards the higher of the two thrones and indicated that this was her place.

From her seat she looked down on the multitude of anonymous faces. They were still turned to her but now all hands were raised, palms outstretched. Eventually, the murmuring died down to become the soft hum of a ritualistic chant.

Confused by an intoxicating mixture of fear and excitement, she was startled when one of the two young male slaves came forward and, from a reverential kneeling position, offered up a silver platter on which there was a goblet of wine. Thankful for this opportunity to slake her nervous thirst, she took the goblet and lifted it to her lips, startled by the roar of approval which greeted her simple action.

The liquid tasted sour and she was glad that the flickering candles helped her to disguise her involuntary shiver of revulsion.

Even as her stomach churned, she saw Sylvie offering up another goblet, this time of crystal. The liquid inside was as clear and colourless as its container, and thankfully she felt her palate being cleansed by a musky white wine.

Still unsettled by the first potion, she looked to Helge who was smiling beneficently on her with open and total approval. Feeling she had passed a crucial test but still nauseously wary, she waved away the plate of roasted meats that the other young man offered to her.

This refusal seemed to signal a change of mood. The music, emanating from some hidden source, became immediately lighter and gayer. The whole mood of the gathering seemed to change and they returned to the banqueting tables, which had been previously hidden by their crowding forward to greet her.

Helge leaned in and took her hand. 'Splendidly done,' she murmured above the rising sounds of revelry.

Isolated high above the multitude, she could now see that the chamber was built solidly of stone. The candles which flickered on the tables were augmented by flaring flambeaux which were fixed to the stone walls by iron brackets. Directly opposite her, somewhat ominously, loomed giant sculpted figures of two men, naked and ferociously aroused.

The figures framed a dais exactly like the one on which her throne sat but the space between their outstretched arms looked worryingly empty, as if awaiting a spectacle that had yet to be played.

Vanessa, high on her throne, felt isolated – as if she had been caught up in a game in which all but her knew their places and their roles. Her thoughts isolated her further from the gathering and created a deep well of uncertainty about their expectations of her.

A great clash of cymbals announced the entrance of two male dancers costumed in feathered headdresses which seemed to be faintly African although their costumes were theatrically garish in design.

Each carried an Ali-Baba basket, half as tall as themselves, which they laid down in the centre of the cleared space. The arrival of the two dancers was greeted with great applause by the onlookers, and as the two men whirled skilfully with great spinning leaps, the enthusiastic applause continued. It reached a crescendo as two lithe and totally naked girls, both black, appeared from the baskets and insinuated themselves, serpent-like, to the stone flagged floor. The applause which had greeted the appearance of the two girls died into almost reverent silence as the music, matched perfectly to the dancers' movements, became more sinuous and erotic.

The two male dancers came towards the girls as they rose slowly to their full height and seemingly floated from the floor as the two men lifted the perfectly matched pair up high. Then they walked in different directions around the room, showing off the girls' perfect young bodies to the enthused revellers.

So skilled were they, their movements so perfectly harmonised, that it looked to Vanessa as if she were watching, not two, but one pair of dancers and their mirror image. The two men slowly closed on her throne and, showing great control, they lowered the girls to the floor, where they slithered to the foot of the throne and lay stretched out before her feet in homage.

Hypnotised, she watched the girls writhing, then as the music quickened to a more urgent, insistent pace, Vanessa was filled with a breathless sense of expectation.

Her expectation was quickly fulfilled when the two male dancers came forward to take each of Vanessa's arms and, gently but firmly, urged her to her feet.

Vanessa had never thought of herself as a dancer, but she suddenly found her confidence soaring. It was as if she had entered her dream in the forest, where she had come upon dancers in the clearing. Perhaps it was because of the confidence of the dream that she could join these skilled dancers and match them step for step.

As the men lifted her, high above their heads, she felt something approaching the exultation of flying, until she was set down on a raised platform in the centre of the room.

Quickly the two girls joined her and moved about her, their hands, fluttering about her body, creating a surge of response wherever they touched.

Somehow, she found herself able to move with the dancers, as if some inner voice was coaching her, telling her how to anticipate and match the steps. She felt exulted. Even as she moved in pagan-like abandon she knew that this exquisite moment was like no other she had ever known. She and the dancers moved together, as if these perfected movements were the result of weeks of intense rehearsal.

Aware that the two men had closed in on each side of her, taking a firm grip on her upper arms, she heard only the music resonating deep inside her body.

Someone must have given the signal for her to be stripped of the chains as they were removed in seconds, leaving her as naked as the girl dancers. She was now convinced that the spectacle to which she contributed was the most transcendentally beautiful tableau she would ever know.

Euphoria surging through her, she knew that she was as good as the dancers, matching their wild sexuality, their flaring eyes and abandoned nakedness. She *knew* that she was beautiful and wanted all those unseen, silent, watching eyes to have their fill of her.

It was then, at the very crest of her excitement, that she was borne backwards to be laid upon a gilded couch. Once there, she was quickly and expertly spread and her wrists and ankles secured to leave her body open and vulnerable.

She was left barely a moment to be afraid of this bondage before she saw the watching women surging forward to lay gentle caressing hands to each and every part of her body.

As they touched her, Vanessa felt herself writhing and screaming under the caress of hands and lips that sought out every crevice of her, dispensing the most exquisite pleasure sensations she had ever known. These were her peers – women and girls – which made their devotions gentle and sweet. She wanted desperately to return their gifts of sensation but her wildly casting mouth could catch only brief contact with the wall of feminine flesh that surged about her.

Cursing the bondage that confined her Vanessa rose high on a wave of surging orgasm that threatened to continue forever as the lips and tongues about her fought for her more sensitive places.

This, her distracted mind proclaimed, was true worship. As she felt her body rising unashamedly, greedily, to meet the thrusting tongues, she knew that she was loved in the most primal sense which at that moment she felt was the most honest. If she were to be pleasured then let it be as a Goddess and let her be worshipped!

It was at the height of her pleasure that she felt the crowding pressure of the naked women about her lessen. A sudden cessation of sound and movement caused Vanessa to nervously open her eyes.

She saw that they had fallen back from the couch to which she was still secured and in their place stood Helge – but it was not that magnificent woman who took her eye but the hooded king cobra that Helge held in her arms!

Vanessa could not contain the scream of fear that escaped her lips, as Helge came forward, caressing the serpent, so that it all but filled Vanessa's horrified vision. 'There is no reason to fear the symbol of your pleasure,' Helge purred as she laid the snake down on Vanessa's fright-tautened stomach. 'He means you no harm. On the contrary he comes to love you!'

Vanessa stared at the creature in total brain-numbing fear. Its eyes, yellow flecked against green, stared at her. Its questing tongue tasted the air as it reared up before her eyes which dared not blink. Vanessa stopped breathing as the hooded head of the serpent moved ever closer to her face and then, at the height of her terror, she saw it change. Gone was its primeval menace, gone were the poisonous colours, and in their place had arisen the more pleasurable contours of a rearing phallus!

As it came closer to her face and pressed itself against her, she greedily opened her mouth and took its entirety between her lips to thrust hard against the back of her throat.

This action brought forth a huge sigh of appreciation from the watching women which goaded Vanessa to suck even more greedily on the living, raging, muscular presence in her mouth. Eagerly she sought to so excite the flesh as to cause it to offer up its tribute but she was to be denied as her hands and ankles were freed and she was again lifted high into the air. Once more she heard the inward rush of sound and awareness of those about her, then she was carried, back arched, loins spread to many eager eyes, and was brought finally to the space between the two larger-than-life male statues.

The giant figures gleamed, forever fixed in their imperious poses. From their raised hands hung golden chains which, she knew, were to be clipped to the golden loops about her wrists and ankles.

She felt a rush of understanding for all of Helge's efforts to prepare her for this moment. Without her she would, by now, be a trembling incoherent wreck which was not what those many eager faces watching her had been led to expect. This was to be a rite of passage in which she must show the guests how far she had transcended mortal constraint.

As Sylvie and Renate took her wrists to the clips and then spread her legs to the ankle chains, she trembled. Not at the pain she knew was to come but from fear of being found unworthy by the company of women that now stood watching in reverent silence as she was carefully, almost lovingly, prepared.

Having secured her, spread and naked, the attendant girls withdrew to kneel either side of her. Then Helge came forward, eyes gleaming with approval. 'You are beautiful,' she said, 'and worthy of your sex.'

With fevered eyes she watched as the company quietly formed into a line and then, one by one, were summoned forward to place their lips on Vanessa's body and bless her with a five-fold kiss.

Each supplicant would first bend to kiss each of her feet, then rise to touch their lips to the point of each of her breasts before again kneeling to kiss the place Helge described as her 'Gate of Immortality' – her loins.

As each of the women approached her and knelt to make their supplication it produced in her a writhing arousal that demanded to be satisfied. As each woman approached, Helge repeated the same question, 'Shall you be whipped?' until eventually Vanessa was screaming 'yes' in desperate abandon.

Now, as the last of the supplicants joined in the invocation, she saw her male acolytes approaching, bearing the scourges and whips by which she was to suffer. Mentally she prayed that all of Helge's instructions would now be proved true – that she could flee her temporal body shell and so escape the pain that would otherwise be betrayed to all before her in screams.

Helge's face loomed close to her own. 'You are now truly the most beautiful of my followers and all will bear witness to your resolution. Be proud, beautiful one, be ready now to make every woman here proud of her gender, but, above all, be sure that all that I do is done from love.' Helge paused, peering deep into her eyes. 'You understand me?'

In spite of her fear, Vanessa managed to nod.

'Then prepare yourself.' Helge paused and smiled. 'I shall now blind your eyes as I have blinded your body to the coming pain.'

A strip of silk was lowered about her eyes and she found the darkness almost welcome as she braced herself for the coming ordeal.

'Listen to the words of the Great Mother who was of old called by many names: Astarte, Melusine, Aphrodite, Ceridwen, Dana, Arianrhod, Bride, Isis and by many more. They were our example and showed us the way to discovering the true strength of our gender. Let this, their daughter, show the same courage as they, as she prepares to suffer for us all.'

Absorbed behind the silky dark of the mask, Vanessa desperately tried to find courage enough to steel herself against the coming trial. Anxious not to disappoint either Helge or those others that followed in her beliefs, she found her breath shortening, her heart beating faster and clear thought all but impossible as the anticipatory panic gathered like a lead weight in her chest. Knowing she needed to find a focus for her mind, she could only summon up the face of the Count.

She now had no doubt that the assembled women believed her to be an object of veneration and was determined not to disillusion them. If this ordeal was necessary for her to progress on the road to self-discovery, then so be it.

Helge's voice rang out. 'Are you ready, sister?'

Unable to find words from her terrified throat Vanessa simply nodded into the black void the blindfold had created.

As the first searing lash fell upon her naked body, she was forced to bite hard on the gasp that might have escaped her lips.

Again the fire burned across her back but this time a bit deeper. Suddenly she was terrified that she was still in her own body and had not, as Helge had promised, been transported beyond pain to another place. Could Helge know this? Would she lessen the pain if she knew? Or, would she perhaps increase it in order to punish her for an ill-learned lesson?

As the gathering shouted acclaim of her suffering, the sounds of unbridled revelry penetrated her velvety darkness as each of the assembly turned to one another for a pleasure heightened and spiced by the sound of the rising and falling whip that lashed into her body.

As the total blinding pain mounted, it blotted out all

sound and sensation until she had to struggle to understand the words being soothed into her ears. 'Lady, you may scream now!' It had been Sylvie's voice,but she knew the words must have been sanctioned by Helge.

Released from the imperative to be stoical she let her voice rise high above the sounds of joy coming from the others.

In her screaming she found sanctuary and it seemed that the burning of her tormented body began to dissipate. Soon she felt an onrush of pain-deadening adrenalin which flushed through her body, releasing her into a place of pleasure where she was certain she could endure all and everything.

Then, quite suddenly, there was cessation. Not simply silence and stillness but an all encompassing transition to a quieter, pleasanter place. Her only previous experience of such a sensation had been when diving from the side of a boisterously noisy swimming pool into the blanketing silence of the water. Except that here even the rush of water past her ears was missing.

Opening her eyes she felt, simultaneously, great joy and overwhelming incredulity.

Standing before her, as if lit by a blue spotlight, stood the Count – the image that had carried her through the barrier of pain.

Wanting to rush to him she was reminded that she was chained, spread-eagled and naked, yet as if in a dream, she knew that they shared this moment alone.

Then, all at once, the screaming riot of the assembly came back like an avalanche of sound and sensation. Her back and buttocks felt as if a torch was being applied to them.

Somewhere a woman was screaming, 'No more. Dear God, no more!' But this voice, which she now recognised to be her own, was stilled as she felt a man's arms about her. Then her wrists and ankles were freed and she was slowly lifted and taken gently into his arms.

'You were magnificent.' The man spoke and she was thrilled to understand that it was the Count that held her and who was now carrying her from the chanting throng of women.

Brought into a luxuriously furnished room, her mind unable to focus, Vanessa felt herself being laid upon the silken covers of a bed before feeling the loving caress of his hands.

'I shall ease your pains and restore your love,' the Count murmured into her ear.

Instantly responding to his caress, she dreamily murmured her gratitude as her arms went about his body to find delight as they touched his strong back. 'Did you see?' she begged through excited, quickened breath. 'Did you see how I stood the pain?'

In answer, his lips closed on hers, his tongue searching out the inner recesses of her mouth. Feeling him hard and aroused against her willing body, she gasped her urgent need of his penetration.

'Not yet, beautiful one,' he answered and she screamed in a mixture of joy and frustration as his mouth searched out her breasts and nipples, alternatively suckling and nipping them between his teeth.

Now, openly begging that he take her, Vanessa held his head vice-like between her hands as her pleas became desperate. Had the world been about to end she would have had no thought but that she must feel him deep within her, feel again that surging triumphant joining of the flesh.

As her orgasm became so prolonged as to be almost painful, she sobbed again for him to take her and then gasped with joy when he moved to enter her.

'Now!' she screamed, her voice rising to ecstatic hysteria. Then, with a long heartfelt sigh, she felt him pushing inside, consuming her, ravaging her as she vented her joy to the far heavens.

Opening herself for him, she soared on a tidal wave of joy as his flesh seemed to penetrate deep inside her, generating a heat so intense that where their bodies joined she felt touched with flame.

Ecstatic tears and mindless exhortations mingled with the sweat that lubricated them, making more difficult their sliding, gasping and clutching and so adding another dimension to the unreality of such intense pleasure.

Even as her distracted mind sought to reassert itself in this tidal wave of animal response, Vanessa thought she now understood what Helge had meant when she had spoken of self-realisation through orgasmic release.

If this were it, then it was a discovery worthy to take its place among the wonders of the world. Vanessa knew, even as she writhed and wracked in an almost continuous orgasm, that she had found Nirvana and wanted more than a simple, transient visit.

She had begun a journey that she felt was worth any price that Helge might demand.

Never had she felt more alive or more attuned to herself as she plunged into a void of such contented exhaustion that she felt she could, at this moment, die happily.

Chapter Sixteen

'I don't believe this place,' murmured Steven as the almost totally naked waitress laid their drinks on the table.

Grace, watching the young woman walk away murmured, 'I won't ask how they got their dress code through the Health Department!'

The girls waiting the tables wore a tiny apron-like suspender belt, fishnet stockings, high heels and a garter tied round one thigh.

Roz laughed. 'You have to agree their drinks policy is unique.'

Grace shook her head. 'I don't know how they make any money.'

'Could be that making money isn't the point.'

The three sat crammed tight at a tiny table in one of the rambling rooms that made up the Osiris Club. On entering they had found that the club had no licence to sell alcoholic drinks so they had neatly circumvented the law by *giving* them away – each customer was sold a *glass* at a price which was supposed to cover the cost of the drinks.

Grace was sceptical. 'In New York this place would be packed with every alcoholic in the city.'

Steven, who was seated on the main thoroughfare between the bar and the tables, was being buffeted every time one of the waitresses pushed past, and he was getting annoyed. 'What makes you think this place isn't?'

Looking round Roz was less sceptical. 'The incredible thing is the number of young people in here.'

'What worries me,' said Grace, 'is how the hell we're ever going to get noticed just sitting here like this? There isn't room to swing a cat in here, let alone start a scandal.'

Steven, whose drink had just been spilled again as he went up to take a sip, looked up. 'Damn it! If those girls don't stop bumping me every time they pass *I'm* going to start a scandal.'

Roz laughed. 'You're complaining when a young nubile nude girl brushes past you? Maybe they're trying to tell you something.'

Steven nodded. 'I wish they would. That's why we came here.'

Grace suddenly yelped. 'Shit!'

Both Roz and Steven looked at her.

Grace was staring at the paper skimmer which had been laid under her drinks glass. 'What is it?'

Silently Grace pushed the paper to Steven.

'When I come back take my garter. S.'

Steven was about to ask the obvious question when he saw Grace holding a finger to her lips. 'This could be it.'

Leaning in, Steven whispered. 'What does it mean?'

'How in hell would I know? But it's got to mean something, right?'

Roz was scanning the message. 'What happens when you take her garter?'

'Let's find out,' said Grace and waved across the room to the girl that was now serving another table. The girl motioned that she would be with them soon, and Grace turned back to Steven. 'I know that girl. I've seen her before, but where . . .?'

Steven had now had a chance to take a second look. 'She was at the club.' Suddenly excited, he turned to Grace. 'She was with Helge.'

'Damn right she was!' agreed Grace enthusiastically. 'I've got a feeling we're getting a break.'

'But what will taking her garter signify?' asked Roz.

'I don't know, but whatever it is we play along, right?' Grace scanned their faces. 'No matter what?'

Nodding, they both agreed. 'No matter what!'

It was some minutes before the girl they now knew to be Sylvie was able to wend her way through the crowded tables to them.

'Yes, madame?' she asked of Grace.

'What do you want me to do?'

Sylvie glanced around while speaking softly. 'Take my garter to the cashier. You have to pay two hundred guilders and then they send me upstairs to you. There, if you do what I say, we can talk.'

After a glance at Steven she reached out and untied the black silk garter band. Sylvie smiled and then walked away.

Grace, the black silk in her hand, looked at Steven.

'It could be some kind of trick,' he told her. 'That Sylvie was very close with Helge.'

'Isn't that where we want to be?'

'Alright, but I'm coming with you.'

Roz protested vehemently. 'Then so am I! Don't imagine you're going to leave me down here alone!'

'We'll all go!' said Steven definitively.

Grace shrugged. 'I don't know what the house rules might be, but I guess a few dollars in the right place should work it out.'

All three made their way to where a stern-looking woman sat behind a grill labelled CASHIER.

Silently Grace showed her the garter. The woman looked at the three watching faces.

'All of you?' the cashier asked. 'Three with one girl?'

'We'll pay,' said Steven. 'What's the price?'

The woman shrugged. 'The same as if you took three girls upstairs.'

'Six hundred guilders?' asked Steven. 'Listen will you take US dollars?'

'Four hundred American dollars,' said the woman without blinking.

Steven hesitated as he took the money from his wallet. 'Where do you get your rates of exchange?' he asked.

'From the management,' said the woman patiently.

Sighing, Steven counted out all the dollars he was carrying and added a hundred guilder note to make up the difference.

The woman counted the notes, added them to a drawer and handed them a key. 'Room two one six,' she said. 'You have to go out of this building and it's the next door to your right. Second floor,' she added. 'The young lady will join you there.'

Steven led the way, fighting through the crowd at the bar, and out into the street. 'Christ these people have a weird way of doing business!'

They found the entrance to the next building guarded, until they showed the bull-necked man on the door the key. Nodding, he let them pass.

Inside was a long corridor which led to a ramshackle stairway.

They had just reached the second floor hallway and were looking for the room when a door marked LADIES opened and they saw Sylvie urgently signalling them in. Disregarding proprieties Steven found himself in a designated ladies' toilet for the first time in his life.

'I have not much time,' said Sylvie urgently. 'When we get to the room we have to behave like orgiasts, you understand?'

'You mean we'll be watched?'

Sylvie nodded. 'They say it's to protect the girls but really it is to check that we're giving the clients good value.'

Steven was incredulous. 'Are you telling me that Madame Helge runs a brothel?'

'Only to punish the girls. Do you say "humiliate"?'

'I'll say!' said Grace emphatically.

Sylvie was perversely anxious to justify the doctrine. 'In the old religions every woman had to serve at least one day in a brothel. Even the highest women in the land . . .'

Steven got impatient. 'What's all this got to do with anything? I mean we're all here, why can't we speak here?'

Sylvie looked horrified. 'Already they will be wondering

227

what happened to us. Come!' she said and led them out into the hallway.

As they walked down the corridor Sylvie was speaking loud enough for the monitors to hear. 'I'm sorry you could not find me. Here we are!'

Sylvie led the way into a room bare of almost anything but a bed and heavy red damask hangings and a wooden X-shaped whipping cross.

As she shed the few items she was wearing Sylvie went on, 'I understand the gentleman wishes to watch me with the two ladies, is that correct?'

'Er – yes,' said Steven.

Beaming a broad smile, Sylvie went to Grace and wound her arms round her, while whispering urgently into her ear. 'Take me to the bed.' Then as Grace started towards the bed, Sylvie cooed, 'Won't you undress madame?'

Grace hesitated only a moment before stripping down to her skin as Sylvie laid out on the bed with whorish abandon.

Roz saw that Steven was looking nervously about the room as if trying to spot the peepholes. Going to him Roz put her arms round him and placed a kiss on his surprised lips.

'Hey!' Steven's protest was whispered.

'Idiot!' Roz whispered close into his ear while pretending to nuzzle his neck. 'That's the only way we can talk.'

Looking to the bed Steven saw the two girls' bodies were entwined with all outward signs of passion. 'It's what *they're* talking about that interests me!'

'There's only one way to find out!' said Roz, then reaching behind her, she unzipped her dress, stripped down her panties and joined the other girls on the bed.

Steven closed in on the three girls and sat on the bed. Conscious that he might be being watched, he laid a tentative hand on Roz's back, but it was Grace who responded. Reaching out, she grabbed him, pulling him into the mêlée which had developed on the bed.

Lying alongside them, simulating passionate kisses, he listened amazed at the whispering Sylvie.

'You are looking for her, right?'

'Yes!' screamed Grace as if in the throes of passion. 'YES!'

'She is at Helge's chateau. It is on the Dutch border.'

Steven interposed. 'Was she kidnapped?'

Sylvie shook her head. 'No. She is mesmerised into enjoying the Count.'

'She's what?' cried Steven.

'For Christ's sake,' seethed Grace to Steven. 'Look as if you're fucking one of us!'

'Er . . .' said Steven, who was finding great difficulty in coping with the embarrassment and confusion he felt at having to simulate sex with his business manager – a feeling not lessened by Roz's apparent enthusiasm for the pantomime.

'Darling! Fuck me harder!' cried an apparently ecstatic Roz.

'What?' a startled Steven asked of her.

Grace turned to him. 'Listen, just do it alright? Either that or get the hell out!'

'Certainly not!' cried Steven.

'Suck this, you bitch!' cried Grace to Roz, and wound

her thighs about Roz's head while being careful to keep her ear close to Sylvie. 'So how do we get to her?'

Sylvie looked despondent. 'I don't know. It is, after all, a fortified house.'

Realising that the girl he was questioning was desperately frightened, Steven softened his questions. 'Just give us the exact location. We'll figure out the rest.'

Sylvie grabbed Steven and brought his mouth down onto her breast. 'Listen,' she whispered into his ear, 'She is not being kept there by force. Helge can make you be anything or anybody she wants. That woman is pure evil.'

Steven, his voice muffled, whispered. 'Why are you doing this?'

'Because I have come to hate that woman. She used me as she is now using Vanessa. If you don't get her out of there she will become Helge's slave.'

'So why don't you just leave?' asked Grace as she continued to simulate sexual abandon.

'Because she would find me. She is insane. I just want someone to stop her, but I don't know how.'

'Leave it to us,' said Steven, smiling to try and reassure the girl. Then he added, 'You've been a great help to us. We're very grateful.'

Sylvie looked genuinely distressed. 'There is so much more I should tell you, but they will be getting suspicious.'

'Can we meet somewhere, tomorrow maybe?'

'Impossible. I have to go back to the château tonight. If you hadn't come until tomorrow you would have missed me.'

'Tell me something,' said Steven urgently. 'Is Vanessa truly alright?'

Sylvie nodded her head emphatically. 'I promise you.'

Steven was ready to ask many more questions but Grace intervened. 'OK folks, it's orgasm time!'

Grace led the way with a screaming cry, Roz joined in while Steven did his best and Sylvie looked at the three of them bemused.

In the shamefaced silence that followed, Grace spoke first.

'My,' she said, 'that *was* fun! We must all do it again sometime!'

Chapter Seventeen

Each morning one of her attendants – and Renate had soon emerged as her clear favourite -- would attend her bath, along with such other human 'toys' as she requested. Afterwards, she would receive a lengthy, stimulating body massage. Vanessa always asked Renate to bind her wrists since she loved the voluptuous feeling of helplessness in her pleasurably tormented body.

It was Renate who worked on her this morning. The young girl understood better than most the agonies of arousal she induced and was better at bringing Vanessa to the edge of orgasm and keeping her suspended in that most exquisite of torments.

Eyes closed, she could lie back and conjure up visions of the Count, which caused her to remember his fiery touch, the musky smell of his arousal, the steely length of him entering her. As these thoughts stirred her, she began to have her first doubts. Had he really taken her at the previous evening's initiation that Helge had so superbly choreographed in her honour, or had it been merely a dream arising out of her sedated state?

As she murmured appreciatively under the roaming hands

on her body, she indulged herself in memories of her masochist delight at being made to wait, in a state of constant unrelieved stimulation. Everything she presently suffered would make sweeter that moment when the Count would again come to her.

Feeling Renate's lips closing gently on her engorged nipples, Vanessa allowed herself one of the internal convulsions in which she could indulge without giving outward sign.

'Thank you,' she murmured to Renate, fighting down the urge to beg her lips to move to her loins and release the tightly wound spring of her raging libido.

A small cry from Renate disturbed her reverie and the soft landing of paws on her body alerted her to Pluto's arrival.

Opening her eyes she saw the cat looking down at her with such intensity that she imagined for one wild moment that he was about to speak!

'Lovely pussy!' she cooed and then regretted that her bound hands prevented her reaching to caress the beautiful beast.

Pluto played sentry on her body for a moment, striding majestically up and down, his tail held high, each pace carefully measured.

'Renate!' she called to the girl who was cringing back as if afraid. 'What's the matter with you? Untie me, so I can stroke him!'

'No!' Helge's voice came from frighteningly close at hand.

Straining her head to look behind the couch she saw the

ever smiling clear blue eyes of the Countess looking down at her.

'How deliciously vulnerable you make yourself,' she said, before turning to Renate. 'Leave us,' and she dismissed the girl from the room with a wave of the hand.

As Renate scurried away, Vanessa lay under Helge's gaze, recognising the sea shift of emotions that the woman's presence always induced. In the company of her attendants Vanessa was treated with the deference due a supreme being but everyone knew that the real ruler of this chateau was Helge and she had never felt more helpless and at the mercy of a woman whose word was law. Even Pluto's majestic striding now seemed suddenly menacing. He had stopped pacing and, standing four square on her rising and falling chest, stared openly at her as if listening to the conversation.

'I see your taste for bondage is growing. Splendid!' Helge smiled. 'One should learn to experience everything, even before slaves.'

'It's because I don't trust myself,' Vanessa murmured hesitantly.

'Trust yourself?' asked an amused Helge. 'But, my dear, you are here to *indulge* yourself in any tiny thing you may desire.'

'Then let me see the Count.'

Helge winced. 'You should not focus your sexuality quite so finely. You must remember that I have hopes of your coming to represent the ultimate sexuality of all women.'

Helge's fingernails, tracing tormenting trails across her

235

open thighs, were creating sensations that, even now, she could barely acknowledge in herself. 'Pluto seems very fond of you, my dear. Do you know, this morning, I told him to lead me to the person he loved the most and he led me directly to you! Isn't that incredible? You should be very flattered. Pluto isn't always fond of people.' Helge turned her cooing voice to the staring feline. 'Isn't that so, Pluto?' she urged.

Suddenly feeling extremely vulnerable, Vanessa wanted desperately to be free. 'He's a beautiful cat,' she said. 'May I pet him?'

'Of course.' Helge smiled but made no move to untie her hands which had been what she hoped for.

Helge's fingernail was now circling her sensitive navel. 'You are happy with us, aren't you, my dear?'

Suddenly quite frightened, Vanessa could only nod.

'Good,' said Helge, 'because today is to be quite different.'

'Different?' she managed to gasp.

'Very!' Helge looked directly into her eyes. 'You have proved yourself worthy of all things . . .' She broke off, seemingly distracted by watching her own hands trail over the trembling body beneath them, knowing the effect she was creating. Then she continued, 'Except two.'

'Two?' Vanessa asked, the tremble in her voice not entirely due to her sudden apprehension.

Helge nodded, fascinated by the tidal waves she was creating in the helpless girl before her. 'Two matters have been raised by the Councillors. You will remember your meeting with the Count Alonzo in Paris?'

When she looked askance, Helge went on. 'You were unsatisfactory when kneeling to the phallus. You must be further instructed, starting tonight. The Count is not easily satisfied. It may be necessary for you to arouse him time and again to ensure his approval.'

'What must I do?' Vanessa asked, closer now to letting herself go in front of Helge than she had ever been since her arrival in this place.

'You are to learn the true magic of a woman's oral womb.'

'My mouth?' she asked.

Helge nodded. 'I shall personally instruct you,' she said, laying her fingertips precisely on the engorged bud of flesh which she had so far ignored, sending shivers of pleasure through Vanessa's body. 'Following which you will be examined by the Council of Men.'

Vanessa was unable to absorb the full meaning of Helge's words as she was now engulfed in an unstoppable emotional earthquake. 'Yes!' she screamed under Helge's expert manipulation. 'Oh, yes!'

Her cries seemed to disturb the still pacing Pluto who reacted by sinking his claws into her writhing flesh. Helge watched dispassionately before smiling with quiet satisfaction. 'That excess will have to be paid for, of course,' she murmured as her lips brushed lightly across Vanessa's own. 'Meanwhile – ' she added reaching across to loosen the bindings which held her wrists ' – we have something else to attend to.'

When Vanessa was finally freed she saw Renate coming towards her, carrying the very shell-cupped ivory evening gown she had admired in Helge's salon.

Hurrying forward she cried, 'But that's the gown I ordered.'

Helge smiled. 'Complete with the alterations you wished for.'

Turning it in her hand she saw that the awkward clips and eyes had been replaced with jewelled clasps. 'But it's beautiful!' she cried. 'When shall I wear it?'

'Tonight, of course.'

For the moment the gown took all Vanessa's attention as Renate fitted it about her. Its fit was perfect. Turning to Helge she could barely contain herself. 'Oh, it's lovely. Thank you.'

'You can thank me tonight,' smiled Helge, 'by learning your lessons well.'

Helge's eagle-eye had spotted something imperfect in the hem of the gown and ordered it to be removed and taken back to the workshop. Then, summoning the unusually errant Pluto to her side, she turned back. 'Pluto loves coming down here. It's his favourite hunting ground, you see. The old tunnels are simply full of prey and he does love to hunt.' Helge smiled broadly. 'Well, I shall leave you to make yourself beautiful for the Council. They really are the most demanding of men. Until later, my dear. I'm quite sure you won't let me down.' Then, with Pluto at her side, she swept from the chamber, leaving Vanessa with many conflicting emotions.

It was only some time after the Countess had left that she realised she hadn't been told of the second of her shortcomings. Reviewing every aspect of her conduct since coming to the chateau, she tried to divine what other error of conduct she might have committed. Try as she might she could think of none, unless it was the occasional forbidden climax. How could Helge remedy that? She couldn't imagine and so dismissed the thought from her mind. Whatever was to happen would happen whether she was forewarned or not. It was simpler just to give herself over to the moment.

As she luxuriated in her sunken tub, she had the feeling that she was to be surprised yet again. The thought led her to dare a self-caress.

Renate returned that evening to help her with her hair and make-up, to which she submitted with growing impatience. She could barely wait to put on the evening gown and see herself as the Count would see her.

The gown proved the match of her expectations. The golden high-heeled slippers, which Helge had sent along to accessorise it, lifted the hem so that it draped beautifully to the floor. Those and the soft silk stockings were all she wore underneath.

Looking at herself in the mirror, her long black hair falling in a cascade about her shoulders, Vanessa was thrilled to realise that the upward lift of the stiffened cups presented her breasts beautifully so as to give free access to the questing hands of a lover. The Count would only have to slip his arms about her to feel both breasts casually bared to his touch, even in public.

The thought was enough to cause a shiver of expectation to run through her.

'Are you ready, Lady?' enquired Renate's soft voice.

Turning away from the mirror, she nodded to her attendant

who then crossed to open the door, calling to someone outside.

Lars and Rolf appeared before her looking oiled and muscular. Then, bowing in unison, they took burning flambeaux from brackets outside the door and led her along the stone-flagged passages to mount a flight of stairs to a resplendent hallway.

Here the stone-flagging of the floors gave way to polished marble while on the walls hung heavily framed canvases in place of the tapestries that ruled below.

Led along the imposing hallway, Vanessa was brought to huge double doors over which many craftsmen must have laboured long hours to produce the intricate tracery of carving. She had little time to appreciate it though as the doors were thrown open to reveal the daunting magnificence of the room beyond.

Helge came hurrying towards her, but not so quickly as to prevent Vanessa noting the presence of several formally dressed men.

'My dear!' Helge crooned. 'You look devastating!'

Kissed gently on both cheeks, Vanessa was taken to meet the men who had made an informal line in order to greet her.

'May I introduce Baron Rosskind?'

The Baron was a man in his sixties, somewhat overweight, with a roll of fat fighting its way out from his starched collar. He was bowing formally over her hand. '*G'nadige Frau*,' he beamed, using the ultra polite German form of greeting.

Helge moved her to the next man. 'Le Compte Michel.'

Vanessa was surprised by the man before her. His hair curled about an angelically open face, his full lips shaped like Cupid's bow. No, she decided, as he too bent over her hand, he is not handsome, he is beautiful.'

'Our third Councillor,' announced Helge. 'Leopald Harrington. A countryman of yours, I believe.'

Looking at him she could see a man in his fifties who must have been incredibly attractive in his youth but had been impatient to corrupt his looks with experience.

'Enchanted,' he was saying to the back of her hand.

The next man to be introduced was unnervingly young. He looked less than twenty years old. So young, in fact, she wondered if he should be exposed to the temptations of the naked flesh that so often abounded in this place.

Helge introduced him as Ferenc Stavos, but Vanessa would always think of him as 'the boy'.

Only one other man remained for her to meet. The Count had remained apart from the others standing, self-consciously, she thought, by the magnificence of the carved stone fireplace in which blazed several sizeable tree trunks.

'The Count Alonzo Fuego e Meducato,' said Helge formally, as if introducing them for the first time. Vanessa, uncertain whether this was for the benefit of the other men, extended her hand which he bowed to kiss.

Seeing him created an avalanche of feelings which, tumbling about in her mind, made chaos of her emotions. Standing there, dumbly submissive in every fibre, her liquefying loins told her that she was no less ready for him!

Memories of Sheila and the place where all this had started brought an unsettling reality into the fantasy dream world she had lately inhabited, but she shook it off as she thought of Steven, the man she had left behind in that other world.

When he looked up she saw again the glittering emeralds of the Count's eyes and for one truly unnerving moment she imagined that he looked at her through the eyes of Pluto! The shape, even the colour, was a perfect match.

Aware that she had never before felt such total animal lust, it was all she could do to stop her weakened legs from bearing her down to her knees and begging him to be merciful.

Brought into the glittering dining room, Vanessa was conducted to a place of honour at one end of the table while the Count was seated at the other. She noted that none of the men took their seats until Count Alonzo was seated. Obviously he was a man to be treated with the greatest respect even by the Councillors.

As she sought respite from his unwavering gaze by fussing with her heavy linen napkin, she still could not escape the oppression of his eyes. When she looked up she saw that he was not so much looking at her as watching her, as if every nuance of expression was something of great importance.

Throughout the meal, despite the conversations to which Vanessa contributed little, she saw few remarks addressed to the Count Alonzo and none answered. She found she had little appetite for the delicious food. Far more important was the fire raging in her loins. A man such as he could make anyone forget loyalties and allegiances, and abandon all constraint. She wanted that man with an animal lust she could barely recognise as her own. It frightened her to think that she would pay any price to satisfy it.

'My dear!' Helge's voice finally pierced the lustful aura that had blanketed her mind. Vanessa turned her reluctant eyes, aware that she had been called several times before she had found the will to respond.

'I'm sorry.' She smiled. 'I must have been dreaming.'

'For some considerable time I fancy, my dear. You've barely heard a word spoken to you.' Helge broke off to indicate the German Baron seated next to her, halfway down the table. 'The Baron was complimenting you on your bearing and beauty.'

Vanessa felt as if she had been plunged into ice as Helge's words reminded her of where she was, and her reason for being here.

Suddenly she wanted to flee from the knowledge that, at a sign from Helge, she might be transposed from elegant lady at dinner to craven supplicant. But there was nowhere she could run. No place to hide – especially from the blaze of *his* eyes that never, for one moment, seemed to leave her.

She was totally at their disposal. In this company she had no choices and only one question – what was it they meant to do with her?

Vanessa knew it had begun when Helge rose from the table and suggested the company take liqueurs in the adjoining room.

Any doubts that might have been in her mind were instantly dispelled on entering the room. Until now there had been no hint of the abundant sexuality that had run through her life since being brought here. Therefore, it was something of a shock to see that while they had been at dinner the furniture had been rearranged. Now five leather armchairs stood in a wide half-circle before the blazing fireplace, creating a kind of arena. Looking at the ominous arrangement she had little doubt as to where her place would be. Behind each chair stood a totally naked girl with hands raised submissively to her head and thighs spread far apart. Even as Vanessa was led to stand at the very centre of the circle of chairs, she noted Renate and Sylvie among the attendant girls.

Four of the men took their seats in the chairs but Count Alonzo once more stood apart from the rest, by the fireplace.

Helge, standing slightly behind her, began to speak. 'Gentlemen, you have all now had the opportunity to observe our candidate in all her phases. How say you? How will you judge?'

Terror of the coming humiliation caused Vanessa to stare rigidly ahead and she could look none of them in the eye as she waited for their verdicts. She sensed rather than saw that each in turn had raised a hand and nodded their approval – all but one.

Visibly shaking, she was aware that the Count Alonzo had come forward into the circle of the chairs. 'I claim she has yet to prove she has the skill to give and receive the ultimate pleasure!' he said, speaking the first words she had heard him utter that night, and her eyes went to him, opening wide in silent plea that she be spared humiliation. But Alonzo had already turned away to the fireplace.

Instead, the German now addressed her from the relaxed comfort of his chair.

'So, young lady, you have been found wanting in certain areas which, we are sure, you will be anxious to remedy. In order that we, the Councillors, shall be reassured in this matter, you will now submit yourself, in our presence, to practical instruction by your guiding sponsor. We trust that you pay due and diligent attention and amply satisfy the doubts of your peers.'

She stood before them, praying that none of this was really happening. Even in the orgy club she would have been daunted, but here in the quiet civilised surroundings it would be doubly difficult to submit with any trace of dignity. Most especially under those eyes that had so relentlessly fired lust and which now condemned her.

Then Helge was standing in front of her, offering up a shallow bowl to her tremulous lips. Helge's expression was almost sympathetic as she looked at her and spoke softly. 'Drink this, my child.'

Greedily taking the honeyed brew, Vanessa looked into the older woman's eyes and saw quiet satisfaction at the doubts and fears she had induced, but no sympathy – rather a quietly superior delight in her dilemma.

The moment the dish was drained it was passed to one of the attendant girls. Helge's next words rang out with an authority that was confident it would not be challenged. 'Let the candidate be made naked!'

Her arms were taken by the attending girls and, in seconds the gown was whisked from her with the facility she had herself designed into it. Her arms still held, she was left trembling and naked under Helge's gaze. With a nod from their mistress, the girls holding Vanessa pressured her arms until she was forced forward to kneel.

Terrified now, her arms held rigid and strained behind her, she looked up to see Helge standing over her. When Helge spoke it was as if she were savouring every last syllable. 'Prepare yourself to learn the art of pleasuring the male with your sweet mouth. Learn well the lesson I teach, lest your lack of skill bring down on us the derision of our faithful.' So saying Helge stood aside to reveal Count Alonzo.

It was with a violently churning stomach that Vanessa looked into those eyes. They seemed to be piercing through her skin, touching almost directly onto her cerebral cortex with their aloof impassiveness. When the man's hands moved downwards, she found her eyes avidly following their every movement. With an overwhelming sense of *déjà vu*, she watched as they came to the fastenings on his trousers. Hungrily she saw the fingers pull down the zip and then disappear momentarily as they sought the prize within.

Without a flicker of emotion showing on his face, she saw him take out a half-erect column of flesh which, released to her gaze, sprang immediately to electrifying attention.

There was total silence in the room and, with her own consciousness now firmly centred on the rearing cock before her, she had completely forgotten the presence of the others until Helge spoke.

'You will use this flesh to learn the secrets of the ultimate selfless pleasure!'

Even Helge's words could not deflect her attention for one moment as she saw the magnificent man take first one step and then another to bring himself closer to her eager mouth.

When Helge next spoke it was in an urgent whisper close to her ear. 'First you shall take him tenderly in your hands.'

Eagerly reaching forward, she found herself trembling as she cupped the weight of his sac in her hands. He felt velvet to her touch and she wanted nothing more than to take him fully and immediately to her throat, but Helge's voice stilled her, insisting she must do only what she was told.

'Using just the tip of your tongue,' Helge whispered, 'you must slowly trace the contours of his flesh and feel each swollen venous cable of him until you come to the very tip of his staff.'

With devotional awe she carried out the instructions to the letter, tracing each twist and turn of the prominent veins as she rejoiced at the unexpected offering.

'Flick the nib of him with your tongue.' Helge waited to see her orders being observed. 'Now trace the veins down the other side all the way to the sac.'

Feeling that she had been entrusted with a precious holy relic, Vanessa did as she was told. Coming to the heavy dangling sac between his legs she dared initiate an action of her own. Opening her mouth wide she took the entirety of the sac into her mouth and, drawing in her cheeks, did her best to create a vacuum before popping him out again.

'Excellent,' murmured Helge. 'Now the tongue must slowly rise, flicking in and out – just so – as it goes. Once more, it must be used on his nib to tease his most sensitive place.'

Fully aroused now, all Vanessa's instincts were crying out for her mouth to engulf the magnificence under her tongue, but she forced herself to listen instead to Helge, hoping that permission to take him fully would not be long delayed.

'You must learn to love, to cherish, that which is within your hands.'

Almost at the point of screaming out her frustration, she was only stopped when Helge's voice ordered her to make 'pretty lips'.

Her lips already pouting with inflamed arousal, her entire libido aching, she had little difficulty in making her lips rounded and soft. Then, with a silent cry of relief, she was given permission to close them about the very top of the pleasure-risen flesh which, in her mind, had become depersonalised from the man that stood behind it. Thankfully she suckled the tip until, feeling a tiny pressure from Helge's hand, she was able to sink down further on him and feel the strength of the vibrant flesh pressing hard against her gaping mouth.

'My dear – the tongue!' Helge's voice seemed now to be coming from some way off. 'As you sink your lips you must use it to flicker against him. Even as you sink to the very base of the shaft where you will not fail to kiss my fingers.'

Seeing that Helge's fingers were now encircling the base of his shaft she had to steel herself to fight towards them. When, still an inch or so short of her target, she felt him already probing against the opening of her throat, she had to make a huge effort to force him into that most intimate of orifices.

'Breathe through your nose!' enjoined Helge. 'The test is that you do not choke or gag. You won't if you truly love it!'

Desperate now to have the entirety of him, she found that he seemed to be growing even more enormous, forcing her eagerly reaching lips further from Helge's waiting fingers. Finally, her throat relaxing, she had him totally in her mouth and her lips touched Helge's fingers.

Reminded of the need to breathe through her nose, she was nevertheless relived when given the instruction to slowly rise up his shaft again.

'Remember the tongue!' said Helge. 'Keep it working as you raise your pretty lips. Remember to keep the lips firm but soft!' There was a slight pause as she reached the tip, before Helge urged her to plunge again.

Eyes closed, she steeled herself to take the whole of him once more. Her efforts were rewarded when she felt her throat open more readily and, yet again, she was able to kiss Helge's fingers. Her breath now snorting through her nose, she heard Helge urging her to rise again – this time more quickly – only to be told to plunge again to his very base.

'Faster, my pretty one!' said Helge, and Vanessa responded with dedicated frenetic head-bobbing motions, determined now to demolish the flesh throbbing uncomfortably in her mouth.

'Now, the ultimate test!' crooned Helge. 'I want you to keep working the flesh but now you must look upward into his eyes!'

Feeling desperate now, anxious to have him explode in

her, she had to bring him slightly backward and crane her head and eyes upward to look in his face.

He loomed over her, looking down, his green eyes bright with lust. This eye contact broke down the barrier of impersonality behind which she had been hiding. Now there was a man – a person, an individual who she was working so hard to pleasure. His lack of any outward emotion goaded her to even greater efforts. She felt an almost missionary zeal as, her eyes now locked to his, her breath rasping with the effort, she inwardly pleaded for him to come to orgasm, to fill her desperate throat and grant her victory. For many minutes she worked on him with ever-increasing effort but achieved no reaction from his detached expression.

Then came the order she dreaded the most. Helge's voice struck through her. 'Stop!'

Frantically her brain told her to scream protest at being so thwarted, but she had been conditioned to obey so did as she was told, his cock still deep inside her throat and her eyes fixed on his impassive face. For long minutes nothing happened.

Then, barely perceptibly, she felt the very base of his cock throb about her lips, the movement growing stronger as he finally gave in to the pleasure. Hardly daring to believe her triumph, she smiled, for she now knew he was defeated.

His surge rose slowly at first, then erupted, flooding her throat and all but choking her as she fought to contain his voluminous outpouring. Holding on she defiantly soaked up every last drop of him, thrilled with the measure of her triumph.

She was given no time to savour her victory since, even as the last of her mouth's harvest was being gathered, she felt hands lifting her to her feet, distancing her from her prize.

Helge's stern face filled Vanessa's eyes as her wrists were taken above her head and secured so that she could only scrape a toe hold to relieve the weight of her suspended body. Her wildly racing mind sought to judge whether she was being prepared for pleasure or punishment but whichever it was to be Vanessa knew she would be given no choice.

'That was but the first part of your ordeal, my dear.' Helge spoke with a sweet, even tone. 'Now we shall test your resolve in the face of temptation.'

She wanted to scream that they had done nothing but expose her to temptation since bringing her to this place. What more could they do to her – what greater torment of arousal could they inflict?

Her body, stretched taut in its suspension, could do nothing as she saw the Count approach her. His eyes convulsed her. It seemed her recent conquest was returning to the fray. She was held by his wide green eyes as she quivered to the touch of his hands caressing her breasts, cupping them softly in his hands while his fingers flickered firmly across the tip of her hardened nipples. His face swam closer, denying her the sight of his beautiful eyes, as his lips went to the flesh of her throat, where he gently nipped, only occasionally using his teeth. Her body thrilled as he pressed against her and she sought frantically to meet his lips with her own, only to feel the sting of a whip lighting a flame across her buttocks.

It must have been Helge that struck her since it was her voice that spoke to remind her that she must resist temptation.

Closing her eyes, every fibre of her being already tensed against the pleasure seething through her blood, Vanessa felt the Count moving against her helpless body, his hands roaming freely over every defenceless part of her.

Now she could feel him, resurrected, hard and firm, against the flesh of her back. Desperately she returned the pressure, wanting to absorb him as her lust raced to occupy her mind, driving out all rational thought.

'Open your eyes!' Helge ordered. 'Look at me.'

With great effort Vanessa forced herself to do as she was told.

'Ignore what he is doing to you. You must rise above mortal carnality. Be supreme, my dear!'

With the man's arousal pressing against her like a flame, his hands constantly moving and caressing her, it was hard to understand what was being asked of her. Unable to articulate even the smallest sound, instead she shook her head, desperate to convey her plea for mercy. Helge moved in closer reaching out to cup her hands about Vanessa's face. 'You must resist!' she insisted.

'No!' she managed. 'Please . . . stop!' Her words became a scream as she felt the man behind her, ravaging her senses as he bit deep into her neck. Writhing now, her whole body a living flame experiencing sensations her brain refused to process, she could only sob more pleas. Even in her distressed arousal, she knew she was being expertly manipulated – brought time and again to the brink of orgasm only to have Helge intervene or the man withdraw momentarily.

Again Helge forced her to meet her eyes – this time to show her the cane she held in her hands. 'Will it help if I distract you with pain?' she asked pleasantly.

Vanessa's head weaved from side to side as she called out. 'No! I want him – let him finish me – fuck me!'

As she spoke all activity suddenly ceased. The man withdrew and Helge turned away leaving her in cold frustrated humiliation.

'No!' she screamed. 'You can't leave me like this!'

When Helge turned back towards her, Vanessa saw her triumphant eyes and realised that these were the very words they had sought to force from her. Now that they had them, the game was over.

'Does our candidate speak with the words of a whore?' asked Helge, her voice dancing lightly in elation. 'Does she forget her purpose? How shall we remind her?'

As Helge spoke the man who had made a beggar of her body came to stand, fully erect, beside her.

'You can't—!' she began, but broke off as Helge closed the distance between them to loom large in front of her.

'But I can!' Helge smiled. 'I can do with you precisely as I wish. There are certain words you are not permitted. One of them is "can't", another is "won't" and, above all, the word "no" must never pass your delicious lips.' Helge laid a light kiss on her anguished lips. 'Your punishment will be to witness Sylvie's pleasure.'

Vanessa's wild eyes saw that Sylvie had appeared at the

Count's side. Helge turned to Sylvie. 'You will take her place!'

Sylvie, looking terrified, fell to her knees. 'No! Please. If I do that I know my punishment will be terrible!'

'I intend to punish you anyway so you may either season your pain with pleasure or not, as you wish.' Advancing on Sylvie she placed the cane to the terrified girl's cheek. 'Do it!' she said. 'And remember you do it to prove to our wanton candidate she is above mundane carnality.'

Distraught, Vanessa could do nothing but watch Alonzo as he came to stand between Sylvie's closed thighs only to contemptuously kick them apart and sink down to lay between them. Two of the other girls had scurried to his side and began stroking and caressing him, offering up their breasts to his disdainful lips.

Hanging in the chains, Vanessa felt decimated. Sylvie was protesting the very prize she had lusted for but had been denied. Unable to look away, she watched the finely delineated muscles in his buttocks as he drove home into Sylvie, who, knowing now that her punishment was certain, started to meet every thrust with one of her own, reaching up, arching her back so that he might drive deeper. Her protests now turned to wilder cries of pleasure and soon became screams of orgasm, but still the man drove into her as if his movements directly produced her cries.

Mesmerised, Vanessa had forgotten Helge until the whip landed on her buttocks.

When Vanessa cried out, Helge heard it as a protest against pain but, deep within her tortured body, Vanessa knew it was triumph!

Chapter Eighteen

Steven's suite at the Hotel Lancaster looked more like a military operations room. Highly detailed maps of Helge's estate had been laid out on tables, and every available minute piece of data on the woman herself had been assembled, collated and studied but there remained many gaps in the intended rescue plan which were presently concerning Steven.

Silent for a long moment, he suddenly threw up his hands and rose so violently from the table that the two girls had to step back hurriedly. 'There's too much we don't know. For instance, we don't even know precisely where they're holding her.'

'We can make an educated guess,' said Roz. 'Look at this map again.'

Steven again peered down at the map but could see nothing to excite his interest. 'What's the point you're making?' he asked.

Roz indicated the map. 'Just there . . .'

Both Grace and Steven looked but could see nothing.

'What?' asked Steven.

'Caves!' said Roz triumphantly.

After studying his business manager steadily for a thoughtful moment, Steven asked, 'What tells you there are caves there? I can't see anything.'

'That's because you didn't get your Girl Scout map-reading badge!' said Roz triumphantly.

'You *did*?' asked Grace incredulously.

'I did!' crowed Roz. 'And right there, plain as day, the map shows extensive underground caverns.'

The announcement that Michelle had arrived and wanted to see them wasn't greeted with any great enthusiasm until they found she'd brought exciting news.

'I've finally found a girl who knows Helge's château well. She's been there and she was able to give me this.' Michelle produced a rough diagram which showed the interior layout of the castle rooms. After a great deal of initial excited interest, it was obvious it had little practical use.

A brooding silence descended on the room and it was into this that Raoul, the private detective Steven had hired, arrived, his face lit with excitement. 'I have it!' he cried, waving a bundle of papers high in the air as he came forward.

'Have what?' asked a depressed Steven.

Raoul laid out the papers on the table before him. 'Maps,' he said. 'I have a friend who works in the National Archive.'

'But we've got maps!' protested Roz.

'*Modern* maps are what you have. What I have are seventeenth-century maps!' Raoul continued enthusiastically in the face of their scepticism. 'You see here details of the old fortifications. Now what your modern map doesn't show is this series of tunnels. They were made as a means of escape or infiltrating past a siege. You see what that means?'

'No,' said Steven flatly.

Roz spoke up. 'It means that there are ways of getting into the castle from the caves or the other way around. Escape tunnels!'

'Correct!' agreed Raoul. 'And I am willing to bet that even the present owner has no idea of their existence.'

'Or their condition!' said Steven. 'If they were built in the fifteenth or sixteenth century and haven't been looked at since, they'll probably have got into such a state of ruin as to be impassable, not to say downright dangerous.'

'But you are wrong, m'sieur!' cried Raoul triumphantly. 'During the war the Resistance used these very tunnels! If they were usable then, after three hundred or more years, they would be usable now.'

'I have a question,' said Roz. 'What is the French National Archive doing with detailed plans of a Dutch castle?'

Raoul threw up his hands. 'It was necessary, mam'selle. After all, France was always at war with Spain and, in those days, Holland was a Spanish possession. These were obtained in case it was ever necessary for the French to attack the castle.'

'Sneaky bastards!' commented Grace.

Steven kept more to the point. 'I don't see how that helps us much. OK, so we can get a small army in there but, if we do, people are going to get hurt and, as Roz pointed out, they could have the law on their side.'

Raoul nodded. 'I have given this matter a great deal of thought and I have a suggestion to make which you may think is mad, but I ask you to listen to it anyway.'

'Go ahead,' said Steven. 'At this point we're desperate enough to consider anything.'

'Well this morning, quite by chance, I was—' Raoul had hardly started when Grace's voice cut him dead.

'Holy shit!' she yelled. 'What's that?'

Everyone turned to see her staring at a man who had just come into the room. His skin was jet black and he was so tall and wide that he had to duck to get through the door. Grace's eyes were huge as she stared at him.

The man looked up, grinned shyly and spoke with a deep sonorous voice that had a distinctly American accent. 'I was wondering if you still wanted me to wait?' he boomed across at the stupefied onlookers.

Raoul was the first to move. 'Chuck! Yes. I want you to meet some people – please . . .' Raoul was dwarfed beside the black giant as he came across the room and extended his huge hand.

Raoul was excitedly explaining. 'I saw Chuck this morning at a reception for their team . . .'

A bright-eyed and excited Grace interrupted again. 'A team? You mean there's more of them? Would they let me play?'

Slightly irritated by Grace's interruption, Raoul resumed his explanation. 'Chuck is part of a basketball team touring Europe. When I explained our dilemma, he was kind enough to be sympathetic to what we are trying to do. I thought that if we needed a man of his size . . .'

'I'll say . . .' interposed Grace.

'. . . he'd be willing help us out.'

Even Grace, who was herself over six feet in her heels, looked small standing beside the smiling American. 'Hi,' she said, taking a proprietorial hold on his immense arm. 'I'm Grace. Some call me Amazing Grace!'

'I'll just bet you are, little lady,' Chuck grinned.

'I hate to break in on young love,' said Roz heavily, 'but I return to my original point. Impressive as Chuck is we still have no idea how to use him.'

Raoul looked puzzled. 'But surely his strength and size would cause anyone to think twice before opposing us.'

'We can't use overt force,' Steven told him. 'We might all end up in jail. Besides we don't know that any crime has been committed, and even if we did, we don't know if we could prove it.'

'What then?' asked Raoul.

Steven was suddenly highly animated. He turned to address them all. 'OK, there is almost no time and we've a lot to do. First we need to make a list of everything and everybody we're going to need!'

'But *what*?' asked Roz. 'What are you going to do?'

Steven smiled. 'We're going to give them a visit to remember. Exactly what they want!' he told her, then added, 'And what they want is Chuck!'

'I'll say!' said Grace with great enthusiasm.

Chapter Nineteen

Vanessa woke from a sleep that had been much disturbed by dreams. The images of the night still lingered, making her feel unaccountably unnerved.

She had seen the room in which she woke clearly in her dream and for a moment felt she might still be in her fantasy. Last night she had gone to sleep plagued by the frustrated memory of seeing Count Alonzo plunging into Sylvie's body.

Why then should she imagine that Sylvie, the thief of her pleasure, had come to her in the night and urged her to flee? How could her imagination have conjured up the young attendant urging her to use the same tunnels that Helge had told her were abundantly full of prey for Pluto's predatory explorations?

This morning, even Renate's caressing hands could not soothe her. Was it possible that Sylvie really had come to her in the night? It was not, she decided, impossible. Her sleep, aided by the late night draught of herbs, was always heavy and deep, and Renate often had difficulty in rousing her from it. Sylvie might have come and only half woken her, but for what reason?

Jealousy? An attempt to delude her into imagining that some harm was meant her, so that she would run away? If it had not been a dream, to do as Sylvie had urged would be to reject all these weeks of preparation, and why would her sleeping mind have thought to prompt her to do that?

No, she decided, if there was any reality in her dream then it would have been the action of a girl so distracted with jealousy for her pre-eminent position that she had wanted to provoke betrayal.

Dismissing the thoughts as mere fancy, she laid back into the warm perfumed waters and guided Renate's expert hands to tease her breasts.

It was when she closed her eyes that the most horrific vision of that disturbed night returned. As Sylvie, or her shadow, had urged her to wake there had come a most terrifying scream of outrage and out of the darkness had come Pluto, the cat, green eyes flaring.

Like a demented banshee, he had landed on Sylvie's naked body and brought screams from the terrified girl who had been forced to turn and flee. How could she dismiss this as pure delusion when Sylvie's screams still resonated about the walls of this very chamber?

'Excuse me . . .' Renate spoke softly to break her reverie.

'What is it?'

Renate simply pointed.

Following the girl's gesture, Vanessa saw that Pluto had come into the chamber as if conjured from her thoughts. Instead of coming forward to greet her and be petted as he usually did, he was standing in the door, growling and purring, his tail held stiffly erect, staring intensely at her.

Immediately the images of her dream – or was it nightmare – returned. In Pluto's face she could see him to be the predator of the night. It was the first time she had seen him as evil instead of beautiful. Not wanting him to come to her, she stood up and stepped from the bath. Pluto's gaze remained unremitting.

'What is it?' she asked of the cat.

Pluto growled, made small tail-high turns, before going to the door as if to leave. Then he turned back to stare at her again with eyes that, disturbingly, reminded her of the Count Alonzo.

Wrapping Vanessa's body in the warmed towels, Renate joined her in looking at the agitated cat. 'I think he summons you,' she murmured.

Her voice filled with nervous scorn, Vanessa asked, 'Summons me? You think a cat dare to summon me?'

'He is no ordinary cat, Lady. He is the Lady Helge's familiar.'

'But where does he want me to go?'

Suddenly defensive, Renate murmured, 'That would not be for me to know, Lady.'

With Pluto's alert eyes fixed on her as inexorably as had Count Alonzo's, she hesitated one more moment before deciding that, whatever it was, it might make a diverting game. 'Quickly, girl, dry me and fetch me a gown.'

Whether Pluto understood these words or not he showed his approval of them by hurrying to stroke himself against her legs as Renate's hands flew about her body drying up the last vestiges of water.

Finally, with a robe about her shoulders and slippers on

her feet, Vanessa turned to the waiting Pluto. 'So then, furry friend, lead on!'

Immediately Pluto ran to the door where he turned as if to ensure she was following him.

Beginning to warm to the adventure she started to feel more relaxed. Pluto took off down the stone-flagged corridors to a flight of steps where he again paused to look back. The moment she caught up, he purred with pleasure and started carefully padding his way down the winding stone stairs.

Warm from the bath and covered only with a thin robe, she shivered against a sudden chill as Pluto led her further and further into the unexplored depths of the castle.

'Where are you taking me?' she asked of the implacable feline.

Pluto simply growled and kept going down the seemingly interminable stairs, until they came to a corridor where she felt a welcome draught of warmer air. Here Pluto seemed to hesitate and, growling still, looked up at her as if demanding a decision.

Looking round, she could see no obvious destination, only a heavy wooden door set in the far end of the arched passageway. 'There?' she asked. 'Is that where you want me to go?'

Weaving in and out between her legs the cat seemed to consider his work done. With a disconcerting squeal he took off back the way they had come.

Puzzled, she hesitated and looked from the departing cat to the heavy closed doors before her. Going forward she noticed that the flagstones beneath her feet were clean of the dust that pervaded much of these lower depths. It seemed many feet had recently trod this way.

Coming to the door, she saw it was built of solid wood with an iron-ring handle set into it. Her hand, unbidden, reached forward to find it moved easily and the door swung smoothly open on its oiled hinges.

The sight which greeted Vanessa seemed to have sprung from a Medieval torture chamber. There were many people in the room but the one figure that took attention was a naked girl who hung suspended by her braided hair from a hook set into the ceiling, her hands bound behind her back.

Horrified by this vision, it took a moment to realise that Helge was approaching her, her face lit with her ever indulgent smile. 'My dear, you've found us. How delightful!'

Vanessa's startled eyes were still rooted on the image of the semi-suspended girl as she found herself taken by the arm and led forward. Slowly the girl turned and she saw Sylvie – her suspended weight drawing up the face to make her look grotesque.

'We have discovered a traitor in our midst,' Helge murmured. 'One who has dared interfere with our astounding enterprise.'

Guiltily recalling the night's dream, her eyes feverishly searched Sylvie's suspended body. There, about her breasts and belly she saw undeniable evidence of a cat's scratches! Shaken, she realised that her memory of last night was no mere fancy. Sylvie had really come to her with an urgent plea to flee this place. Now she was aware that she might be about to be implicated.

'Punishment must follow as day follows night,' Helge

was intoning, then, turning to the naked men who waited, she nodded her head. Stepping forward, they wielded long whips, bringing them down with mind-numbing impact on Sylvie's already tortured body.

The girl's cries cut through Vanessa like a knife. Held there only by an unwillingness to believe what she was seeing, Vanessa shook her head in silent denial of what was being done.

Helge seemed to have been watching closely for her reaction. 'My dear,' she said above Sylvie's continuing screams, 'you are too compassionate. Your forbearance towards your slaves has been noticed by the Councillors. It is the second fault on which they remarked.'

'Stop it!' she heard herself shout.

The two men, who she now saw to be Lars and Rolf, hesitated in their lashing of Sylvie and looked to Helge who nodded. As Lars and Rolf desisted and fell back from their whipping stances, Helge turned to her. 'You make the Councillors' point for them, my dear.' She smiled. 'But what would you have us do with such a treacherous slave? Surely you cannot counsel that she go free of any penalty?'

'What has she done?'

'Sought to betray us to outsiders and even tried to persuade you that we have anything other than the most benevolent of intentions towards you. We were surprised that you did not immediately report such outrageous treachery yourself.'

Helge's words stung in her ears. It was now obvious that her chambers must be monitored – for sound, at least – and, in coming to her last night, Sylvie had betrayed her too.

'So, you see, we have here an opportunity to expiate both failings at the one time. You, my dear, shall have to prove that you have the necessary moral fibre by deciding how to punish this worthless, wretched girl.'

Aware that whatever she said next would decide many things, Vanessa could only think that she must find some way to end Sylvie's suffering, but she could summon up nothing.

Helge gestured to the men and Rolf responded by coming forward with a terrifying pair of shears which he handed to Helge. 'She must be given some mark of her shameful conduct. I would say that she should be caused to lose something she holds precious. What do you think that should be? A finger from a hand, perhaps? Or a toe from a foot?'

As the awful words seared Vanessa's ears, she found she could barely think. 'She's been punished enough!' her voice rang out. 'Let her down!'

This desperate plea was greeted by Helge with unexpected pleasure. 'Delightful!' she cried. 'What exquisite subtlety you show, my dear. The Council will be delighted with your decision.'

Puzzled as to why her plea should be received in such a way, she turned to stare into Helge's smiling face.

'You have seen the subtlety that escaped me! Of course! The hair!' Moving closer to the softly moaning Sylvie, Helge reached out to touch the strained braids by which Sylvie hung. 'She has such vanity about her hair, always brushing it, always seeking compliments on its sheen.' Turning back, eyes alight, she thrust the shears into Vanessa's hands.

'You shall do it, my dear. Release the wretch from her suffering by cutting her hair! How exquisite that we shall achieve the two aims in one. Truly a worthy decision!'

Looking from the heavy shears in her hands to the strained agonised face of the tortured girl, Vanessa felt only a sickening dilemma. The hair, she thought, unlike a toe or a finger, would grow back and it would end the girl's present suffering but still she hesitated, unable to summon the will to act.

Seeing her reluctance, Helge's voice took on a more steely edge. 'You have made a wise judgement,' she was saying, 'but perhaps you think she should first suffer more? Should we add weights to her legs until the hair tears itself out of its roots?'

'No!' she heard herself answer and then, before she could change her mind, she stepped forward and with three quick cuts severed the surprisingly resistant braids.

Sylvie, released, crumpled to the stone floor, her bound wrists preventing her from doing anything to soften the fall.

Helge called to the men. 'Fetch me the hair!' Lars and Rolf immediately lowered the chain that had held Sylvie suspended and unhooked the braids which they handed to Helge who next ordered the men to lift Sylvie and carry her off.

'Where are they taking her?' Vanessa demanded. 'Her back is bleeding – she needs treatment!'

Helge's smile was indulgent. 'Of course she will be treated.' Coming forward she reached out her hands to Vanessa's face with a touch that repelled her.

'What an extraordinary girl you are,' said Helge. 'Such

compassion combined with such a deviously clever mind. I made no mistake in recognising you as our true candidate.' She smiled indulgently before going on. 'Don't you understand that what I did was done with great sadness? I love Sylvie and she loves me. What happened here this morning will soon pass away to be lost among the many sweeter memories we both hold.'

Looking into Helge's face, the thought that the Countess must have gone mad came into her mind. Or perhaps *she* had.

'Come, child. Let us go to my apartments, have some wine and contemplate the joys of life.'

Finding Helge's arm about her extremely discomfiting, Vanessa followed, knowing that she now had something of her own to say.

Helge's excited voice stilled her. 'I've just had the most wonderful idea!' Turning to her, she presented the thick braids of hair so recently cut from Sylvie's head. 'I shall have this braided into the most exquisite many thonged whip. Sylvie will be so delighted!'

Vanessa found herself transported back to the first time she had ever seen Sylvie. Then she had seemed a carefree, almost feral wild child of nature, dancing with abandonment before an attentive audience of voyeurs. It had been with the same hair that Sylvie had lashed her audience that night. Seeing it now lying in Helge's hands she imagined she saw the corpse of aspiration.

Her mind was jolted back to the present when they found Pluto confronting them on the stone steps. In his angry sounding murmurings and his wild accusing eyes, she felt she saw some measure of her own predicament. As she saw it, she had two options: to either continue along the path already subscribed for her by the madwoman at her side, or to call a complete halt and leave.

'Pretty Pluto!' cooed Helge as she bent to pick up the fearsomely beautiful animal. 'What have you been up to today?'

Mounting the steps and following Helge, she could only reflect that it was a question she might well have asked of herself.

Once inside Helge's apartments she went directly to stare out of the window, keeping her back firmly turned towards Vanessa, as if sensing that the young woman had something to say that she would rather not hear. For reasons not entirely clear, Vanessa felt suddenly apprehensive but, nevertheless, she was determined to speak.

'Helge . . .' she began, hoping that the Countess would now turn to her. Disappointed, Vanessa ploughed on, 'It's been absolutely marvellous here. An incredible experience . . .' Once more Vanessa broke off, unable to continue addressing Helge's turned back.

Helge spoke so quietly that Vanessa had to strain to hear her. 'But, my dear,' she cooed, 'you speak as if it is over . . .'

'Well, yes . . .' said Vanessa. 'As I said, it's been a wonderful time and I really think . . .' She broke off as Helge finally turned, still stroking the purring Pluto.

'But it is *not* over,' Helge said with simple insistence. Then, in the face of Vanessa's surprised silence, she went on. 'I simply cannot allow it to be over. I have far too many hopes for you, my dear. I'm sorry but I must insist.'

Astonished, Vanessa stood in silent surprise as she watched Helge cross to a bell rope and give it a firm tug. 'Surely you don't mean to keep me here?' she asked.

Infuriatingly, Helge's smile was filled with patient confidence. 'I had hoped you would stay with us out of love or, failing that, simple pleasurable indulgence. However, if that is not to be, then I must take other measures.'

Vanessa found her rising anger tempered by sudden fear as she realised that Sylvie's warning had been no dream and that she could easily suffer the same treatment that unfortunate girl had experienced. 'But why? Why would you want to keep me here by force?'

Helge shrugged, her smile not a whit diminished. 'Simply because you have not yet fulfilled your function.'

'What function?' Vanessa demanded.

Helge paused, as if considering how best to phrase her answer, when the door opened. Turning, Vanessa saw the Count had entered.

'My dear Count Alonzo.' Helge's greeting was effusive. 'It seems our dear friend Vanessa has taken it into her head to leave us. Surely you, above all men, can persuade her otherwise.'

As the Count approached, Vanessa felt her determination deserting her. His eyes were impossibly green, his face never more appealing. He came to stand close in front of her.

'Surely not?' he murmured as he reached out and placed his two hands on her temples. 'Leave us? How could you contemplate such a thing?'

As his fingertips moved gently on her forehead, Vanessa felt something akin to an electric charge surging through her body. Facing him, looking into that impossibly beautiful face, she realised that her lust for him was as strong now as it had been that first night. As he leaned in to brush his lips gently against her own she gasped with a sudden hunger.

'Can you not be dissuaded?' he asked.

Paralysed by her desire, Vanessa was hardly aware of Helge standing close behind her, her hands reaching out for the robe and gently but firmly opening it. Vanessa, unable to resist, dropped her arms and the robe slid from her, leaving her naked. Her decision to leave suddenly seemed ludicrous.

Helge's voice, huskily insistent in her ear, only added to her confusion. 'She must be punished,' Helge was saying. 'She has to be taught humility.'

Hearing these words, Vanessa did not object. On the contrary, held as she was in the spotlight of the Count's eyes, she knew that she was totally lost and that they could do anything they wished with her. Not only that, but she desperately wanted them to.

The Count, his eyes alight with confident triumph, tightened his grip about her face and started to press Vanessa down. 'The proper place for a penitent,' he said, 'is on her knees.'

Willingly, grateful almost, Vanessa allowed him to press her down until she was kneeling before him. Knowing the treasure that was now within inches of her hungry mouth, Vanessa felt nothing but excitement, heightened by the thrilling knowledge of helpless humiliation to which she was being subjected. Waiting only for permission to seek him out and pleasure him, she was surprised to see hands other than her own reaching round him and opening the front of his trousers. Mesmerised as his magnificently aroused flesh was revealed, Vanessa barely questioned whose hands these had been. It seemed irrelevant that others had come into the room. Lars and Rolf stood just outside her vision as Vanessa tentatively reached forward with her lips to enclose the beautiful flesh that had been revealed to her.

Suddenly enthused with the confidence that Helge's instruction had given her, she twirled her tongue about his pulsating staff and brought into play every nuance of Helge's instruction as she sought to ensure that this time she would not be robbed of the ultimate prize.

Taking him deeply into the back of her throat and then wanting him even more deeply down into her very depths, she gagged and controlled her throat muscles until she heard from Helge that which she dreaded most. 'Seize her!'

Immediately Rolf's and Lars' hands were on her, dragging her away from that most precious object of desire, her protests ignored. Borne backwards, she was laid on a couch and joyously realised that the Count had followed. Even as Rolf and Lars spread her thighs, she understood that she was being opened to the Count's penetration!

Filled with desire, she spread herself wide to receive him, uncaring that others were there to vicariously share this moment of triumph. Vanessa rose to meet his every thrust, enjoying even the pain as his hugely aroused flesh struck home deep within her.

Soon she was riding her own roller-coaster of orgasmic delight. When her hands were taken from where they encircled his thrusting body, she put up only token resistance. Nothing mattered now but that the ecstasy she drowned in should continue. Finding her wrists trapped, she was able to gain even greater leverage of her body and she strained to spread herself even wider, begging him to engulf her, drown her, in his pleasure.

The Count needed no such spur. He pounded relentlessly, remorselessly, into a body which was wild with delight and near hysterical with its screams. Still he went on, each thrust seemingly reaching deeper inside until she feared she was to be cloven in two.

'Now!' she was screaming into his face. He loomed above her as he levered himself up and held himself at arm's length, the better to see the torment on her face. 'Come!' she screamed as she felt his invasion becoming unbearable. 'Please!' she called as her entreaties became ever more desperate. Realising that his pleasure had become punishment, she felt her loins protesting and her flesh becoming tender and painful.

'No more!' she begged, but then realised that he had no intention of stopping and that her cries for mercy would go unheeded.

Helge's voice, her breath harsh and warm on Vanessa's tear-stained face, hissed into her consciousness. 'There is no mercy for those that spurn me. No more for you than there would have been for Imogene. He took her from me and then sent back the used-up traitor. Had she succeeded in coming back, she would have suffered as I intend you shall suffer. Just as that man will suffer when he knows of his loss.'

Vanessa's distracted mind absorbed nothing and registered little of what was being said to her. She only knew that what had begun as a highly desirable excursion in pleasure had now turned to torture. Her voice rang out, begging for a release that she knew was not to come and she lay sobbing out her pain as her nightmare continued without pause.

She was hovering close to unconsciousness when she suddenly felt the deluge of his release and understood that the frenetic battering of her thighs had ceased. The moment he withdrew, Vanessa wanted to curl her ravaged body into a defensive ball but was given no relief. When her wrists were released from their fastenings, she put up no resistance as she was lifted to her feet and spread-eagled by the arms between two chains that now dangled from the ceiling high above her head. Her ankles were similarly fastened before her confused mind understood what was happening. Her body spread wide into a vulnerable X shape, Vanessa understood too late what was now intended.

Helge, her face bristling with triumph, stood directly before Vanessa and, catching up her sunken chin, insisted she looked directly into her eyes. 'How different it could all have been. If only you had wanted to stay with me instead of deserting me as Imogene did. You see, I took you from Steven, just as he took Imogene from me. Since he is not here, it is you – the woman he cherishes most – that will suffer.'

Stepping back from Vanessa's terrified gaze, Helge

nodded to some unseen person behind her captive's helpless body, and the first of the whip strokes landed on the exposed flesh of her buttocks.

Begging for mercy would have served no purpose but the greatest cruelty for Vanessa was to realise that the Count was standing before her, his elegant hands tormenting her nipples even as the fire was spread across the entire expanse of her imprisoned flesh.

'No more!' she heard herself begging, but there was more.

Much more.

Chapter Twenty

'Here!' whispered Raoul as his torch pierced the darkness beneath the cellar of the ruined farmhouse. 'I'm sure this is it!'

Steven – together with Roz, Michelle, and Grace and Chuck, who had insisted on coming along despite Steven's objections – crowded forward to look into the hole in which Raoul had already climbed.

'Yes!' the detective said, as triumphantly as his whisper allowed. 'This is the beginning of the tunnels. Come down. It's quite safe.'

'Jesus!' breathed Grace. 'It's like a sewer down here – only colder!'

Raoul's torch was revealing narrow arched passageways built of mildewed brick, glistening and dripping with their permanent coating of water.

'I told you to dress in something warmer,' Roz reprimanded Grace.

'Yeah, well I figured Chuck would keep me warm!'

Steven turned to her. 'Let's try and keep our minds on the job in hand. It could be a matter of life or death.' Steven turned to the others. 'What we have to do is find somewhere dry to spend the night.' He looked to where Raoul was studying the map by the light of his torch. 'Do you know where we are?' he asked the Frenchman.

'I know where I *think* we are,' he replied, adding ruefully, 'but the map doesn't show where the dry spots might be.'

'Then we'll just have to keep going until we find one. One thing's certain – we can't lie down in the wet.'

The tunnels ran in deliberately tortuous directions and, after taking a succession of fruitless diversions only to be confronted with the rubble of a fallen roof, everyone was beginning to despair.

'There has to be somewhere dry – or drier, at least!' sighed Steven.

Raoul nodded. 'What I was hoping to find was some kind of storage chamber. There must be some somewhere.'

A frightened yelp from Grace had him swinging the torch in her direction. Its beam lit up rows of grinning skulls stacked in rows behind a corroded iron grill.

Grace was recoiling in horror from the discovery. 'Jesus! We've got into a graveyard!'

'A catacomb,' Raoul assured her. 'Probably the victims of some long-forgotten battle.'

'Yeah?' said Grace. 'Well, would you mind just making sure they're all dead?'

Raoul's torch lit up something that caused him to swear.

'What is it?' asked Steven.

Raoul indicated with his torch. 'That door in the grill,' he said. 'It's open.'

Grace was ready to panic and grabbed hold of the ever-attentive Chuck. 'You mean they can get out?'

'No!' snapped Raoul. 'But it does mean that someone has been here.' Moving the torch further he indicated some white stubs. 'Look – modern candles have been burnt and they're not even dusty. Someone had been here quite recently.'

Michelle was shivering. 'Perhaps it is not such a good idea to spend the night down here,' she offered.

'We all agreed it was better to get into the castle by daylight,' Steven reminded them. 'People are likely to be less alert to possible intruders then.'

'At any rate we cannot stay here,' Raoul said.

'Can't say I'm disappointed,' mused Grace, who was still warily eyeing the long-dead bones.

Steven, obviously thinking some firm leadership was called for, spoke a little sharply. 'I didn't think it was a good idea for any of you girls to come in the first place, but since you're here, you're stuck with it. I'm not even sure we could find our way back if we wanted to.'

'You're sure we'll be able to find a way into the castle from here?' asked Roz, not bothering to disguise her own scepticism.

'Of course we will.' Steven's attempts to sound reassuring were carrying less and less conviction. 'Come on, let's find somewhere to bed down and make some coffee or something.'

'You got my vote!' said Grace, adding with yet another nervous look at the placidly grinning skulls, 'If I ever got to look like that I'd kill myself!' Then she wondered why everyone was laughing.

As they moved away from the catacombs, they found

themselves confronted by a series of divided passageways, some of which, they soon discovered, were deliberately 'blind' to confuse any possible attackers.

It was while exploring one of these apparently dead ends that they stumbled upon one of the storage chambers that Raoul had theorised about. It was behind a stepped wall and although the roof had fallen in somewhat the resulting rubble had created a natural drain for the water seepage and so it was still relatively dry.

'*Voilà!*' cried Raoul in triumph, as they all clambered thankfully into an area where they could, at least, sit down.

Raoul had brought along solid fuel pellets and lit two of them under cans of soup and water. The bag he carried, with what he promised were sufficient rations, was small but as more and more was pulled from it, it seemed bottomless.

As Raoul worked his camping catering magic, Steven called a war conference. 'Now I know we've been over this many times already but it'll do no harm to run it past once more. It could all go wrong and turn nasty in there.'

'It won't go wrong,' said Roz confidently.

'I said could,' Steven reminded her. 'We should all know what we're doing in case it does. Now the plan is for us to somehow infiltrate the castle, locate wherever it is they are holding Vanessa and, somehow, get her out.'

Grace's voice rang scornfully about the walls of the tunnel. 'I do like a plan that's carefully worked out and conceived in fine detail.'

'What do you expect? We have no idea where they might be holding her, nor what state she'll be in.'

'Or, even . . .' Roz said ominously, 'if she'll want to leave.'

'Why wouldn't she? I'm sure she's not there of her own free will.' Steven shrugged. '*However*, we don't know what we might have to do and I personally don't care as long as we pull it off. This is no time to go coy on us.'

'I wasn't getting coy,' said Grace a touch acidly. 'I was just thinking of the cold winter night out there.'

'Maybe they'll make it hot for us,' smiled Michelle.

Steven reasserted control of the conference. 'We have to play it by ear and there'll be no time for any of us to look back, so keep up tight at all times.'

'Devil take the hindmost?' asked Grace.

'Precisely,' said Steven. 'Nobody said this was going to be a picnic.'

Roz spoke up. 'For God's sake, Steven, don't say "I didn't want you along" again. We'll be there for her! Don't worry.'

Steven smiled. 'I know you will. I'm not worried about you girls but I am very grateful that you all care that much.'

'You don't have to worry about me,' said Grace. 'I've been to wilder parties than this is likely to be.'

'Me too,' said Michelle.

Raoul called quietly to tell them all that he had done his best with the cooking and all thoughts turned to that as they each took their share.

Soon they were drinking hot soup with bread and cheese, followed by coffee, a bar of chocolate and a warming cognac. Spirits soared as if they had enjoyed a gourmet banquet.

With an experience born of camping with the Girl Guides,

Roz suggested that they all huddle up close – Grace claimed
Chuck as her own for extra warmth – and settle down for
what promised to be a very long night.

Chapter Twenty One

Nightmares usually ambush the sleeper but as Vanessa slowly began to come round she realised that her torment was only just beginning.

Looking around, she saw that the luxurious apartments she had first been given had been replaced by the chamber in which she had seen Sylvie punished. Only a solitary flickering candle lit the ragged stone walls and the stone-flagged floors added to the hopeless desolation of the otherwise empty room.

Hanging in a helpless X shape from the chains that held her arms and thighs, Vanessa felt numbed.

This realisation that her situation was hopeless acted on her like an anaesthetic, numbing the pain of her contorted body and clearing her mind of all thought other than the simple animal instinct to survive whatever it was that Helge had in mind for her.

With her clarity of thought came the realisation that it had been rebellion and the raw sexual desire for a man now found to be unworthy of her that had brought her here. But she knew that she could not allow despair to engulf her or she would have no chance. Vanessa accepted that only total submission could now be of any possible value to her. Her hatred of Helge had to be disguised so that she could convince that madwoman that she was once more worthy of her favour. The thought of sublimating her hatred into a facsimile of love turned her stomach but there was, she realised, no alternative.

Having found the strength to decide what she must do, Vanessa was left with the thought that she would never get the opportunity to put her plan into action. The very silence of the walls became oppressive to her. She could be left here to rot as others might well have done. Nobody knew where she was. Helge, even if anyone were to question her, could simply deny ever having known her. The game Helge played was power and, from what Vanessa had seen since coming to this place, it appeared that those around her happily fed the woman's delusions.

No, she decided, there was only one way out of this nightmare and that was to play Helge's game and simulate submission while looking for any opportunity to escape back into the saner world.

The grating of the door as it was pushed open on its aged hinges brought Vanessa's head up. The first thing she saw was Pluto stalking into the room, his tail held proudly high and his eyes centring immediately on Vanessa's naked body. The cat stopped and stared alertly at her as if surprised to see her there. Then Vanessa's eyes were drawn higher as the door was pushed further open and Helge entered, accompanied by Rolf and Lars.

The Swedish woman's eyes flashed contemptuously over Vanessa and she came to stand directly before her, letting out a heartfelt sigh. 'You are still beautiful, my dear. How different it could all have been.'

Looking directly into those pale eyes that had once seemed so wise and sympathetic, Vanessa wondered how she had ever missed the fire of insanity that now seemed to be so patently obvious. Knowing that this was the opportunity to speak, to begin her stomach-turning return to Helge's favour, Vanessa found instead that her throat was closed and that she was unable to utter a single word.

Smiling now, Helge snapped her fingers towards Rolf who came forward with a velvet-lined box in which sparkled what first appeared to be earrings. Taking one in her hand, Helge ran her fingers over Vanessa's breasts before taking her left nipple between two fingers.

'I intend to make you even more pleasing to my eye,' she said as one of the 'earrings' was clipped to the pressure-roused nipple.

The first stab of pain quickly gave way to a dull, numb ache as Helge turned her attention to the other nipple.

'There!' sighed Helge as she stepped back to admire the effect she had created. 'They look quite attractive like that. Not too painful . . .?' she enquired in mock concern as she smiled into Vanessa's face.

Vanessa found she still could not summon any words and settled for simply shaking her head.

'Of course, there is to be more.' Helge turned to one side and took a step back from Vanessa before turning to face her once more. 'You, who I would once have elevated to be my closest friend, are now to be the lowest of my slaves.' Relishing her total control, Helge returned to stand dauntingly close. 'You will amuse both myself and the Count. I have instructed my more favoured slaves to devise a form of entertainment in which you will serve as the centre of attention. I most particularly have instructed them that there are to be no limits to the games they may play with you. I think that is fitting retribution for your betrayal of my freely given love and affection. It will also provide my other slaves with an amusing opportunity to revenge themselves on the person who once dominated them. What do you think of that?'

Vanessa finally found voice. 'I agree,' she managed.

Helge's eyebrows shot up with surprise and astonishment before relaxing into amusement. 'Your *agreement* was not called for. Precisely what is it that you imagine you are agreeing to?'

Summoning every last ounce of strength, Vanessa managed to look Helge directly in the eye. 'My punishment,' she murmured. Then, finding a stronger voice, she continued, 'And the opportunity to realise my greatest fantasy.'

Now Helge did look genuinely surprised. 'Your *greatest fantasy*?' she asked in an astonished voice. 'And what might that be?'

Knowing that everything now depended on convincing this woman of her sincerity, Vanessa drew a deep breath before managing to say, 'To suffer just punishment at the hands of a terrifyingly beautiful woman.'

The words seemed to genuinely disconcert Helge. The dominant fire that had until now burned in her eyes was visibly softened and she raised her arms involuntarily, as if to embrace Vanessa. Just in time, she managed to catch herself and let her arms drop away.

'A pretty speech,' she said disparagingly, obviously having to make an effort to sound harsh. 'One that almost tempts me to test you in a more agreeable manner.' Helge paused, giving rapid consideration to what she might do. 'However I have already made promises to my more loyal slaves so we shall proceed and see if such dedication can survive whatever it is they decide for you.' Turning abruptly away, Helge snapped at the two waiting men. 'Prepare her for your pleasures. The Count and I will expect you to attend us within the hour and we will not be best pleased to be disappointed by lack of imagination. I trust you understand that the penalties for wasting our time will be extremely severe!'

So saying, Helge stalked haughtily from the room. Despite being disappointed at the apparent failure of her ploy, Vanessa felt that her words had had some small effect on Helge's resolve and that there was still hope. Then she found herself staring into the grinning faces of Rolf and Lars and that hope diminished.

'Hello, beautiful bitch!' seethed Rolf as his hand ranged over her defenceless body. 'Remember us? Remember what you had us do for your amusement? Well, now it's our turn.' And Rolf's fingers closed on the clips clamped to her nipples where he squeezed them together about the sensitised flesh.

'*Merde!*' breathed Raoul as he scrambled back over the fallen debris where the others had waited for him. The detective had earlier set out alone to find a way through the tunnels that would lead them to the 'backdoor' entrance of the château.

'What is it?' Steven voiced the question that was anxiously on everyone's lips.

'Men,' he said. 'Two of them – searching the tunnels.'

'They're coming this way?' asked Steven.

Raoul nodded. 'What can we do? If we try to run away down the tunnels they will hear us even if they do not see us . . .' He picked up a heavy rock. 'That leaves us with only one other choice. You take one and I'll take the other.'

Roz spoke. 'I thought the idea was that nobody got hurt?'

'Maybe they won't look down here. Why should they?' asked Grace.

'There is another way,' said Michelle. 'If they do come here, maybe we could behave like communicants ourselves.'

'Great!' said Grace, her voice edged with nerves. 'Who shall we gangbang?'

'Them, if we have to!' said Steven.

Raoul hushed them to silence as they heard the distant, indistinct sound of the two men talking as they went about their routine task.

All listened, hardly daring to draw breath as the voices came closer, then stopped. One of them took a noisy leak against the rock right by the entrance to their tunnel. Then they heard the men move off and the sounds of their voices receded.

'That was close,' sighed Roz.

Steven was consulting his watch. 'It's daylight out there

now.' Directing his question to Raoul, he went on. 'Did you find the way into the castle?'

'Not yet. I'd gone some way when those men started searching and I had to hurry back here to warn you.'

Steven was less than cheered as he considered what else they might do. He was about to speak when Raoul hushed everyone to silence. Their keen ears heard faint but unmistakable sounds of the two security men returning.

'Everyone keep very quiet and hope our luck holds,' whispered Steven.

As the voices came closer, they all froze as both men flashed their torches down the blind tunnel in which they were hiding. They seemed to be having a disagreement over whether or not they had already looked down there.

After a heated discussion, the men started moving away, leaving Steven's party much relieved. Grace might have said something but Steven motioned her to be silent until they were sure the men were not coming back.

Finally, he relieved the tension with a whisper. 'Come on, let's find that damned entrance.'

Rolf and Lars worked diligently on Vanessa's make-up, anxious that they should present her in the best possible light at the forthcoming entertainment. She had been left spread-eagled in the chains as they painted her breasts and body in lurid Day-Glo colours. She had no choice but to listen as, deliberately speaking in English, they planned what they might do with her body to amuse Helge and the Count.

'I think it would be good,' Rolf was musing, 'for her to

go down on one of us while the other thrashes her arse with a whip. What do you think?'

Lars was doubtful. 'Too ordinary for their tastes,' he mused, tracing Vanessa's mouth with his finger. 'We need something a little more original.'

They worked silently for a moment before the silence was broken. 'I've an idea,' said Lars. 'Why don't we suspend her by the ankles – upside down – with her mouth at crotch height? That way she could give us oral service while her spread legs would leave all her tenderest parts open to the whip.'

'Better . . .' agreed Rolf, still not sounding totally convinced. 'It just needs something *special*.' Rolf broke off and forced Vanessa to look at him by taking firm hold of her chin and turning her to face him. 'You got any ideas?' he asked tersely.

'Go to hell!' Vanessa answered and would have spat in his face had she been able to summon the spittle from her fear-dried mouth.

Rolf's face tensed with anger. 'I'd like to fuck you right now, just as you are, hanging in chains.'

Uncaring about her vulnerability and anxious only to assert herself, Vanessa hissed back, 'I'd *have* to be chained up to let you near me!'

Infuriated, Rolf drew back his hand as if to strike her, but Lars caught it. 'Save it!' he cautioned. 'We'll have plenty of time for that upstairs.'

Rolf reluctantly allowed himself to relax and stood back a half pace. 'That bitch is going to pay for that,' he told Lars.

'Of course she will. You heard Helge. She's ours to do anything we want with. So let's contain ourselves for just a little bit longer and then she can scream for us all she wants.'

'By God she's going to scream!' said Lars in a teeth-clenched hiss.

Despite her resolve to keep as much self-respect as her situation allowed, Vanessa quailed in the face of so much naked hatred. Why, one small part of her mind was asking, was she doing this? She was provoking the men who Helge had licensed to inflict upon her the worst atrocities they could devise. It was something she decided to think about later. Meanwhile, the two men were inspecting the job they had made of her face and body and seemed pleased with the end result.

Rolf spoke. 'We've got about thirty minutes before we have to take her up. Time to get ourselves cleaned up and ready.'

Lars shook his head. 'One of us had better stay and watch her,' he mused.

'Why?' asked Rolf. 'Where do you think she's going?'

With a laugh Lars agreed that his caution was unwarranted. 'You're right. Come on then. I can't wait to get my hands on the bitch.'

'So let's go and prettify ourselves. We don't want her getting all the attention.'

Watching the two leave her in the candlelit desolation, Vanessa felt her carefully nurtured courage leaving her. Believing herself to be totally alone in the world and at the mercy of a madwoman, she was startled to hear a soft padding sound and then feel soft fur being rubbed against her ankles. Straining to look down, she saw Pluto had stayed behind throughout. The sight and feel of the sleek bundle of fur caressing her calves brought a surge of hope flooding back into Vanessa as the cat's affection made her feel that she was not entirely alone and deserted. This moment of relief was shortlived when the dungeon door once more creaked on its ancient hinges. Looking up she saw Sylvie slip into the room – her shorn hair hidden under a bandana.

'We've got to get you out of here,' Sylvie whispered.

Stunned by this sudden development, Vanessa felt hope returning. 'How?' she asked.

Sylvie was already working on the screws that closed the leather manacles about Vanessa's wrists. 'I don't know, but I do know if that bitch Helge gets started on you she could go completely out of control.'

As she spoke, Vanessa felt one of her wrists come free and, as the arm dropped to her side, felt a numbing ache as the blood rushed through her veins. 'Why are you doing this?' Vanessa asked as Sylvie turned her attention to the other wrist.

'You helped me when they might have maimed me for life. I'm returning the favour. Besides there are others who know where you are.'

'They do?' asked an astonished Vanessa. 'Who?'

'That man you were with at the French club. I saw him and the French girl in Amsterdam. They came to this club Helge runs there.'

Vanessa gasped as the other wrist was released. She

tried opening and clenching her fist to get the circulation moving again as Sylvie turned her attention to her ankle tethers.

'You mean Steven?' Vanessa asked the moment she got her breath back.

'Yes, him and the French girl.'

'Michelle . . .?' asked Vanessa.

Nodding, Sylvie went on. 'And another English woman. I think someone called her Roz.'

Feeling as elated as if she was already free, Vanessa's sigh was truly heartfelt. 'Thank God someone knows where I am.' She paused. 'But what can they do? They can't just march in here and demand my release.'

'That I don't know,' Sylvie said. 'But that man of yours, judging by the lengths he was going to, must be pretty determined to find you. You can bet he'll find a way.'

Her ankles freed, Vanessa took her first tentative steps in what seemed a very long time. Everything, she discovered to her relief, appeared to be in working order. 'What do we do now?' she asked of Sylvie.

'We get out of here. We can't go up through the main house, but there are old tunnels under the castle. We'll have to find a way out through them. At the very least we'll be able to hide down there and hope they think we've got clean away.'

Vanessa hesitated. 'Have you anything I could wear?' she asked.

Sylvie's answer was scornful in the extreme. 'Make your mind up – you want modesty or freedom?'

'Freedom!' said Vanessa vehemently.

Sylvie moved to the door, cautioning Vanessa to be quiet. Peering out into the dungeon corridors and satisfied they were alone, Sylvie waved Vanessa forward to follow her.

Neither noticed that Pluto was trailing along with them as Vanessa felt an almost painful chill striking her bare feet as she padded across the stone-flagged floor in Sylvie's wake.

They followed some steeply inclined steps until Sylvie came to an ancient-looking arched doorway. Try as she might, Sylvie alone couldn't budge the rusted hinges and Vanessa had to come forward to help.

'Where does this lead?' Vanessa whispered as she peered into the chilly darkness beyond the door.

'Freedom, I hope,' said Sylvie, stepping through the door.

Vanessa had barely placed one foot over the threshold before she was blinded with the glare of sudden flashlights.

'Well, well . . .' crooned Helge's voice from beyond the blinding glare of the torchlight. 'What have we here? More treachery?'

Panicked, Sylvie tried to run back past Vanessa but only succeeded in reaching the dungeon hallway before she was firmly caught up in Rolf's arms. Beyond the subdued attendant, Vanessa saw the grinning face of Lars as he made his way towards her. Seeing that resistance was useless, Vanessa dropped her eyes in submissive acceptance of her fate.

Stepping into the corridor from where she had lain in ambush, Helge, now dressed in a head-to-foot form-fitting black rubber costume and accompanied by Renate, turned to look from Sylvie to Vanessa. 'Now we really do have cause to punish.' She smiled. Turning to Sylvie, Helge's face turned to thunder. 'As for you, it is obvious that you are incapable of learning a lesson. I'm finished with you,' she snarled as if she had just delivered a death sentence. Then her tone softened as she turned to Renate. 'And thank you, Renate. Obviously I have under-appreciated your worth to me. I shall make amends, my darling, you'll see.'

The simpering traitor received a peck on the cheek before Helge started off up the narrow stone steps. 'Bring them upstairs,' she snapped to the two men. 'I shall see to these two personally!'

Her last hope gone, Vanessa shook off Lars' hands which sought to hold her and walked with as much dignity as she could muster towards what she now considered an inevitable fate.

'Dammit!' snapped Raoul 'Another blind tunnel!'

'If we don't find it soon, it's going to be too late,' murmured Steven. 'Let's try another tunnel.'

With more hope than purpose, they retraced their steps and pushed into one of the smaller tunnels they had earlier rejected as unlikely.

No sooner had they turned into it than Grace yelped.

'What is it?' Roz asked.

Grace was pointing ahead. 'There's a monster up there!'

Following her finger they saw ahead of them what at first seemed to be twin green lights peering out of the darkness at them.

'Shit!' cried Grace. 'It's a giant rat!'

Raoul was scathing. 'If so it's the first green-eyed rat I've ever seen.' Going forward he shone his torch closer.

'It's a cat!' cried Grace. 'Now where did he come from?'

They all gazed at the big black cat who seemed totally unafraid of the intruders and determined to hold his ground.

'It must be from the castle,' suggested Steven. 'If we could turn him round we might chase him back there and if we could follow . . .!'

'Never try to chase a cat,' admonished Roz. 'They're too smart and will always do the opposite to what you want them to do. Let's see if we can get closer.'

Going forward, each of them making a variety of mewing sounds, they came within a foot or two of the indomitable feline.

'Jesus,' breathed Grace. 'Look at that collar! Are those real emeralds?'

'Looks like it,' replied Roz.

'Whether they are or not, this is a very important animal,' remarked Raoul.

The cat suddenly started growling at them, warning their inquisitive hands not to come too close, then, tail held high, he turned and stalked proudly back the way he had come.

'Let's follow him,' said Steven excitedly. 'He obviously knows where he's going.'

'Which is more than we do,' Grace remarked. Taking firm hold on Chuck, she continued, 'Stay close to me. I feel better with you around.'

'Be sure not to frighten him,' cautioned Raoul. 'We don't want to lose him.'

Carefully keeping their distance, they marked the progress of the cat as he stalked forward just at the edge of the beam of light.

Helge regarded the two girls with great satisfaction. 'Now doesn't that make a pretty picture?' she asked of the attentive Count, lounging close by. The Count nodded his approval of the tableau before him.

Vanessa and Sylvie, facing each other with their hands firmly bound behind their backs, were joined by two cords which trailed from cruelly pinching clips on their nipples.

Helge, confident that she held total mastery over her victims, stood back. 'So, what do you suppose is going to happen next?' she asked. 'Well, to find out what you both must do is bend forward.'

When they hesitated, Helge nodded to Rolf and Lars, each stationed behind one of the girls. The men immediately lashed out with the canes they were holding and spurred the girls into obeying Helge's last order. Leaning towards each other, their heads almost touching, they watched with growing trepidation as the Countess attached a pretty flower basket to the centre of the cord that joined the girls by the nipples.

'There,' sighed Helge. 'Now all we have to do is add to the basket.'

Vanessa watched with dread as she saw Helge place some heavy-looking weights into the basket.

'Now, the rules of this game,' Helge was saying, 'are

very simple. All you have to do is, on my command, unbend and stand up straight.'

Each of the girl's snatched a fear-filled breath as they realised that, on straightening, the weighted basket, which presently rested on the floor, would bear directly on their clamped nipples. It was the anticipation of the intense pain that would result that rendered them all but paralysed.

Helge's amused voice reached their strained ears. 'Obviously you both need some encouragement.'

Bracing herself for the sting of the rattan canes, Vanessa was startled to feel the swish of a bunch of pliant plants across her strained and exposed buttocks. It was only later that she realised that the plants were ferocious stinging nettles whose action, though delayed, was extremely painful. The plants fell again and again on both her and Sylvie until they started to lift the weighted basket from the floor. The pain was immediate and intense but Helge was not satisfied.

'You will straighten your backs!' she yelled at them, accompanying her order with rapid downward strokes across their already pained breasts.

'No! Please. No more!' It was Sylvie that had broken and was now begging for mercy. Vanessa, although equally desperate for relief, was determined not to give in. Unfortunately, Sylvie's plea served only to goad Helge further.

'But, my dear,' cooed Helge in mock solicitous tones, 'I have barely begun!' Now the nettles were used in upward strokes between their wide-spread legs.

Sylvie gasped and Vanessa held her breath, waiting to feel the stinging plants laid on her most sensitive flesh. So she was surprised when instead she heard Helge give them permission to lower the weighted basket to the floor.

The relief that flooded their tortured bodies was instant but shortlived as they felt hands on their buttocks and fingers searching out and lubricating them. Fearing they were about to be violated by the two men, they were little comforted to see Helge approaching them with a monstrous dildo attached to her costume.

'Now,' she hissed, 'which of you shall I have first?' Helge paused as the desperate girls' eyes strained upwards. Smiling at them in turn, Helge finally turned to Sylvie. 'On the principle of saving the best to last . . .' she murmured, before lunging forward with full force.

Sylvie's humiliation echoed about the chamber as Vanessa wondered where this nightmare was going to end.

Steven stopped dead in the hallway to which the cat had led them. 'What's that?' he asked.

'Sounded like someone shouting,' said Roz.

'Let's go!' He would have rushed forward but for Chuck's huge restraining hand on his arm.

'Hold it,' Chuck grunted with an untypical burst of eloquence. 'We don't know what we might be rushing into.'

As Steven was about to reply, further noises could be heard reverberating down the hallway. 'I don't care anymore!' Steven yelled and moved rapidly off in the direction of the sounds, the others following quickly behind him.

* * *

'Now, my pretty one . . .' Helge was cooing as she prepared to address Vanessa, having finished with the sobbing Sylvie.

It was then that Steven burst through the door and all hell broke lose. He went directly for Helge and, with an arm about her throat, dragged her backwards before throwing her across the room where she landed heavily and banged her head on the wall.

Rolf and Lars, both initially frozen in shock, now roused themselves and had just started to go to Helge's defence when Chuck burst through the door. He came up behind them and efficiently caught them about their necks, banging their heads together. Both of the men went staggering away dazed and with all fight stunned out of them.

Steven meanwhile had turned to face the Count who, pale-faced and ashen, had risen to his feet and was holding out placating hands towards him as the girls hurried to tend to Vanessa and Sylvie.

Freed of the clips that had so painfully tethered them together, Sylvie immediately flew across the room to where the treacherous Renate crouched defensively. Grabbing the terrified girl by the hair, she swung her round and launched her across the room, ripping large tufts of her hair from her head in the process.

Roz and Grace, meanwhile, lifted the still-dazed Helge to her feet and stared at the false appendage attached to her rubber suit.

It was Grace that dragged Helge forward as Chuck seized the Count, bringing them face to face with Vanessa. 'What do you want done with these two?' the American asked.

Confused, Vanessa shook her head and turned towards

Steven who offered his jacket to cover her. Going towards him, Vanessa was suddenly overcome with emotion and, instead of simply turning to accept the jacket, she found her legs giving way. It was almost a relief as unconsciousness engulfed and she felt his reassuring hands catch and hold her.

The moment Steven had carried Vanessa from the room, Grace and Roz turned their attention to the shocked and terrified Helge.

'You were playing games with my friend?' she asked. 'Well, I can dig that. I *love* to play games. Matter of fact I got one in mind right now.' Turning to Chuck she snapped, 'Bring pretty boy here, Chuck. We need him.' Turning back to Helge, she smiled with all the warmth of a serpent as she indicated the dildo strapped to the front of Helge's rubber costume. 'Interesting piece of equipment you got there. Love to see you using it!'

Chuck had brought the Count to stand before Grace and, with an athleticism that delighted him, she executed a karate kick which ended with her leg wrapped around the Count's neck, bringing him breathlessly to his knees.

Straddling the Spaniard, Grace squeezed his head between her thighs, making it impossible for him to move. 'Rip his pants off, Chuck,' she told the grinning giant.

Chuck's hand took hold of the Count's trousers and with one heave they were shredded.

'Hey, will you look at that pretty arse?' Turning to Helge she smiled, 'Don't it tempt you, dykey lady?' Helge, pale with shock, could only stare dumbly at Grace, who continued, 'Sure hope it does, 'cos that's where you're

301

going to use that rubber stick you're wearing!'

The blood draining from Helge's face, she stood paralysed in shock until Grace indicated to Michelle and Roz that they should take hold of her.

'Do it bitch!' Grace snarled as she applied additional pressure to the helpless Count's head. 'Do it or I'm going to rip pretty boy's head off!'

Michelle joined in the chorus of insults that showered down on Helge as Roz pushed her into place.

It was the Count's anguished howls that told them that Grace was being obeyed!

Chapter Twenty Two

It was hot.

The sun burned out of an azure sky while the palm fronds of the trees behind her stirred lazily in the breeze.

Standing naked on the broad wide curve of white sand, her eye was caught by the blades of the helicopter flashing in the sun as it closed on the island. She had been watching it for some time before the sound of the motors reached her. Only then did she turn to pick up the sarong and, winding it around her, started towards the house where the helicopter landing pad stood.

It had been a year since Vanessa had last seen Grace and she was looking forward to a long gossip.

Vanessa and Steven had found this island in the Indian Ocean on their honeymoon and, almost on impulse, they had decided to buy it. She revelled in the splendid isolation of what amounted to their own kingdom. Here they could be totally alone except for the couple that looked after them – Maria took care of the house, while Imran tended the vegetable and fruit gardens, sharing the fishing with Steven, who had developed a taste for plundering the surrounding ocean for fresh fish.

became too much to bear they
by taking the helicopter, which
to fly, to the main island of Mahe.
onal airport could take them anywhere in
y desired. They enjoyed these trips enormously,
as a means of reminding themselves that paradise
s not only attainable but also had an address known to
the postal authorities!

Vanessa stood well back as the helicopter came in to
land. She had learned the hard way that a landing helicopter
stirred up a choking cloud of sand that could make the air
unbreathable for ten or more minutes. Standing there, eager
to see Grace step down, she reflected, that, try as she might,
she could find no flaw in her happiness.

After his spectacular rescue of her from Helge's château,
Steven had whisked her off to a Swiss clinic where she had
been examined for narcotic dependency. To their relief, the
drug in the honey-sweet brew turned out to be a mild
euphoric of the cannabis family and had no lasting effect.

Steven had then asked the doctors to search out any
possible psychological damage that might have been inflicted
by her ordeal. The Swiss doctors had enthusiastically
embarked on a lucrative exercise of investigations but could
find no sign of any damage. Steven, on the other hand,
noted a marked increase in her sexual demands but, after
consideration, decided there was no need to seek a cure for
them!

They had married in Switzerland and had gone directly
to honeymoon in the Seychelles, before returning to London
to see what had been happening to his business in his two

month absence. There he found Roz in perfect control of everything.

Deciding to make a return to their island in the Indian Ocean, Steven had suggested they should live there.

Never one to refuse a new adventure, Vanessa had enthusiastically agreed.

When the helicopter's motors were turned off there was only the swish of the slowing blades to disturb the tranquillity she now thought of as their right.

As the dust began to settle, she could see Grace fumbling with the cabin door that Steven was constantly promising to get fixed. Unable to contain herself a moment longer, she took a deep breath and plunged into the last of the dust cloud.

Grace was laughing as she stepped down from the helicopter, missing her footing on the awkward step and almost falling into Vanessa's arms.

'Jesus!' Grace was crying, 'Talk about limousine service!' Then, stepping back, Grace's eyes grew in exaggerated astonishment as she looked down on Vanessa's swollen belly. 'My God, what you got in there? A whole basketball team or what?'

'Speaking of which . . .' said Vanessa significantly as she saw Chuck unwinding his huge bulk from the rear seats of the helicopter.

Grace chuckled as they looped arms and started out towards the house. 'How long is it now?' Grace asked as they went.

'Seven months,' she answered happily.

'Isn't it time you started getting closer to a hospital?'

'We are close to a hospital! That chopper will get me there in less than half an hour. That's quicker than most suburbanites could drive there.'

Taking a deep breath of the air free of the dust, Grace looked around to see the ocean sparkling through the extravagantly coloured shrubs and trees and turned to her open mouthed. 'Is this the place they modelled Heaven on?' she asked.

'The Garden of Eden, anyway.'

'Right!' said Grace. 'So we got an Eve and you sure as hell have an Adam – what does that make me? The Serpent?'

'You can be anything you want to be!' Vanessa laughed happily as they walked arm in arm to the house. 'Our island is your island!'

Steven, having brought the bags to the house, led the newcomers to their room.

Grace, bubbling with excitement, was amazed by it all, while Chuck was impressed with the extended bed which Imran had specially adapted for his particular needs. It now took two six by four mattresses laid sideways across the specially widened frame.

Grace couldn't wait to get out of her travelling clothes and into the shower and then she and Chuck joined them for drinks on the terrace.

'You got yourself a piece of paradise alright,' said the unusually animated Chuck. 'There's space enough here for a man to breathe.'

Looking round, Grace shook her head, 'Nothing can be this perfect! How's the crime rate?'

'Dreadful!' Vanessa answered. 'Just yesterday I was raped on the beach!'

Grace laughed. 'So what did you do?'

'Rounded up the usual suspect and made him do it again!'

'She runs a harsh regime here,' said Steven. 'Imran and I have formed an escape committee. Trouble is we can't think of a single place we want to escape to.'

Grace had news of Michelle. 'She's turned into quite an investigator. Raoul is impressed – especially with the way she gets divorce evidence!'

After the Great Escape – as their rescue mission had now come to be known – Michelle had started working full-time for Raoul's agency and they were getting along marvellously.

Curiously impatient with these newsy intrusions from the outside world, Vanessa took Grace by the hand and told her she had something to show her.

Grace, anxious to get down to some serious girl-talk, let herself be led away from the men and down a winding sandy path to a beach house built on spindly bamboo poles.

'Close your eyes,' Vanessa told her friend as she led her up the steps into the hut.

There, given permission, Grace opened her eyes to a display of canvases whose riot of colour made her gasp. 'Steven's?' Grace asked.

Nodding happily, Vanessa said, 'Did you know his work before?' When Grace shook her head she went on. 'If you had, you would see just how much his style has changed. Before his subjects were always threatening – sombre, dark. This – ' Vanessa waved a hand about the canvases glowing with vibrant life ' – is happiness.'

Grace looked in wonder from one painting to another. They had mostly only one subject – Vanessa explicitly naked. 'They're gorgeous.' Smiling she added, 'But it's a shame the guy's so obviously limited in his choice of models!'

'Would you pose for him while you're here?' she asked. 'Steven's got a show coming up in London in a couple of months and I'm going to feel awfully lonely hanging on the walls all by myself.'

'Love to,' said Grace. 'Hey, maybe I could get Chuck to pose – although getting him to be still for five minutes isn't easy.'

'What happened to all your resolutions about men?' Vanessa asked.

'Gone!' cried Grace. 'I got to say that man is something special.' Drawing close, Grace whispered in her ear. 'And *everything's* in proportion!' She giggled.

It wasn't until they sat down to dinner that night that Helge was mentioned.

'I'll never forget the day you went missing!' Grace yelped. 'Steven was like a madman – screaming down the phone at everybody. The whole of Paris came to a complete stop. Nobody was safe! We all thought he had gone nuts. Then Chuck turned up and the moment I saw him I knew I had to have him.'

'Except when I'm in training,' observed Chuck.

'I go crazy when he turns monastic on me!' Grace laughed, laying her hand on Chuck's leg. 'Of course you never saw what I made that Swedish dyke do to your Count,' she added.

Mention of the Count brought a flush of guilty memories flooding in to embarrass Vanessa and she tried to change the subject. 'Would anyone like more wine?' she asked.

Grace, however, was not to be diverted. 'That Spanish guy was down there squealing like a stuck pig and that bitch Helge was sure giving it to him.' Grace, totally unaware of Vanessa's discomfit, laughed and went on. 'You know something? I think we made a conversion that night. Wouldn't surprise me one bit to hear that he'd had the operation! That would sure give everybody something to talk about!'

'Nothing like giving the public what they want,' smiled Steven.

'Or anyone else,' Vanessa said with such sudden solemnity that both Grace and Steven looked at her. 'Helge was crazy but there was one thing she did for me.'

'What was that?' asked an interested Grace.

'She made me unafraid.'

'She was building you up only so she could make a slave of you. Michelle told me stories about her that'd make your hair curl. Jesus, girl, that crazy lady planned to send you to Hell.'

'And, instead . . .?' Vanessa smiled, indicating all about her.

'You sound almost grateful,' murmured Grace.

Rising from the table, she walked through the open doors onto the moonlit terrace. 'I suppose, in some perverse way, I am,' she called back into the room.

'Tell me about it,' said Grace rising to join her.

She smiled. 'Look back into that room, at that man. He started it all. When I first met him I didn't trust him, but how wrong I was. He gave it all back to me. Sure, without him, there would have been no Helge but there would also have been no island.' Turning to Grace she smiled. 'And no Grace.' Then reaching out a hand to caress her friend's face, she added, 'Amazing Grace.'

Rejoining the men, they found Chuck yawning. Soon, the two Americans, tired from their flight – or so they said – were anxious to turn in. Just as the two women exchanged goodnight embraces Vanessa asked, 'How is Henri these days?'

'He's fine,' said Grace. 'Working hard and happy.' Then, she wished everyone a goodnight and led Chuck off to their room.

Steven turned to confront Vanessa. 'Well?' he asked and waited one agonising minute before she spoke.

'Grace will pose for you.' She smiled. 'But, knowing how excited you get when you work, I intend exacting a price that will have to be paid in advance . . .'

As the last of the candles flickered out on the terrace, there came, wafted as if drifting on the perfume of a thousand tropical flowers, the soughing sound of a cane rising and falling on naked flesh . . .

Adult Fiction for Lovers from Headline LIAISON

SLEEPLESS NIGHTS	Tom Crewe & Amber Wells	£4.99
THE JOURNAL	James Allen	£4.99
THE PARADISE GARDEN	Aurelia Clifford	£4.99
APHRODISIA	Rebecca Ambrose	£4.99
DANGEROUS DESIRES	J. J. Duke	£4.99
PRIVATE LESSONS	Cheryl Mildenhall	£4.99
LOVE LETTERS	James Allen	£4.99

All Headline Liaison books are available at your local bookshop or newsagent, or can be ordered direct from the publisher. Just tick the titles you want and fill in the form below. Prices and availability subject to change without notice.

Headline Book Publishing, Cash Sales Department, Bookpoint, 39 Milton Park, Abingdon, OXON, OX14 4TD, UK. If you have a credit card you may order by telephone – 01235 400400.

Please enclose a cheque or postal order made payable to Bookpoint Ltd to the value of the cover price and allow the following for postage and packing: UK & BFPO: £1.00 for the first book, 50p for the second book and 30p for each additional book ordered up to a maximum charge of £3.00. OVERSEAS & EIRE: £2.00 for the first book, £1.00 for the second book and 50p for each additional book.

Name ....

Address ....

....

....

If you would prefer to pay by credit card, please complete:
Please debit my Visa/Access/Diner's Card/American Express (Delete as applicable) card no:

Signature .... Expiry Date..............